D0355128

# The Everlasting Rock

DISCARDED

DISCARDED

# The
# Everlasting Rock

FENG ZONG-PU

translated from the Chinese by
Aimee Lykes

A THREE CONTINENTS BOOK
LYNNE RIENNER PUBLISHERS
BOULDER & LONDON

Cover art adapted from an illustration by Hilary Tham Goldberg,
© Lynne Rienner Publishers, Inc.

Published in the United States of America in 1998 by
Lynne Rienner Publishers, Inc.
1800 30th Street, Boulder, Colorado 80301

and in the United Kingdom by
Lynne Rienner Publishers, Inc.
3 Henrietta Street, Covent Garden, London WC2E 8LU

© 1998 by Lynne Rienner Publishers, Inc. All rights reserved.
Translated from *San Sheng Shi,* first published in 1980 in
China, © Feng Zong-Pu

This is a work of fiction. Names, characters, places, and incidents are the
products of the author's imagination or are used fictitiously, and any resemblance
to actual persons (living or dead), events, or locales is entirely coincidental.

**Library of Congress Cataloging-in-Publication Data**
A Cataloging-in-Publication record for this book
is available from the Library of Congress.
ISBN: 0-89410-781-X (hardcover)
ISBN: 0-89410-782-8 (paperback)

**British Cataloguing in Publication Data**
A Cataloguing in Publication record for this book
is available from the British Library.

Printed and bound in the United States of America

∞  The paper used in this publication meets the requirements
of the American National Standard for Permanence of
Paper for Printed Library Materials Z39.48-1984.

5  4  3  2  1

# Contents

APR - - 2000

# Introduction

≈

In writing about an author, deep cultural sources are hard to describe at a stroke. In sum, the author of this work, Feng Zong-Pu, can be said to be fortunate. This wise and brilliantly expressive woman was born into the family of a prestigious Chinese philosopher and historian, receiving as a matter of course a thorough education and rigorous training while immersed from childhood in the nurturance of China's age-old cultural traditions. She graduated from Qinghua University's Foreign Languages Department; for a lengthy period after graduation she was engaged in editing foreign literary works, nourished by and steeped in both Chinese and Western culture, becoming one of the most well-informed, educated, and talented writers in China.

Zong-Pu has lived all of her life in the peaceful seclusion and beauty of the campuses of higher educational institutions. Throughout her creative work she strives to express the lives and thinking of China's intelligentsia (*zhi shi fen zi*). Standing at this window, she overlooks the distant lives of a vast society. Many of her characters are comparatively cultured and accomplished intellectually, especially the female intelligentsia. From her wealth of learning, from her experience of the joys and sorrows of her characters, she has created moving works of literature, one after another. Her rich cultural background has resulted in tensions within her spirit between traditional eastern morality and Western humanism, a kind of cultural accumulation producing a quiet and solemn art of high elegance, making her an outstanding Chinese example of the learned woman writer. This quality has given her, among the swarms of famous authors arising in China for several decades, a bright and lasting artistic charm.

Zong-Pu began to write in the 1950s, making a name for herself with the short story "Red Beans." As soon as the story was published, the talents and feelings and the scholarly elegance characteristic of this woman intellectual won her readers. "Red Beans" overflowed with that era's youthful flavor. In this work, Zong-Pu began to treat humankind's search for life's meaning and its eternal emotional pondering. Although "Red Beans" passed through the invasions and attacks of an era of trials and hardships, it is nevertheless a proud memory of Chinese literature.

After this, Zong-Pu, like most Chinese writers, was so pressed by the Cultural Revolution that she stopped writing for many years. In 1978, when she once again met readers with "A Dream on the Strings," the reserve and elegance unique to her artistic craft were still vividly displayed. Inspired by abundant life experiences, this piece, with its completely beautiful and restrained gracefulness, also conveyed despair. This was a period of very vigorous creativity for Zong-Pu. In quick succession, she published a series of noteworthy short stories. The spirit and aims of the Chinese intelligentsia permeate these writings deeply. For example, in "The Tragedy of the Peach Tree" the writer uses "the self-defense of the weak," a kind of resolute aloofness, to shield the dignity of human personality. The piece's protagonist and her peach tree share their trials and tribulations; in the end she is forced to cut down her beloved tree, bringing about the tragedy of a "useful gift that cannot after all have a natural life span." The writing carries the full measure of the author's indignation, embodying the Chinese intelligentsia's traditional character and strength and its resistance to the alienation of contemporary life.

In "Lulu," the little dog's fate touched how many people's hearts?! "Who Am I?" and "The Snail's House" draw on the techniques of Western writing, twistingly telling us the special feelings of individuals in unusual circumstances. These works have profoundly inspired the transformation in the techniques of contemporary Chinese novels.

The novel *The Everlasting Rock* was the important work of this peak period of creativity. It uses the Chinese Cultural Revolution as its background. We have here not only sincere romantic love but also genuine friendship. In traditional Chinese culture, friendship is one of the five relationships and is taken very seriously. In *The Everlasting Rock* it is given ample expression. The heroine, Mei Puti, her father, Fang Zhi, and Tao Huiyun—all are gentle members of the intelligentsia; all suffer extremely unjust attacks and persecution. Added to the surprise attack of a serious illness, catastrophes follow one after another. Relying on their faith in life, and the power of supportive love and friendship, the protagonists meet the challenges of fate with dignity and serenity. Within *The Everlasting Rock*'s cramped little

Spoon Court, there are splendors of human sensibility. Tao Huiyun personifies selfless and committed friendship, almost religious in its devotion. Her great sufferings, weighing down on her extraordinary patience and self-sacrificing, loving spirit, are almost more than she can endure. In the midst of this physical and spiritual overload, the writer lets us feel and know Huiyun's goodness and honesty and her superlative capacity for steadfastness and generosity.

*The Everlasting Rock* also tells the story of Mei Puti's and Fang Zhi's true love in the midst of hardship. It is just as Fang Zhi says: He feels that if he discusses his love with his friends, none of them will support his choice. Nevertheless, he relies on his heart to guide him, to bring him to Puti's side. It is because of Fang Zhi's love that Puti's drifting boat henceforward anchors on the everlasting rock, gaining courage for life. At a time when people were in desperate situations without hope of saving themselves, this kind of approach through the heart, this bonding, brought a gleam of light into the night's deep darkness.

This novel truly mirrors the miseries the Cultural Revolution brought upon the Chinese people; it is historical, emotionally charged, and hued with rich romantic themes. Zong-Pu is the kind of writer who sets a target for her purposes, and persistently pursues this target. In her own work she always painstakingly expresses her persistent search for human emotion and the spirit of humanity. In *The Everlasting Rock*, the author places this searching against a backdrop of misery, expressing it in an even more moving and sorrowful way.

Yet another demonstration of Zong-Pu's wide-ranging talents is her series of long novels, *Ye Hulu Yin* (Pull on the Wild Bottlegourd). The first volume of this, *The Journal of the Southern Crossing*, and the second, *The Journal from East Zang*, have been published. These works again tell of a large family of intellectuals, with scholars and officials versed in both Chinese and Western learning. They are touching tales of what happened after the fall of Beijing to the Japanese in 1937–1938. The elegance of style, the moderation and faithfulness of the writing, are indeed rarely found in contemporary Chinese writing. Blended harmoniously with these, a spirit of morality and sincere conviction are achieved by the writer. These long novels are profoundly beautiful and stylistically unique.

Zong-Pu is not only a novelist. She is also celebrated in today's China as an essayist, and her outstanding novels and essays are equally well known. She endows her prose with a special experience of life. It manifests clearly a cultured tone and a sensitivity to the beautiful in a literary style created by the long nurture of an environment of disciplined learning. In her essays, she gives expression to the more traditional prose subconsciously in the Chinese character, including the prose of the May Fourth movement. It can be said that throughout her work she consistently conveys great depths of spirit with the art of traditional prose.

Zong-Pu's journals of scenic travels emphasize objective description, succinctness, and superiority of style. They demonstrate the profundity of the written language. Writings expressing emotion are not "carved ornaments"; they are a realistic outpouring of deep human feelings. Like the writing of her father, Feng Youlan, her style is distinctive and poetic.

The 1950s first brought fame to Zong-Pu. Now, her creative work has spanned almost half a century, and new works still appear steadily. As human affairs give way to change, she consistently observes "honesty" and "elegance," two words guiding her writing; she painstakingly cultivates her own garden. All of her writing—her novels and essays, children's stories, poems, and songs, as well as commentaries and translations—come from a great field of vision, a wide angle displaying the author's comprehensive and resourceful artistic skills.

*Chen Su Yen*
*Research Fellow of the Chinese Literature Institute,*
*Chinese Academy of Social Sciences*
*(translated by Aimee Lykes)*

# Characters in the Novel

(in order of appearance)

*Mei Puti* the central character; professor at Y University

*Mei Lian* father of Mei Puti; professor at Y University

*Zhang Yongjiang* professor at Y University; leader of the faction there implementing the Cultural Revolution

*Fang Zhi* doctor at Z Hospital

*Tao Huiyun* professor at Y University

*Chen* a doctor who assists the Meis

*Qin Ge* son of Tao Huiyun; his given name is Huaisheng

*Qi Yongshou* student at Y University

*Han Yi* suitor of Mei Puti; an engineer

*Shi Qingping* wife of Zhang Yongjiang

*Zheng Liming* professor at Y University

*Sister Huo* nurse at Z Hospital; member of the faction there implementing the Cultural Revolution

*Aunt Wei* patient at Z Hospital

*Elder Sister Qi* patient at Z Hospital; mother of Qi Yongshou; worker at Y University

*Cui Zhen* professor at Y University; one of the faction there in favor of the Cultural Revolution; patient at Z Hospital

*Chen Yuan* deceased husband of Cui Zhen

*Chen Li/Cui Li* daughter of Cui Zhen and Chen Yuan

*Old Qi* official in the District Court; husband of Elder Sister Qi; father of Qi Yongshou

*Xiao Wei* son of Aunt Wei

*Xin Shengda* doctor at Z Hospital; leader of the faction there implementing the Cultural Revolution

*Xiao Ding* nurse at Z Hospital

*Han Lao* doctor at Z Hospital; father of Han Yi

# The Everlasting Rock

# 1

# The Diagnosis

E VERYONE MUST DIE. HOWEVER, NO ONE HAS EVER RETURNED TO DESCRIBE this universal experience. A few people have experienced a suspended death sentence, which they have been able to talk about after the event.

Mei Puti, riding a dilapidated bicycle, sped toward Z Hospital. It was a day of gentle wind and radiant sun, the air still a little chilly, but long past the harshness of winter. On the tips of poplar and willow branches a hazy layer of fresh and tender green rippled without interruption toward the open country, stirring mind and spirit. "Spring has come," Puti said to herself, and drew a deep breath of spring air. She felt a flash of happiness; for an instant she seemed to forget her situation. At this time her status was that of a "bad" person who had been discovered, which as a political judgment could precede political death. One of the reasons: her father, Mei Lian, had been a "reactionary academic authority"; although he was dead, the lingering "authority" was still enough to shroud her life in shadow. A second reason was that she had taught school rather intensively while also being a Communist Party member, so she naturally had to be a revisionist. An even more important reason was the one she didn't want to think about. Briefly, she had lived at the "cowshed"[1] for over seven months.

---

1. In Chinese mythology, "cows' demons and snake spirits" assumed human form to do evil. When recognized by humans as devils, they resumed their original shape. Mao Zedong first used the phrase in 1957's anti-Rightist campaign to describe intellectuals who only seemed to support the Communist Party. By the time of the Cultural Revolution, the term was applied to nine categories of enemies: former landlords, rich peasants, counterrevolutionaries, "bad elements," Rightists, traitors, spies, capitalist-roaders, and intellectuals of bourgeois family origin. Often the phrase was shortened to "cows." The places where these "enemies" were exiled or confined thus became known as "cowsheds."

Whereas, as far as ordinary life was concerned, she had become a sick person awaiting diagnosis. She had come to the clinic to find out whether she suffered from an incurable disease: cancer.

Seven days earlier she had undergone a slight surgical procedure: a small piece of tissue would tell whether she had cancer. During the surgery she had heard the doctor murmuring to himself: "Not too good, all adhering together." His tone had been both harsh and astringent. After a bit he had said: "Broken, broken! I'm going to a meeting." The tumor had probably been what was bad. When the doctor had finished suturing the cut, he said loudly, "It's finished." Puti instantly thought that she was probably finished, too.

Over many years, because of her father's age and ill health, Puti had developed the habit of reading medical books. She had thus known that she needed surgery, and moreover that her condition mandated a frozen tissue study. If a laboratory test, done immediately after a tissue sample was taken while the patient was still on the operating table, indicated cancer, major surgery to prevent the cancer's spread could be done right away. But during these days of disorder, one felt endlessly grateful even merely to be examined. The director of the rebellious faction, Zhang Yongjiang, put it this way: "Permission to enter the clinic is a profound parental favor from Chairman Mao." Only after bowing three times toward Mao's portrait had she been dismissed.

Puti had waited one week after her tumor was found to have spread. At first she had thought she would be worried and fearful, but strangely she had felt an extraordinary peacefulness. Thinking that poisonous fluids were trickling through her body, she even felt some excitement. After the blows she had received in the confused world of the spirit, this had seemed like *terra firma;* at least she could think about cancer and not feel bewildered.

In the examining room people crowded around a thirty-plus-year-old doctor, each shouting loudly to bring up some matter. Calmly, he dealt with each. When Puti's turn came, she explained she had come for the test results. The doctor looked carefully through the patient records; there was no test report.

"You'd best go search for it yourself." The doctor was still calm. "The pathology department is in the rear." His steady and profound gaze gave his face a serene look, as though for him there was no disorder that was not a common occurrence. As Puti passed through the pathology department, she saw a large number of persons weeping—for a while she did not know why. When she did come to know, she felt that those who wept were very fortunate, for they were many

weeping together. Bereavement and other griefs, so shared, were easier to bear. She thought back to the time, more than two months
ago, when her father had died and she had wept alone; it seemed to
her that her grief encompassed the whole world. Alone she had
borne that pain pressing down on her. The pain in her heart had
welled up, welled up unceasingly; even the whole world had not been
able to contain it.

She must not think about that! Of what use was thinking about
it? Puti found the pathology department; she paused outside the sin-
gle-story building, then went in.

In the pathology department was a gray-haired man who looked
very much like a doctor. After learning why Puti had come, he quickly
brought out a glass slide and a paper from the cabinet. Obviously the
verdict had already been written. The old man smiled apologetically.
Puti, however, knew that he was definitely not the one responsible
for the report's being left here. Carefully he placed the glass slide
under the microscope and examined it. "Would you like to look?" he
asked Puti kindly, as she stood silently beside him. He pulled out a
seat. "Is this your mother's slide?" Puti did not answer as she got up
to have a look. During her first year at the university, in general biology, she had looked through a microscope. She could easily discern some deeply colored cells. They seemed very tough. What was
most strange, they imparted a feeling of ferociousness. Puti suddenly
felt as though she had touched snakes and scorpions, and she started
to tremble all over. To think these poisonous creatures were in her
body! "And now look at this one." The old man put another slide on
the microscope. "This is the normal cell." The normal cells' color
was soft; as one looked at them they seemed to exude a warm,
smooth kindness. Puti, gazing silently, felt her terror evaporating.

"There's no mistake." The old man stuffed the pathology report
into the case history envelope and handed it to Puti as he said comfortingly: "It can be cured."

The doctor in the examining room glanced at the report and
quickly raised his head to size up Puti. His look was still steady, but
his sallow face betrayed solicitude and sympathy, the intimacy of
common kindness. "Go right away and get a shot." He quickly wrote
out a prescription. "After the shot we'll talk again."

Puti saw what the medicine written on the injection slip was and
that in the space for the doctor's signature were two clearly written characters: "Fang Zhi." Doctors' signatures were usually in a self-invented
scrawl, as though the doctors feared that if they signed legibly a
loudly accusing army would burst forth. From the two exceedingly

legible and neat characters, it seemed the doctor who wrote them must be kind and calm.

When she returned from receiving the injection, the prescribing doctor asked: "Did someone accompany you here?"

"No."

"You're thirty years old?"

"I'll soon be forty."

"You need major surgery."

Puti silently watched his face, waiting for him to say the word "cancer." He did not, but only added, "Will you go along?"

Puti smiled faintly. "Do whatever must be done."

Taking the hospitalization slip, she saw that in the column for the diagnosis of the patient's condition, next to the words "breast cancer biopsy," in large letters was written "URGENT!" She knew that death was no longer a remote possibility, but a real concern. The man in charge of hospitalization, however, did not seem aware, from the gravity of the large characters, that anything was amiss. "All he knows is to write 'URGENT'! The corridors are filled up, where is there a place? Bookworm!" With frowning brows and angry eyes, he poked a paper over to Puti: "Put down your address and telephone number. When we have a bed, we'll notify you!" As Puti left she could still hear him saying angrily: "So many people have cancer, it's especially difficult for us here!"

When Dr. Fang heard there was no bed, he quickly rose, wanting to go himself to negotiate. Then he suddenly sat down again: negotiating himself would be useless. Calmly he wrote out another prescription. "Return for an injection; by no means should you stop the medication. You won't have to wait long—we'll notify you when you may be hospitalized." He smiled slightly.

Puti's heart quivered. For seven months not a single person in her department had given her even the tiniest smile. She was familiar with only the accommodating expression of her neighbor and fellow sufferer Tao Huiyun—actually an extremely tired expression assumed in an attempt to comfort Puti. She seemed to have forgotten what a real smile was like. In these days of insanity, with most acquaintances hurling accusations and counteraccusations, there could still be some warmth between strangers!

When the time came to return home, Puti felt unable to ride her bicycle. But if she didn't, how would she get home? There was nothing for it but for her to exert herself and slowly push down on the pedals. The reawakening countryside gave off an aroma of spring earth. "So if I just go to sleep for a long time, what kind of experience will that be?" Puti felt a touch of sadness. She recalled a line from Shakespeare:

> The undiscovered country from whose bourn
> No man returns . . . [2]

Since no one could return, no one could tell of their experiences. If she were able to believe that after death the soul fared better, then she might also be able to believe that death was only a journey to her beloved parents. After death one might actually encounter one's dear ones, and who knew what other joys? But this was the secret land of the spirit from whence no man had ever returned, could not return! Could not return!

She finally arrived home, in one of the most run-down sections of the school compound. Originally a private garden for a prince of the Qing dynasty, its shape greatly resembled an old type of key, and it was also quite small; thus it was known as Key Garden. There was a pond, some rockery, and several tall pavilions. This had originally been a delightful scene. However, over the years the site had suffered long neglect; also, it had experienced half a year of the "revolution," so that broken tiles and ruined walls everywhere produced a scene of desolation. Long years since, a disheveled mass of reeds had overgrown the pond. Puti presently lived in one of two small, shabby rooms beside the reed pond. In front of the room was a short wall that unexpectedly gave out onto a tiny courtyard, the entrances to which were in the shape of vases. There had originally been a lilac tree in the yard. When the Mei father and daughter had been driven there, the Red Guards had dug up the lilac tree, and designated the little courtyard a garbage dump. However, most people continued to dump their rubbish at the gates to the public lands. Some dumped outside the gate to the little yard. No one entered the yard to dump. The little yard was quite bare; only a large rock, about as tall as a man, rose high and graceful beside the wall. It had the appearance of recoiling from a precipice.

After Mei Lian died, a Spanish teacher from the Western Languages Department, a woman, Tao Huiyun, now labeled an "active counterrevolutionary," had been brought to live in the other room. The door to her home was always unlocked. She herself said this was "to facilitate confiscations."

---

2. *Hamlet,* Act III, Scene 1.

When Puti came through the compound gates, she first pushed open the door of Huiyun's home to put away the old bicycle. The relatively new machine that Puti once used had disappeared without a trace during her first confiscation. Huiyun's bicycle, so old no one wanted it, was still passable to ride. The old bicycle fit the atmosphere of the room, which otherwise contained only a camp cot and an old chair. The quilt from the cot had been pulled in a heap to the damp floor; a disorderly pile of things lay on the chair. There was also a small bench on which Huiyun often sat. Puti sighed softly and went into her own place. She felt unable to take another step and promptly lay down.

The rebel leaders, suspecting some kind of scheme in Puti's recent illness, had done another confiscatory investigation of her little room. The square space displayed their achievement: a chaotic mess, as if no one had lived there for a long time. The window curtains were pulled half off, deliberately smashed teacups lay here and there, some face up, some up-ended. Coal ash and torn scraps of paper covered the floor. But from the doorway to the little bed, thence to the table, there was a kind of triangular track, resembling a little garden footpath. This little path made Puti think of the flower garden of her former home. The Mei family had for many years lived in the school's best residential section; each little Western-style house enclosed a uniquely patterned and styled garden. The Mei garden had had a bamboo paling. There had been a three-cornered area between the dense bamboo and Puti's room, an area containing some very fine sheepbeard grass, of such a uniform green that in the sunlight it had resembled shimmering waves, soft to walk on, but still resilient. These things were no more; all had turned to stupid paper scraps scattered on the ground and trampled upon.

Puti rested for a while, then felt she had the strength to open her eyes. The first thing she saw was the urn with her father's ashes, or, strictly speaking, the pot with her father's ashes, since it was an extremely simple earthen pot. These earthen pots were the crematorium's best for "bad" people. Fortunately, she had his ashes, obtained thanks to the mysterious compassion of a nameless rebel leader. The jar with the ashes was placed on a board nailed into the wall; a cup of clear water often rested in front of the jar. Puti remembered that her father had loved best of all to drink tea; after his "ferreting out," there were times he could not obtain tea leaves and had to drink plain water. She was, naturally, unable to hang his portrait, much less a photograph she did not have. Such things had all gone. Puti, however, felt no regret on this score. She had such a clear image of her father, memories of the past were so abundant, that it seemed no visible reality could replace the dear one in her heart.

As Puti looked at the jar of ashes, scenes of her father's illness and death rose before her eyes. It was a little more than two months ago, in the midst of Beijing's bitter cold season. There had been no real snow since the beginning of winter, but that day the sky was heavily overcast, and scattered snowflakes of various sizes were falling; the ground of the run-down little compound was hard and slippery. Puti was then living in the room Huiyun now had. Early in the morning she had seen the snowflakes falling and had gathered several bricks from the road to prepare a path for her father. Opening the door to her father's room, she saw that the old man was still lying in bed, moaning. "Dad's ill!" Puti instantly bounded to the bedside. She saw that her father had both eyes tightly closed, his skin was moist and flushed, fine beads of perspiration spread over the grizzled old face, already half comatose. He was gasping deliriously: "*Ci . . . ! Ci . . . !*" Puti's dead mother's name. "Dad! Dad!" Puti cried out loud. Although his forehead felt cold to her outstretched hand, this did not mean there was no high fever. But there was no thermometer! She pulled out a towel and wiped Lian's forehead twice, then threw down the towel and ran from the room.

The sky was very dark; it was as much like dusk as early morning. A bone-chilling cold wind swirled the snow against Puti's face, taking her breath away. Never slowing her pace, she ran as fast as she could to the school infirmary. Snow sprinkled on her hair and face. Her eyes were wet, her vision blurred. When she took off her glasses, the wet and slippery road felt as if it were shaking. She used the front of her jacket to wipe her glasses, and then put them back on. The road was long and difficult. Wiping her eyes, replacing her glasses, wiping her eyes, replacing her glasses, she ran into the infirmary.

When the people there heard that it was Mei Lian who was ill, some were indifferent, and some "rejoiced at misfortune and enjoyed calamity"; a bald person spoke of "feigning illness to avoid reform through labor"! Puti, using her jacket front to dry the wet snow from her face, felt tears suddenly well up. She did not understand how relationships between people could become so heartlessly cruel; moreover, this was considered the highest type of revolutionary ethics! Finally, a person in his thirties walked over and agreed to send an ambulance. Puti, following him to the telephone, heard him say in a low voice: "I heard your lecture, selected readings of Tang poetry; you spoke well." Puti looked at him. She seemed to remember him as a pharmacist, for the past few months serving as a doctor in the Ear, Nose, and Throat Department. Looking at Puti wiping her tears, he said: "Don't come here, there's no doctor. Go to the city."

Puti had no time to thank him before he turned and left. She knew that talking to someone like herself was not advisable for anyone. She composed herself a bit, then called the History Department to ask for leave for her father. The person answering went for instructions; returning, he said coldly: "Go for treatment." She replaced the phone, then called the Chinese Department. The person who answered chanced to be Zhang Yongjiang. This Zhang Yongjiang was very fond of letting people know his name: "Zhang Yongjiang. *Yong* means to sing. All my life I've been 'Yong Jiang.'" He really had foresight, Puti had thought on each of the several occasions she had listened to his introduction, for he had early known that the "Jiang" would someday need "Yong."[3] Zhang Yongjiang then said: "Ill? You are taking him to the hospital? Okay." What he said was not improper, but his tone was cold and hard, sounding rigid and tough. Puti got into the ambulance. As if grasping a lifesaving celestial force, she was now more in control of herself. When the ambulance started up, however, she felt a new rush of bewilderment, realizing she did not know how her father was. Was he having a cerebral hemorrhage? Could he have fallen out of bed? How could the ambulance go so slowly? Would Dad die waiting for it to arrive? How could he die leaving her behind all alone? Puti wiped her glasses with her jacket front, while snow swirled against the car window. They were there! Puti, rushing in, saw her father open his eyes. With great effort he asked: "Where did you go?" The sound was barely audible.

Dad was alive! Puti quickly hugged the old man to her, sobbing: "The ambulance has come; we're going to the hospital." She hurriedly dressed him. "Where do you hurt, Dad?"

"I . . . I haven't urinated for two days." Seeing Puti's reproachful look, the old man added painfully: "I was afraid to worry you, so I didn't tell you. And time off isn't easy to get. . . . "

The old man exerted himself to the utmost to help his daughter, leaning on her with one hand, against the wall with the other, groaning loudly as he dragged each step forward, the cold wind and snow biting into his sleeves. After no more than ten steps of an indeterminate duration, they climbed, with great difficulty, into the ambulance. He again sank into a half coma. The neighbors had come over and stood in the doorway; everyone had stopped to watch the ambulance. Some people said quietly: "Mei Lian is ill." The softly spoken words and sympathetic looks gave Puti a feeling of warmth in the cold wind.

---

3. Jiang was the surname of Mao Zedong's wife, Jiang Qing.

The emergency room of the hospital, in the heart of the city, overflowed with people. Like refugees, some were lying, some sitting, some standing. After many setbacks, many entreaties, it was finally ascertained the old man suffered from an enlarged prostate and could not urinate. Already, it appeared, there was toxicosis, extremely dangerous. Puti carefully and cautiously asked a doctor wearing black-rimmed glasses: "How do you think it should be treated?"

"We aren't taking him. There's no bed." The doctor adjusted his glasses with his hands and spoke with cold severity.

"He is so ill, if there is no treatment, what will happen?" Puti was half inclined to throw herself on her knees before the doctor.

"We have no beds! Go to another hospital!" The doctor answered unequivocally.

"How can you serve the people like this?" Puti wanted to ask loudly, but what she actually said was: "Please, doctor, be kind, have sympathy for a man of the people."

"What man of the people?" The doctor smiled coldly. "Mei Lian! Who doesn't know! Reactionary academic authority! The papers mentioned his name long ago. We are not serving class enemies." As he spoke, he left the emergency room. Nor would anyone else help Puti, no matter how she reasoned and pleaded, tears streaming down her face. The doctors seemed made of stone; there was no flexibility, no latitude. Of what use was weeping? Of what use hate? Every minute, every second counted for her dear one's life. With difficulty Puti supported the old man with her hand and they climbed into a three-wheeled car. On the soil of their ancestral country, in the city of Beijing where she had been born and raised, she could only feel an inhospitable vastness, with no place to shelter them! There was only the piercing cold north wind, spraying them liberally with snow.

In the end, however, a hospital did take Mei Lian. The decision was made by a Dr. Chen, wearing a military uniform, who ran it. He declared: "But there is no single room." Puti, looking tearfully at this savior, thought to herself that he had probably participated in the War to Resist U.S. Aggression in Korea.

Bladder surgery was performed at once. After a couple of hours Mei Lian was pushed into the ward. He was asleep, breathing regularly, his high fever already abated. Dr. Chen said that after a week he would operate to remove the prostate, completing the treatment. Puti very much wanted to grasp his hand and thank him for saving her father's life. However, she had already become accustomed to not extending her hand. She only smiled slightly at the doctor, her eyes filled with tears.

After Mei Lian's surgery he urinated without obstruction; his symptoms diminished daily, but he still ran a fever. Puti attended him for three days without changing her clothes. On the afternoon of the fourth day, she went home to get some things and cook a little broth to help strengthen her father for the major surgery. The bus still had one stop before Y University when she heard heaven-rending thunderous sounds coming from the loudspeaker: "Learn from the Shanghai rebels! Salute the Shanghai rebels!" On the bus several young people were discussing how *Wan Hui Bao* and the *Liberation Daily* had "charged out" first; after that, the rebels had seized power in the Shanghai Municipal Party Committee. How had they seized it? Puti was not at all clear about this. She only felt her heart quiver at the sound of the slogans, making her long to cover her ears. She only thought of one thing: using all her strength to help her father recover; other matters did not concern her. But if big events were in the offing, it could certainly influence millions of people's destinies. No matter if one wanted to hide, one could not. Those who decided great things did not always consider the consequences, this much was certain.

That morning, when Puti hurried back to the hospital, Dr. Chen called her into his office to talk. "Last night, revolutionaries took control here. They said that taking in Mei—your father—was wrong in principle. I have already completed self-criticism. They want you to sign a pledge saying that you will leave the hospital in three days and will not seek prostate surgery." Dr. Chen pronounced each word clearly, speaking so plainly that his peasantlike face took on a stupefied expression.

Thus three days later Mei Lian left for home, with a rubber tube inserted in his bladder and wearing a glass bottle at his waist. Despite the torments of his illness he had remained in good spirits. As he walked into the compound gate, he halted and moved his face closer to the wall beside the gate. He seemed to be looking for something.

"What are you looking for, Dad?" Puti, supporting him, had to stop too and look toward the wall.

It turned out that in this wall was a glossy brick, with two tiny characters engraved on it in seal style: "Spoon Court." Mei Lian had discovered them. After father and daughter had been expelled to their poor little rooms, Lian, after his daily forced labor, and after writing explanatory materials, had always loved to bring his face close to the wall, carefully studying each brick. No matter that he was very nearsighted and his vision extremely poor; he nevertheless meticulously studied the walls on the three sides of the compound. When he discovered the two characters, the old man's happiness knew no bounds and he talked to Puti about them for quite a while. Although the name of Key Garden was still in use, few people knew of these inscriptions in the garden. The original name of this earth mound had been "Key Hill," and the reed pond's original name "Spoon Pond." The little place had probably once been intended for tea water; surprisingly, it was also inscribed with a name, counted as one scene in the garden. One could do worse than be banished to a place like this.

Lian lightly stroked the two seal characters with his hand and said, sighing: "I really didn't believe I would come back." What he had also not known was that he would return so briefly.

That evening father and daughter talked late. The old man was still feeble, but spoke frequently off and on, his heavy Hunanese accent now even less understandable than before. He said: "I can live with wearing the urine bottle. I have the energy to go on. I have gone through so many years of reform, and now this assault. I should use what I have learned to study Marxism-Leninism and write another history of the Qin and Han dynasties."

Poor Dad! Still to be thinking of reform, of writing another book! Puti asked: "How would you treat Emperor Qin Shi Huang? If you evaluate him in a 'matter of fact' way, you could be labeled an active counterrevolutionary. You overall approve of him. Is this whole-hearted?"

"Ultimately this is historical research. Why must it always be mixed up with current politics?" the old man muttered. "The great Cultural Revolution—this great cultural revolution—I believe Chairman Mao always has his reasons."

"I believe Chairman Mao has his reasons": this was a sentence Mei Lian often spoke. He said this, and believed this, as did hundreds of millions of Chinese.

"Under the heaven of our holy ruler, all things turn to spring, but I in dark ignorance have destroyed myself."[4] Puti quoted two lines from a poem by Su Shi written when he was imprisoned in Wu Tai, then quickly bit her lip.

"You say my thinking is feudal?—possibly." Mei Lian did not consider blaming her. He said thoughtfully: "You're a Communist Party member. Your faith must be steadfast. I always feel honored for you." Puti did not answer. She certainly did not anticipate that these words would be Mei Lian's last.

---

4. Burton Watson, translator and editor, *The Columbia Book of Chinese Poetry* (New York: Columbia University Press, 1984), p. 304.

Next morning Puti quietly attended to household details. She emptied the urine bottle, sterilized the catheter. Her movements of hand and foot were so nimble that the old man was only dimly aware of them. He remained in a muddled sleep, without waking, only giving frequent groans. Puti planned to ask for time off work so that she could return home and attend to her father's meals. She was trying hard to dig in the frozen ground—frozen ground that seemed much more approachable than people's faces. She thought of the pot of gruel sitting on the stove—it probably wouldn't be ready until after she returned. Could it have boiled over? Perhaps it wasn't boiling at all? The urine bottle could have overflowed; in that case the sheets would need to be changed immediately or Dad might catch cold.

Suddenly came the piercing sound of a whistle. "Fall in! Line up!" The loudspeaker vibrated with heaven-rending tones. "To celebrate the proletarian revolutionary groups' victorious takeover of my school, a special great criticism meeting for the whole school has been called, to thoroughly expose and criticize the counterrevolutionary revisionist line!" To the din of the loudspeaker, the reform-through-labor group fell in line, walking silently and ponderously, as though to an execution ground.

During those days, if an important matter arose, or merely a sentence communicating the latest quotation,[5] a mass criticism rally was called, for a session of tormenting the "targets of dictatorship." Puti, as one of that group, felt as though humans were still controlled by ancestral gods demanding sacrifices—often great sacrifices. If the gods knew, they must surely be especially happy.

The meeting place was usually in the dining hall. Several rows of people, the school's first-rank criticism targets, were already on stage: party members from the school, political leaders, and reactionary academics. Puti saw at a glance that her father stood among them. Her aged, pale, weak, feverish father, who had just had surgery, stood there, held by two Red Guards.

"He's ill! My father is ill! He's still wearing a urine bottle!" Puti said urgently to a woman teacher in charge of the session.

"None of your tricks! You want to go up and join in too?" The Shanghai accent answered shrilly, a sound like long fingernails scraping some household container.

"I'll go in his place!" Puti said with determination.

---

5. It is understood that this refers to Mao Zedong's sayings.

Two male students instantly grabbed her arms and yelled loudly: "No disturbing the meeting!"

Those on stage had consolidated. The Red Guards pushed the "criminals'" heads down as far as they could, their two hands pulled as far as they could to the rear. People soon submitted, their heads quickly touching the ground. Only Mei Lian, no matter how he was pushed, could not bend down. "The bottle, the bottle," he muttered feebly, as he stumbled to the floor. Cuffs and kicks fell like raindrops on the old man's body. "Bring a whip, see if he'll get up!" Then a female's high-pitched tone began to yell slogans; the piercing hate-filled sound clutched at all hearts. "Down with counterrevolutionaries! Sweep away all class enemies! Carry out the great proletarian cultural revolution to the end!"

Indeed, all had been done in the name of the revolution. Mei Lian did not get up. He had thought he had the strength to go on living, but he was actually very feeble, unable to withstand the insults of thrashing. He did not get up again.

As he was brought into a room at the school infirmary, he was near life's end. There, in a flash of awareness before dying, his last thought was: "Men—they are indeed frail."

Septicemia rapidly spread throughout his body. As he fell into a coma he spoke deliriously: "*Ci . . . Ci!* Little Ti . . . Little Ti . . ." He called the two names over and over. He continued to murmur frequently. Puti heard a couple of phrases that sounded as though they had come from the *Book of History:* "I have a good wine vessel, and you and I will divide it," meaning "I have good wine, I'll share it with you." And, "It's going to finish soon, it's going to finish soon." Puti used a damp towel to wipe away the cold sweat pouring from his face, and whispered comfortingly.

With Puti's painstaking care, his life was prolonged a few days. But on January 25, in the deep of night, with the north wind howling violently and the window lattice shaking, he began to breathe in agonized heavings, the tragic effort of a man approaching the end to hold fast to life. Puti, her face bathed in tears, opened the door to find help. Directly before her in the corridor sat a large black cat, its lime-colored eyes gleaming. When she and an exceedingly reluctant doctor returned to the sick room, her father had already breathed his last.

"Now there is only me." Puti was still gazing at the jar of ashes polished to shining. She rose slowly. "Only me, and I am not going to live either. . . ."

The door opened gently, and Tao Huiyun came in. She seemed to have resolved before entering to leave the day's worries outside the door; her withered, wrinkled, and gaunt face wore the exhausted but smiling expression of Huiyun.

"How's it going? Do you know the results?"

"It's definite." Puti handed her the injection sheet. On it indeed was written: "Breast cancer, live test."

Tao Huiyun opened her already oversized eyes wide and stared at Puti's verdict; the "cancer" character's three mouths[6] leapt up compellingly before her. "It's not often a doctor writes that clearly." Having seized the pretext, she let the point rest for a long time. Suddenly she raised her head and burst out: "If I could only have this illness instead of you! I'm willing!"

Puti, moved, looked at her, was silent for a moment, and then said comfortingly, with a smile: "Perhaps I can win. I believe people should prevail over disease, not disease over people." She remembered the cancer cells' fiendish appearance, and quickly turned her gaze out the window, resting it on the strange vertical rock. "Who knows what will happen? But I believe . . ."

She rose, leaning against the table, and appeared to study the rock in the dusk. "People should be the strong ones."

---

6. The Chinese character for cancer contains three *kou* or mouth characters.

# 2

# Hidden Grass

THEY WERE SILENT FOR A LONG TIME. PUTI CONTINUED TO LOOK OUT the window at the rock. Although the dim light of dusk was not easily penetrated, the rock was still discernible, standing tall and straight, its beautiful outline as clear as always. Gazing thoughtfully, Puti suddenly cried softly: "Tao Hui!" This was the name Tao Huiyun was commonly known by. Puti used it as well. "Look! Can it be that the Everlasting Rock described in my book was like that?"

Huiyun, startled, quickly took careful measure of the rock: "Perhaps. I hadn't thought of that."

"I've been living here half a year and I, too, only just thought of it. You know, the tradition of the Everlasting Rock was originally a eulogy of friendship—of course, there are people who say it is superstitious propaganda."

"All the same I feel that your version of the love story is a good one. I've really liked that book of yours right up till now," Huiyun said sincerely.

"I've paid such a high price!" Puti grimaced in bewilderment.

The book known as *The Everlasting Rock* was the main reason Puti had become a "class enemy."

The two friends of Spoon Court had been acquainted for many years but had had only casually friendly encounters. Although both had worked continuously at Y University, they had belonged to two different circles. Mei Puti had originally been an outstanding student in the Western Languages Department. Because of the scholarly influence of her family, she also knew the Chinese classics. After she graduated from school, as a result of her interests, she had taught in the Chinese Department, serving concurrently as a Party general branch committee member.

In the 1950s this kind of person belonged to both the "red" and "expert" categories, and was quite highly thought of. She herself had been filled with a love of life, filled with faith in the Communist cause, respecting the Party as if it were her father and mother, always trying to reform herself, to work hard. By 1957 her fellow students had one by one all married off. Attending their weddings, she had discovered for the first time that there was a three-day wedding leave, which she thought exceedingly strange: how could one spend three days' working time to go on wedding leave! Wasn't that frittering away one's time?

However, Puti was at heart a person of feeling, often dreaming of a perfect love. In 1956 during the great mass fervor of the Hundred Flowers, she chanced to publish *The Everlasting Rock*, a novel adapted from an ancient legend. The original legend was from the Tang dynasty and was about Li Yuan's taking the Buddhist monk, Yuan Guan, as an intimate friend.[1] After Yuan Guan's death, he was reincarnated as an ordinary man and, unaware of his former role, met Li Yuan beside a large rock in Hangzhou. The rock thus became known as "the everlasting rock." In this district there was some superstitious belief in the Buddhist *samsara*, or transmigration of souls. But Puti had discarded this aspect of the story and just written about two friends' loyal and steadfast love, unswerving in life or death, love that looked forward to eternal life together, and thus the story's title: *The Everlasting Rock*.

Soon after the story's publication, before the great cudgel fell, it was criticized as a "bourgeois theory of human nature," making "personal love supreme," and "undermining the foundation of socialist society." Puti herself believed that she had problems arising from erroneous thinking about art and literature, emotions that were not healthy. She had often criticized herself in her teaching and research unit. Her colleagues of many years knew her and after a while had stopped criticizing her. However, she had been less busily involved in her department at school, her social activities had been far fewer, and she no longer held the post of Party general branch committee member. By nature indifferent to fame and fortune, she had simply given up writing while continuing to engage seriously in teaching and research. She had remained in the respected professional circles of the Party; life at that time was still a splendid garland from which she could day by day select blossoms. But in the wake of the criticism her heart had gradually hardened. She was no longer sentimental.

---

1. The story seems to refer to two men.

She would no longer tremble and bow her head before "engrossing poems," or with grieving heart gasp in admiration. She tried hard to find "limitations" in poems. Hearing those tunes that could move one to tears, her now-experienced heart grew quite impenetrable to the waves of "melody."

Things being so, she still had not been able to "transcend life," life's great unseen hand ultimately directing the road to the grave. Puti felt that a traveler on this road, even while still alive, was shown a glimmering of the hardships of hell. During these years, what had changed least in Puti's life was her appearance. The traces left by time on her looks did not nearly match the many scars left by the world on her spirit. Despite having passed most of the year in suffering, she looked not yet thirty, although she was already thirty-eight.

Tao Huiyun's life had taken a totally different course, a path on which the sufferings of existence were like land mines, lying hidden until the time came for them to explode. Now forty-eight, she looked as if she were approaching sixty. Her father had been the pampered son of a grand bourgeois household in Tianjin. Her mother had died of puerperal fever. She had been in the constant care of an old nurse who believed in the doctrines of Confucius and Mencius; she too had accepted these Confucian teachings. Her stepmother had been Spanish, so although English was what she had studied at college, later on in life she had depended on Spanish to make a living. Her husband, on the geological staff of the Resources Committee during the Kuomintang era, had fallen into a crevasse while exploring a glacier; his body was never found. Huiyun was then less than thirty. In the half year after her husband's death, she had given birth to his child. The stepmother had wanted to bring up the child, but said that if it were given to her to raise, it should remain entirely under her care; Huiyun should not concern herself with it at all. But Huiyun had asked, looking at her child in swaddling clothes: "Why should I let her raise you to become a foreigner? We're Chinese!" Alone, she thus performed both maternal and paternal duties, painstakingly raising her child to adulthood. The son naturally took his father's name of Qin; his given name was Huaisheng; this was afterward changed to Qin Ge.

Huiyun's husband, in addition to leaving her a posthumous child, also bequeathed to her the status of "wife of a suspected spy": it was alleged that some of those on the Resources Committee had been on a special mission. After Huiyun had been living as a widow for a year, several people urged her to remarry, saying that she would not only lighten the various burdens of daily life, but by so doing would also improve her political status. And everyone thought there were several suitable men. However, Huiyun avowed publicly, "I will remain the traditional widow."

When her child was in elementary school, he wrote in a composition, "Sunday morning, Daddy and Mama took me to the park," explaining that all his little friends wrote this way. Ordinarily Huiyun taught the child to be extremely accurate, but when she saw this composition, she only wiped a tear from the corner of her eye and said nothing.

Huiyun had been just an ordinary teacher. Each day she had conscientiously taught school; she was no budding talent beyond this. Torrents from the violent social storms of the period were not yet drenching her. In the personal struggles of Huiyun's department general branch secretary, according to what was said at the time, it was she herself who had "skipped out." With social relationships so complicated, she had had the audacity to stick up big-character posters, using a red brush for large calligraphy: "The general branch secretary is a good person!" Then all sorts of labels began to fly about in quick succession. Since Huiyun's parents had left China a couple of years before the Cultural Revolution to settle in Switzerland, in recent months charges began to circulate that she "had had illicit relations with a foreign country" and was a "spy." In a confession she was compelled to make, Huiyun had spoken sincerely, saying that, having considered Chairman Mao's "Ode to a Plum Blossom" carefully, one line could have a few words changed. She took the line "the precipice is already a hundred *zhang* of ice, there will be branches of pretty blossoms" and changed it to: "Just as the precipice is one hundred *zhang* of ice, there'll soon be branches of pretty blossoms."

This was sacrilegious. Huiyun's status immediately changed to that of an "active counterrevolutionary"; she was even taken under escort to the Bureau of Public Security. At this time people were brought to the Bureau of Public Security in great numbers. It was said there weren't quarters for them all. After a few days she was freed and returned to the school to be part of her department's "reform-through-labor" team.[2] Since she was considered to be an "active counterrevolutionary," she had to endure even worse conditions than the average team member.

---

2. During the Cultural Revolution, "reform-through-labor" teams were composed of people with political problems who were assigned to physical labor instead of their usual occupations.

In the daytime, those ordered to reform-through-labor cleaned toilets. When the pipes were blocked up, it was always Huiyun who stretched and shook her hand in the feces-ridden cavity. In the evenings she had to work on all sorts of strange self-criticisms cooked up just for her. She was incessantly engaged in struggle, forced to bend down several hours at a time. None of this did she take to heart: "Whoever named me Huiyun meant 'gloomy fate'!"[3] she would say, mocking herself. One day, however, her eighteen-year-old son, Qin Ge, turned against her, making a clean break. Criticizing three generations of his ancestors, putting what he considered to be a fitting hat on each, he left the house, never to return. Huiyun wept bitterly for several nights. Her thin, weak body became thinner and weaker; she looked very much like a slender blade of grass. Her face was small, her eyes large. In her youth she might have been beautiful. But, now, her face was small with withered creases, her eyes large but lifeless. These proportions did nothing to improve her appearance; they were only somewhat intimidating.

Zhang Yongjiang had always had an eye on the two-room apartment that Huiyun originally occupied. Immediately after Mei Lian's death, with the help of his cronies in the department, he drove Huiyun to Spoon Court. She was, moreover, only allowed to take the necessary items of clothing with her. Puti and Huiyun had not been neighbors very long before they were secretly congratulating themselves on their good fortune. From that brutal world, from those dirt-laden winds whipped up by knives, they only needed to come "home" to find a small, green haven where they could nurse their bruised and toil-worn spirits.

On this night neither of the occupants of the two little rooms could fall asleep. Puti counted "one, two, three, four" over and over to relax, but the more she counted the more wide awake she became. So she sat up, propped her pillow behind her, and, half leaning against the wall, opened her eyes wide toward the darkness.

"Puti! Are you asleep?" Huiyun tapped on the wall from next door.

"I can't sleep."

"I can't either."

Huiyun seemed to have gotten up. In a little while she entered Puti's room, turned on the table lamp, and sat down on the dilapidated cane chair.

---

3. This is a play on an alternate meaning of *hui yun.*

"Oh, you're already sitting up." Huiyun, still exhausted, smiled slightly. "You should have a big pillow, a big pillow sewn all around with crepe."

"The big-character poster mentioned it. It spoke of my bourgeois way of life." Puti also smiled a little, picking up her eyeglasses from beside the pillow and putting them on. "To tell the truth, I really wasn't worthy to be called a real Communist, far from it! I was a petty bourgeois—or, say, bourgeois intellectual. The changes that came about were overdue. But I never thought that the day would come when I would be seen as an 'enemy.'"

"So many old revolutionaries who have been through life-and-death struggles have been labeled counterrevolutionaries. We have not been wronged as much as some," Huiyun philosophized.

"It could be that the leadership has a lot of serious problems," Puti pondered, "and the intellectuals have many hateful points. But how can these kinds of assaults make things right? I remember when the movement hadn't been under way very long, the leading Party groups were paralyzed, and there was no one running the administration. Several meetings of Party members were held in the department. Everyone conscientiously discussed the situation, wanting to comprehend the Party's general and specific policies as best they could, in order to take on responsibilities that had to be shouldered. How I wanted to try my hardest to do a tiny bit of good for the general situation! But all of a sudden, within a few days, many of us were dragged out as enemies of the state." Puti smiled bitterly.

"It's so strange," Huiyun murmured. Like millions of Chinese, she had trusted the Party and Chairman Mao deeply. Since she and so many good people—like Puti—had become enemies of the state, her kind and honest heart could no longer comprehend what was happening.

"It's really something that puzzles me, despite much thought," Puti observed. "Now that I'm an enemy of the state, why do I also have to be an 'activist'? In fact, I have no right to be 'active.' I can only take part in writing confessions. Dad worked hard for reform. In the midst of his illness he still thought about activist work, but he didn't even have the right to have his illness treated. I hate this kind of 'revolution'! I don't want to go on reforming."

"You absolutely mustn't talk like that!" Huiyun, frightened, began shouting. "Better not think like that! Thinking won't stay hidden. At least, for people like you and me—"

"I was only letting my thoughts wander, that's all." Puti laughed without concern. "It may be I'm wrong, because the support for this revolution is great. How can I confirm that I'm right? If I really have the convictions of an enemy of the state, so be it."

"Speaking frankly . . ." Huiyun paused, then said: "I, too, feel we are like the windmills in Don Quixote's eyes, crushed to pieces for no reason."

"Windmills can be repaired," Puti thought. "And those shattered souls?"

In those days, Puti felt as though her soul lived in the midst of so many shattered glass fragments, blood flowing ceaselessly. How did it all begin? Naturally, when the storm broke, the first to bear the brunt of it had been her father. After her father's "ferreting out," many people no longer spoke to Puti, but the comradely concern of a few friends continued to brace her self-confidence. Little by little the atmosphere became heavier and more terror-laden. Sheets of big-character posters were stuck up all over the corridors: "The thousand-gold-pieces daughter of the reactionary academic authority," "Black go-getter," "The black novel *The Everlasting Rock*'s black author," and so on. Big-character captions glared angrily from the walls. The three characters "Mei Puti" were soon covered with red stab marks. When Puti saw this, she only thought mechanically, "How can they add 'black' in front of Miss Thousand-Gold-Pieces?"[4]

In the department no one dared talk to her; the best that could be had was a glimpse from the roadside—and if someone walked beside her on the road, they certainly could not look her in the eye. Finally, at a meeting of the whole department, the rebel leaders called loudly, "Mei Puti! Come forward!" Mechanically, Puti took up a position at the front of the stage; the general branch secretary of the Party was already standing there, as was the department chair and almost all the professors and several lecturers, along with an assortment of problem persons who had been brought along. Puti was still not standing steadily when a full spittoon was emptied over her head. "Some people grow tall so they can be useful like this," Puti again thought mechanically. Then a dunce cap was turned over. Below the stage loud cries were repeated: "Put it on! Grab her head!" "Teach her a lesson! Teach her a lesson!" as if only by such shouting could people demonstrate their revolutionary conviction.

Puti was not frightened. She was just not willing to have other people's hands touch her, so she crouched from the waist, shrinking into herself with all her might. Shrinking and shrinking, the four words "cannot hide from shame" suddenly came to her. The phrase

---

4. Black symbolized reactionaries.

described shame. But what had she, Puti, to be ashamed of? What had she to apologize to her country, to her people, for? What criminal law had she violated? She was just an ordinary industrious person, an honest, unpolished member of the intelligentsia, and yet it was this very humanness which was responsible for her being forced to undergo torment in purgatory.

"Mei Puti!" The sound was a great howl. "Confess your crimes!" The confession of crimes was part of the routine formula for persons "ferreted out" as Puti had been.

"In teaching I disseminated capitalist and revisionist thought," Puti said forcefully and clearly. "Disseminated capitalist and revisionist thought! You said it very glibly! You are vicious, vicious! Do you hear?" A beautiful male voice shouted with ferocious hatred. "White paper and black characters, you cannot escape!" This was the rebels' ringleader, Zhang Yongjiang, the least popular man in the department who had now become its leader.

"*The Everlasting Rock!* Remember, you wrote *The Everlasting Rock!*" The resonant sound mounted until the voice became hoarse. Puti felt she would remember the sound even when she was eighty years old. Naturally, if she lived to be eighty.

Following quickly with the program, an unstable person who had been a student for years, Qi Yongshou, climbed up onto the stage to blare out accusations. He held a copy of *The Everlasting Rock* in his hand.

Puti had helped Qi Yongshou with his schoolwork. She knew that though he was at times confused, at other times clear-headed, he was nonetheless a good person. Puti did not hear clearly what he was now saying, and thus couldn't determine if he was clear-headed or confused. She could only fix her gaze on her book, not feeling unkindly toward him. Finally, Qi Yongshou, as had been prearranged, tore the book apart with all his strength, and then ripped up the fragments, trying hard to fling them right at Puti.

"Sweep away all class enemies!" the slogan sounded in accompaniment.

From that moment on, Puti felt her spirit demolished, as her book had been, beyond restoration.

"We all still care about politics!" Huiyun, who had been looking at Puti a long while without speaking, sighed with emotion.

Indeed, concern about politics had been the achievement of many persons working for change over many years. Puti, revising the pattern of a temperament that did not seek fame or fortune, had steeled her delicate spirit to produce combative sparks—a hard-won achievement. But neither she nor anyone else had realized what awaited her: the title "enemy."

"Actually, what you should concern yourself with is just one thing," Huiyun continued.

"To cure my sickness, to go on living, right?" Puti turned toward Huiyun's small, wrinkled face. That face, under the table lamp's dim light, flashed hope with a surprising gentle radiance.

"Of course. But I was referring to marriage. You—you should have a home."

"Home!" What a lovely sound! Puti had once had a happy home, a home filled with her parents' profound boundless love, and with material comforts. She had also once longed for a home created by herself; a thousand times she had mentally arranged a place with a man. But neither past nor future made up the present. Now there was only Huiyun sitting at the dilapidated rattan table looking at her with grave concern.

If only the word "concern" were used to describe what Huiyun felt, the word was clearly inadequate: her "concern" was too deep and dedicated. From her childhood, Huiyun had loved many persons. She had loved her father and her stepmother, although they treated her with indifference. She had loved the old nurse who passed on the doctrines of Confucius and Mencius. She had even more stubbornly loved her natural mother, that being who had so early ceased to exist, that ill-fated woman cut off by Heaven who, excepting Huiyun, had left nothing behind her. On each of her mother's birthdays and on the anniversary of her death, Huiyun always tore the page from the calendar and put it safely away in an old embroidered bag, as though the thin paper represented her mother's frail life. After some years had come a fitting cremation: she burned the pages.

Huiyun loved the Communist Party. Moreover, she considered the general secretary of the department's Party branch the Party Incarnate. She loved many teachers in her department. However, beginning with the secretary of the Party branch, many people regarded Huiyun as one of the old intelligentsia. Like a factory worker of the old regime kept on after Liberation, she was clearly different from the general population, although just how was never explicitly stated. It went without saying that she loved her son, but another's feelings are often a burden to adolescent sons, let alone in such days sparing no mercy for noble moral characters! Now, her emotions, having passed through torment, physical suffering, and even greater tempering, had come to focus on Puti's life. She was mother, sister, comrade, and friend to Puti. Just as Puti was willing to exert herself to the utmost to see her country prosperous and her people at peace, so Huiyun was willing to exert herself to the utmost to shield Puti from trials and hardships. Naturally, neither succeeded.

Puti did not answer. Huiyun hesitated and finally said: "I think tomorrow evening I'll go see Han Yi."

Puti quickly sat upright: "I think that might not be necessary."

"Although he didn't come at the height of your father's illness, he did come afterward. Furthermore, your father's illness lasted a short time: you didn't write him a note."

"We still need a note!" Puti, looking at Huiyun sitting at the dilapidated rattan table, tried hard to recollect the image of Han Yi sitting before her. However, perhaps his last visit had been purely a formality (naturally it had not been easy either); she really could not think of what he had said. Perhaps he had actually not said anything much. "The relationship never reached the stage of real friendship, it will never do so," Puti added. "I have a strange idea I've forgotten for many years. Actually this isn't only an idea. . . . When I was in Chongqing one time, I went for fun to Pan Xi. In the stream there were many beautiful stones . . ." Puti turned silent: she could not clarify the recollection. Strangely, beginning she could not remember when, many beautiful past events had become hazily remote, blurred and hard to distinguish.

Huiyun waited a moment, saw that Puti was not going to speak, then, smiling a little, said: "How can it be rocks again? Be realistic. You'll meet 'Mr. Right' by chance."

Over many years Puti had become accustomed to stressful jobs; she had long since ceased to leave space for soft feelings. In the 1950s she had mistakenly seen marriage leave as a waste of time. Such sentiments had left her by the 1960s. By that time she no longer had to take part in wedding ceremonies; those who were going to marry had already done so. But without reason, in the empty spaces of life, sometimes at work, sometimes at study, she would often feel a kind of faint distress; an involuntary feeling of loneliness would envelop her.

Although Puti was nearly forty, before June of 1966 there had been several men seeking her hand and heart. After the "unprecedented Cultural Revolution," these men had one after another withdrawn. Only Han Yi was left, still keeping up a mildly friendly relationship.

Puti and Han Yi had known each other a couple of years, and had never gone beyond this mildly friendly relationship. Han Yi was a building engineer, a specialist in sheet metal construction. His interests were broad; his appearance handsome. His father, it was said, had been a famous doctor; he would be considered a good match. Many people had advised Puti to quickly seize this marriage opportunity. Puti had tried her best, but when she was with Han Yi she always felt as though he were measuring her worth from some sort of calculated posture. His pale, open, elegant face looked proudly at her and seemed to say, as though he were using some mathematical formula: "Your Party membership, professional work, looks, all make the grade; added together, they're even above average." Their time together had not been brief, but it had failed to produce that mysterious emotion to which one could entrust one's lifetime.

There were moments when Puti thought: "Can it be that my emotions have already faded away with my youth?" When this thought came to her she felt a kind of dread, as though, looking into her own warm and sensitive heart under its layers of protective calluses, she could see the resplendent colors of flesh and blood slowly withering away.

Puti was sitting upright. Darkness shrouded the little courtyard; the outlines of the Everlasting Rock had become blurred. A damp, cold wind blew in through the door jamb. Looking idly out of the window, she sighed deeply. "There's already enough reality, too much reality. My soul's long since turned worldly-wise; it can't give out radiance. It is callous. My heart is hard. I am infected with this disease."

"Oh!" Huiyun uttered the sound she made when she was dissatisfied, but quickly covered her mouth, so as not to startle Puti. She paused a little, then said gently: "How can you talk like that! You're a person who knows a lot about emotions. Love can become the expression of a melody; it was just with me that it became a dirge!"

"A dirge?" Puti felt her heart contract. It was a new thought. "A dirge is sacred," she murmured.

"A dirge can't be altered." Huiyun's great eyes shone faintly in the lamplight, the soft glow of her face becoming focused in her eyes, transforming her expression into one of both bitterness and determination. "That was my pledge. On my wedding night, we both pledged. At that time, work on geological explorations seemed as dangerous as flying. My pledge was: if I didn't have a child, on the day he died I would die. If I had a child, come what might, I would raise that child."

Tears started from Puti's eyes and coursed down her cheeks. The child had been raised, but where was he? Could the white bones in that bottomless crevasse know of Huiyun's present bitter fate or of the child's whereabouts?

They fell silent for quite a while. Then Huiyun said softly: "Have I made you sad? I certainly want to go and have a talk with Han Yi. Don't worry about it! I, I only wish you happiness!"

Puti, feeling touched, could not bring herself to answer. Perhaps if Huiyun could make that effort, she might feel better. Best let her go. Huiyun gently switched off the table lamp, opened the door, and said briefly: "It's raining—rest," then quietly pulled the door to behind her.

The sound of the raindrops filled the little room; through chinks in the window tiny currents of chilly air blew in.

Early the next morning when Puti opened her door, a clean, cold, moist gust of wind blew into her face, raising her spirits. In the moonlight, mist enveloped the branches of the willow tree outside the courtyard gate and the pond reeds in a shroud of thin smoke. Glancing here and there about the small court, Puti noticed that a layer of dark green bryophyte had sprung up overnight on the damp earth. She suddenly thought of the words from the poem of Du Xunhe: "One rain has turned the fishing-place into a layer of moss." Indeed, beneath the frosty knives of ice lay the spring days to come. In the cracks on the crooked stone steps, tiny sprouts of green grass had appeared.

# 3

# Burning the
# Manuscripts

O N THE THIRD DAY AFTER PUTI HAD BEEN DIAGNOSED, HER DEPARTMENT
ordered her to go at once to the office supervising the department's role in the Cultural Revolution.[1] Beginning in January, those
modeling themselves on the Shanghai pattern had seized power in
one unit after another. In clinics the takeover resulted in such re-
fusals to give treatment as Mei Lian had experienced. At Y University it resulted in severe supervision, disciplining, and denunciation
of all sorts of "class enemies." In this state of affairs Mei Lian's was of
course not the only life ruined. The Chinese Department at Y University was under the rebels' control; the takeover there had facili-
tated Zhang Yongjiang's becoming first in command of the rebels'
group.

When Puti arrived in the department she saw only Zhang Yongjiang and two other persons sitting in the room that was originally
the office of the general secretary of the Party branch. One of them
was a teacher of modern literature. His professional work was said to
be quite outstanding. Because for many years he had taken the bus
without buying tickets, he had been detained for investigation; however, this had provided him with important evidence with which to
denounce the Legal Department. The other person was Zhang
Yongjiang's wife, data-gatherer Shi Qingping. She thought that for
her to be only a data-gatherer was a grave injustice. With the beginning of the Cultural Revolution she displayed her talents to the full,

---

1. At the beginning of the Cultural Revolution in 1966, such supervisory
offices took control in many work units.

accusing, pasting up expository big-character posters all over the walls. She signed her name as Shi Qingping.[2]

At that time Puti still did not know where this new signatory had come from; only after a time did she find out this was Shi Qingping's new name. Shi's figure was emaciated, like a perpendicular stick. Zhang Yongjiang's was just the opposite: he was heavy. Recently he had put on even more weight. He now sat ponderously in his chair.

"Sit down." Zhang Yongjiang spoke with apparent friendliness.

Puti answered: "I'm used to standing."

Zhang Yongjiang, knowing that Puti had consistently been insubordinate, did not argue. He only said coldly: "In that case, stand. The clinic has sent notice that you're to enter this afternoon. I now admonish you, representing the leaders and masses of the Cultural Revolution! Your crimes are serious. You have persisted in Mei Lian's reactionary position. You yourself have given much currency to poisonous ideas and up till now have not clearly justified yourself. After you've been to the clinic, you won't be permitted to speak or act carelessly. The self-criticism and confession will continue; we'll still criticize and denounce you as the occasion demands! Do you hear?"

Puti, also looking coldly at Zhang Yongjiang, felt it would have been better to have the wooden block ancient judges had used to maintain order. The bellowed-out words "Do you hear?" had the same impact as the clap of the wooden block.

"The instruction is finished!" The teacher of modern literature now took the role of the wooden block.

"I don't have money to go to the clinic." Puti hadn't finished from her side. "My money was all taken by you people; I've only had living expenses for each month."

"If you don't have money, that's your problem!" Shi Qingping's Shanghai accent rang out; the shrill voice made one shudder. "You're still so arrogant! Do you think we're afraid of you? That we can't punish you?"

"You, too, need the wooden block," Puti thought.

But Zhang Yongjiang changed his wife's course, saying: "You can borrow from the accountant!"

So Puti "borrowed" two hundred yuan and went home. On the way she met more than one acquaintance, but no one hailed her or greeted her. Passing by the lake, she ran head-on into the teacher of

---

2. The last two characters, written differently but with the same sound, could mean "celebrate peace." She changed them to mean "green apple."

ancient Chinese: Zheng Liming. He was on a bicycle; after looking to the right and the left and seeing no one, he turned the bicycle around, first riding into a grove of trees. Waiting until Puti walked by, he said: "I've heard you're ill?"

Puti raised her eyes to look at him and nodded.

"You should be careful." Zheng Liming had originally been Puti's fellow student. In 1949 he had enlisted in the army, gone south, then later returned to teach. To date, no charge had been made against him, so he was still part of the revolutionary masses.

"Things are very confused right now; anything can happen. Several days ago Qi Yongshou made a comment to Zhang Yongjiang; he got a thrashing."

"What should one be especially careful about?" Puti asked.

"There isn't any special thing." Zheng Liming again looked right and left. "Only you absolutely must not write in a diary or suchlike. Any bit of writing can be used to frame a charge. Take care of yourself." As he spoke he mounted the bicycle and rode off, the trees soon hiding his swaying silhouette.

Puti, however, was quite calm. She began pondering how matters had developed. Zhang, Shi, the two really hated her to the marrow of her bones; that was common knowledge. At the time of the 1962 teachers' promotions, among Zhang Yongjiang's proclaimed literary works had been a research paper on the *Elegies of Chu*.[3] The paper had been beyond his academic level, undeniably a plagiarism—and discovered by Puti. The Puti of that time had not been able to remain silent.

"Am I too rigid?" Puti said to herself on the road. "No, as far as Zhang Yongjiang is concerned, I was right. But why is that type of person so self-satisfied? Does one have to be involved in political trickery to engage in politics? In the kind of situation we have now, if those who come to the front are not blockheads, they are cheats!" When this great traitorous idea rose in her mind she immediately glanced left and right, to see if anyone had noticed her silent thought.

"How can I prove these opinions are correct? I am powerless. I— am dying." Puti fixed a frustrated look on the still bleak and desolate reed pond. Someone was just dumping garbage beside the pond at the front of Spoon Court.

---

3. A famous anthology of poems attributed to Chu Yuan (340–278 B.C.E.) of the Warring States Period.

When she came in the gate she, like her father, unconsciously glanced at the two characters "Spoon Court" engraved on the bricks. This tiny Spoon Court! For how many years, how many, many people had lived there, had died there. Like her father, like herself, like the cracks in the stone steps, like the little patches of grass under the scattered coal cinders. Green moss! Green grass! When her father was alive, they had still not appeared; now all were there. Seductive greenery breathing fresh life had sprung up, spread tendrilled vines and dyed the whole world, bringing spring! But Puti was about to depart.

It was only necessary to take a few things to the hospital: Puti was ready quickly. There was just one matter she wanted to arrange before leaving. Zheng Liming's words had strengthened her resolve. She stood a moment in the courtyard, then, pulling out a coal shovel by the handle, she unlatched the yard gate, and began to dig in the place where the lilacs had grown. As she dug, a slimy paper package appeared from the muddy ground.

Puti carefully undid the wrapping. Actually, there wasn't the slightest need for such solicitude. Inside were her writings, familiar writings that summed up her life. One was the manuscript of *The Everlasting Rock*, which had produced such disaster for her. She herself often wondered how those tiny character traces could have had such an overwhelmingly powerful effect, so that ten years before so many readers had written to her pouring out their feelings. She did not know what had happened to these deeply moved people; she wished they had not been involved. Another manuscript was an unpublished novelette, *The Roc's First Move*, its subject the life of a group of students before graduation. After experiencing all sorts of intellectual struggles and psychic twists and turns, these had finally spread their wings to fly where their motherland needed them. But now? Would their wings have been broken in the stormy skies of the motherland?

The third manuscript was a 180,000-character literary biography, *The Life of Su Shi*.[4] Puti deeply loved Su Shi's writings and admired his genius. For example, she meticulously described Xuzhou's river and water control, Dingzhou's military exercises. In bygone days, she had once joked: "If Su Shi were alive, I'd marry him." But Su Shi could not live again, and Puti herself was leaving the world.

---

4. Su Shi (C.E. 1037–1101) was a writer and painter of the Northern Song dynasty.

"My whole life I haven't met anyone like my Ding Po."[5] Puti picked up the manuscript, a kind of bemused regret arising within her.

The fourth manuscript was a paper discussing the works of the Austrian writer Kafka, relating him to a Danish philosopher. Puti, turning over several pages, suddenly felt as though she were in another world. How could she have criticized that morbid writer as she had? He described without inhibition the depths of despair felt by people with no way out. Was it only after she herself had no way out that she could understand him?

It was decided, why deliberate? The novel, the biography, the treatise, her thoughts and emotions, what she had loved and what she had hated, what she had suffered and what she had enjoyed—she would commit them all to the flames, to become mere ashes and smoke.

Puti, trembling all over and holding the manuscripts in both hands, stood beside the Everlasting Rock. She had not been a mother, but she felt that the manuscripts were the children she had borne, her very flesh and blood. Who does not love her own flesh and blood? Who does not want to leave her flesh and blood in the world even unto eternity? She, nevertheless, was about to execute her own flesh and blood.

Wouldn't leaving them behind enable people to sit in judgment of her, with their bloody criminal accusations? Wouldn't it enable people to take her crystallized heart's blood to make her cross? No! She would rather die than allow her bones and blood to be abused in this way. There was only one way: she must destroy first!

Puti struck a match, first igniting the manuscript of *The Everlasting Rock*. The image of that young pair of friends had long ago become part of people's memories. Let it have another baptism in the fire's blaze! Soon the other three manuscripts were also dropped into the curling red tongues of the burning pyre. Puti's tears flowed drop by drop onto her jacket front as she gazed at the black ashes still shaped like sheets of paper in the leaping flames. Could they become phoenixes after nirvana? Could they triumph over death and be resurrected as butterflies?[6] How could they? There was only the destruction, only the finality of the ashes. Ashes drifted out of the

---

5. Another name for Su Shi.
6. This calls to mind a well-known Chinese folk tale in which two young lovers become butterflies after death.

little courtyard, some even settling on Puti's hair. Her shining jet-black hair lifted lightly in the draft from the flames, sparks from the papers' ashes flashing against its beauty.

The courtyard gate opened. Huiyun entered, a letter in her hand. The little withered face brimmed with concern and astonishment: "How could you burn these things up so high-handedly? If they find out, it could give them a handle to grab hold of, even keep your illness from being treated!" As she spoke, she reached out her hand to pick the ashes from Puti's hair.

"Do I still have something to fear?" Puti murmured, raising a face bathed in tears.

"Have a look at this letter." Huiyun hopefully, anxiously, and fearfully handed over the letter. It was from Han Yi. Huiyun had gone to visit him two days before, had told him Puti had cancer, had—it seemed—begged him to give Puti some psychological support. Han Yi had expressed polite concern and had sent the letter.

"Oh." Puti glanced at the envelope indifferently. "You read it." As a matter of fact, Huiyun wanted to read it. . . .

"I don't feel like it." Puti continued to poke at the fire, already almost burned out.

Huiyun at once ripped open the envelope, and holding the letter, read: "Puti: I know you have contracted cancer. I'm very concerned, very sorry. My perils are also numerous. I could possibly stir up trouble for you. I can't come to see you anymore. Take care of yourself. Han Yi."

The two characters for "comrade" had originally appeared at the beginning of the letter after "Puti." Han Yi probably knew Puti was no longer a comrade and had wiped them away; the wiping traces were still visible.

"Oh." Puti, still indifferent, glanced at the letter.

"Men, how can they be so rotten, so cruel!" Huiyun, struggling to hold back her tears, tore the letter to pieces and threw it in the fire.

Puti, turning gracefully, nimbly picked out the torn pieces of paper and threw them in the garbage can.

"The letter would burn to ashes, and dirty my manuscripts," she explained in a low voice, smiling gently at Huiyun.

"You have a weakness for cleanliness, I know," Huiyun said with disappointment. "You have ideals, you can't bear filth or foulness, I know—"

"But the big-character posters all said I had a 'filthy soul.'" Puti continued to tidy the pile of ashes. The fire had gone out.

"I don't understand! I really don't understand!" Huiyun helped Puti bury the pile of ashes. "You—don't think of anything but concentrating on curing your illness, curing your illness! You must make up your mind to go on living!"

"I want to live. Only alive can one know whether or not one's thought is really 'out-and-out reactionary.'" Puti looked calmly at the manuscript grave. She gazed for a while, then went into her room, took down the jar containing her father's ashes, and hugged it to her. Stroking the jar, she seemed to be stroking her father's emaciated arms. She even unconsciously put the jar to her ear to listen, saying slowly to Huiyun, "It looks as if it won't be possible to bury Dad and Mother together. If I die, find a place to put Dad—Xiang Shan,[7] the Cherry Dale, even in the school yard; there are many good places."

"You're going to come back! Going to come back!" Huiyun had only these words to say. Her eyes had long since filled with tears, her pale lips quivered uncontrollably.

"I won't necessarily die on the operating table. But it's hard to say what'll come after," Puti said thoughtfully. "Your situation is even harder, but if you just have a chance, if by any chance I . . ." She didn't go on.

"You . . . will come back—"

"I'll come back, I'll come back." Puti, smiling slightly, repeated Huiyun's words. Internally, she cried loudly: "I will live! I will live!"

In the afternoon, the Western Languages Department held a criticism meeting. Huiyun had to go to be criticized and naturally could not ask for leave. Puti, carrying her blue cloth holdall with a package of miscellaneous items in one hand and a thermos in the other, left for the hospital alone.

---

7. Fragrant Hills, a famous scenic area near Beijing.

# 4

# The Ward

⟹

QUOTATIONS HUNG ON ALL FOUR WALLS IN THE SURGICAL WARD LOUNGE of Z hospital. As one entered, the unusually large characters of the quotation on the right-hand wall, encased on all four sides in a wooden frame and occupying the entire wall, mandated attention. This quotation was: "Men all must die, but the significance of each death is different . . ."[1]

A graceful figure wearing rimless gold eyeglasses, a woman still youthful, stood in the middle of the lounge looking the quotations up and down. She continued to carry a holdall and a cotton bundle in one hand and a thermos in the other. She was waiting for the nurse to assign her a room, and turned her head frequently to look out of the lounge toward the nurses' desk in the corridor, where no one had appeared for twenty minutes.

Puti stood in this manner for a while, then looked for a seat with a view of the nurses' desk. The awesome quotation occupying the wall also occupied her mind. "Men all must die," she mused. "Men all must die—however, if they die from cancer, it can be taken as lightly as a goose-feather." This realization came to her suddenly. A thought then flashed. "If I had charge of this room, I'd write: 'Live on, you may see the truth.' Peaceful landscapes would hang beside." This heretical opinion caused her to feel surprised and frustrated. "This is thinking foolishly. . . . All right, this proves I have plenty of courage to go on living. . . ."

---

1. The quotation is from a famous funeral oration of Mao Zedong in which he stated that the death of a humble patriot was weightier than Mount Tai, while the death of one not serving the nation could be taken as lightly as a feather.

A white-jacketed form flashed past outside the door. Puti stopped meditating and walked quickly to the front of the nurses' desk. A plump nurse of about forty was just about to sit down with several voices already calling her: "Sister[2] Huo! Sister Huo, come here!"

Puti hurriedly handed over the hospitalization card. Sister Huo glanced at it, looked Puti over, and asked: "Your family background?"[3] as she picked up a pen and bent down to write on the hospitalization card.

"Professor." Puti had researched Party documents in an effort to deal with this "problem" of her family background. "Professors," belonging to an independent occupation, could loosely be called "staff persons," but when Puti, in a routine assessment of her family background, had used the term, she had brought down upon herself fierce accusations that she was concealing her class status. After that she had always said "professor," although using the word usually provoked needless difficulties.

"Oh . . . ," Sister Huo said in a rising tone, as if to say "It's obvious you are not a good person." She raised her head and glanced at Puti, then asked, bending over to write: "The problem?"

"What problem?" Puti deliberately retorted.

Sister Huo's expression became serious, and on the left side of her forehead a red mark suddenly appeared. She put down the pen. Just at that moment the slight, pretty form of a nurse squeezed past, saying: "Bed 30's veins are very hard to find. Dr. Fang wants you to go. The needle's still not in. It won't be finished tonight and there's no one watching him." Speaking, she gently pushed plump Sister Huo out, and herself sat down at the desk.

This nurse's complexion was fair and clear; she looked like she was in her twenties. At the desk she first rummaged about a bit, then said to Puti, "The medical record hasn't come yet. First go to the ward, Room 308, Bed 2." Still with the appearance of doing official business according to official principles, she smiled a faint, almost invisible, smile, then went to deal with someone else.

"At last, I can go and settle down." The bag in Puti's hand and the warm thermos suddenly felt indescribably heavy.

Room 308 faced south, with good light. Four beds were ranged side by side in the room. Counting from the door, the first and third

---

2. The use of "Sister" as a form of address is common in China.

3. During the Cultural Revolution, family background was a person's primary identifying category.

beds had patients lying on them. The last bed, against the wall, was also obviously occupied: On a little table at the head of the bed were books and orange juice, and the quilt was turned down; hanging over the foot of the bed was an old wool sweater. Puti went over to the empty Bed 2, and slowly put down her things, sitting on the edge of the bed.

One of the patients called out to her in a friendly way: "Where are you sick, girl?" This was an older woman from the countryside, with shriveled skin, white hair, and a kindly face.

"I have breast cancer." Puti smiled. "And Aunt?"[4]

"Me? It's my lungs are bad. Actually nothing to shout about. It's just that I've coughed some blood."

"Aunt looks on the bright side," the person in Bed 3 volunteered. She looked forty-plus, her face dark of complexion or by circulation. "Not like me. I'm nothing but anxious." Then she introduced her illness: "Mine is cancer of the nose and pharynx. This is the second time I've been in the hospital; they've already done surgery. For the second time."

Puti couldn't refrain from carefully studying her face, but couldn't make out anything.

"Breast cancer isn't serious. As long as it's discovered early, it can be cured." The person in Bed 3 gave friendly comfort.

"How is it no one brought you? Did you come to the hospital by yourself?" After a while, the older woman, seeing Puti continuing to sit alone, questioned her solicitously.

"There's no one at home anymore," Puti said simply. The older woman questioned no further. Not from politeness, but out of sincere concern; she feared to stir up painful memories.

It didn't take ten minutes for Puti to know that the older woman's name was Wei, that she was from a nearby farm village of Huairou County, that she had been in the hospital four days, and that they had not yet decided whether to operate on her. The woman about Puti's age was named Qi; she was a housewife who often did temporary jobs at Y University, and her husband worked in the district court. The results of her second surgery had not been good; her head ached badly. There was another wardmate, also a teacher, who had rectal cancer; ten days after surgery, she was doing well. "She

---

4. A common Chinese term of respect for an older woman, translated here as "aunt."

knows a lot, she knows how to take care of herself. . . . Whatever has gone bad, can be controlled," the older woman said.

Just as they were speaking of her, the wardmate came in. This person's figure was well proportioned; although she was middle-aged, she was still pretty, except for her deathly pallor. Looking closely at her, Puti was startled: this was Cui Zhen, from the university's Biology Department!

Cui Zhen was also astonished: "Mei Puti! You have cancer too!" Knowing Puti's situation, she said: "You should have a correct attitude toward illness. Don't be afraid. I didn't worry a bit. I got well quickly." When Cui Zhen spoke, she always sounded like an instructor. "Rectal cancer is much more troublesome than breast cancer— excrement is a real headache. By my way of thinking, this is a struggle, too. Cancer is really a class enemy!" Cui Zhen's comment was in dead earnest.

Puti was not well acquainted with Cui Zhen. She only knew she was celebrated for being strict with herself; in other words, she had long been reputed to be heartless and cold. After the Cultural Revolution she had done several things to keep up with the times and was said to be famous among her peers. Cui Zhen's husband had been Party general branch secretary of the Biology Department; after he was exposed to criticism she quickly divorced him. At that time the court, somewhat confused and disoriented before the rising tempest, said it must seek advice from a higher authority and withheld approval. Cui Zhen upbraided the court: to withhold approval was to take a capitalist-road position; she wanted to appeal to the Party. Without knowing whether she had actually appealed, the court quickly gave approval. After this the general branch secretary committed suicide by hanging himself from a beam.

The department had held a special criticism meeting, inviting each department to bring persons undergoing reform-through-labor to attend, so as to let them know that death could not balance the score. Puti was also present on that grand occasion. A crude and simple cinerary casket had been placed on an ordinary teaching desk; behind the casket was a vertical white paper streamer, and on it in great black characters was written: "Death to unrepentant capitalist-roader Chen Huan!" Only after a time had Puti realized that this was a denunciation of the dead man. Having been transformed into ashes, the battle must continue even into decomposition. One by one, impassioned speeches shot like arrows toward the dead Chen Huan. Last on the program was to be Chen Huan's daughter, Chen Li, criticizing her father. But as the time approached, she was nowhere to be found; the upshot was that Cui Zhen herself gave

forth with a speech, loosing a flood of invective against her husband
of twenty years, as if she yearned to have him die over again. Many
people at the meeting could not hold back their tears. It wasn't clear
whether they were moved by her principles or by sympathetic feelings for the dead man aroused by her callousness. Toward the close
of the meeting those in charge had scrutinized each person's face attentively. Anyone with a hint of tears was penalized with two hours
of standing. Puti was naturally among these.

Now when Puti heard Cui Zhen speak she felt touched again. Expressions of mutual sympathy between the ill arise out of the living
experience. She could not, however, think of anything to say. To
make conversation she looked at the books at the head of Cui Zhen's
bed: "You're still reading so many books!"

"Naturally. Why not read?" Cui Zhen got into bed, took up an anthology of Marx and Engels, and stretched out unconcernedly, as
though on display. As she picked up the book, she instantaneously
gave her whole attention to it. Those beside her looked at her ex-
pectantly, thinking she would make some comment. After a while she
said to herself: "Xiao[5] Li still hasn't come. She promised to bring
Red Guard newspapers." Her daughter had already changed her
name from Chen Li to Cui Li.

"Xiao Li is a good girl," Aunt Wei enthused. "She's good-
natured."

Cui Zhen immediately spoke up: "Aunt, don't talk personality. In
fact, I dislike Xiao Li's softness; she has no spunk."

Elder Sister[6] Qi scoffed: "Really, Aunt, don't say she's good-
natured. These days, only good nature turned a bit evil is of any use."
She added: "If you're talking about good nature, Dr. Fang is great,
one in a hundred. He hasn't forgotten that a doctor should treat the
sick! But I think he, too, is out of favor."

"I just hope Dr. Fang operates on me." Aunt started to cough as
she spoke, and lightly thumped herself on the chest.

Cui Zhen agreed that Dr. Fang had the proper professional standards and sense of responsibility. "But his principles are not strong."
She discussed principles. Patients discuss doctors much the way students discuss teachers.

-----

5. "Xiao" is a common form of address for young people, meaning
"young" or "little."

6. This term, in Chinese, refers to a woman only slightly older than
oneself.

Puti only listened; she had no right to speak. But a calm and profound gaze arose before her eyes, a pale face nevertheless wearing a very serene and kindhearted expression. She wanted to ask whether Dr. Fang also looked at outpatients, but just then a nurse popped her head in the door and called Puti to come to the examining room.

Seated in the examining room was the very Fang Zhi who had seen Puti as an outpatient. When Puti saw him, a feeling of happiness flowed through her like water from a spring. She said spontaneously: "Dr. Fang is on the ward, I am reassured!"

Dr. Fang smiled slightly at Puti in a friendly way and said briefly: "That day I saw outpatients, I was substituting." Then he began a skillful, unhurried examination. After asking pertinent questions, and finally writing in her chart, he said: "Your tumor is at the side. The best thing would be to do radical surgery going beyond it; otherwise we're not safe." Seeing Puti looking at him in bewilderment, he explained: "That is, we need to cut out three ribs and remove the lymph nodes in the breast, to take care of any hidden tumor cells."

"The doctor knows what should be done, so let it be done," Puti answered directly.

"But won't you discuss it with your family?" Fang Zhi took out a form and placed it on the desk. Puti, as she was in the habit of doing, closed her eyes. Behind her lenses these became two curved arcs, her eyelashes lowered, as though she wanted to block the entry of questions from the outside world into her inner depths. This was an expression she often wore when thinking deeply. Usually she also gently closed her mouth, while on her cheeks a careful little smile appeared. This time, however, her expression turned completely to one of perplexity, of suffering. She thought of Huiyun. Huiyun was now her parent, sister, close friend, the closest person in the world to her. But if it came to filling in a form, she didn't even count. Why add to her worries? She was already overburdened with her own concerns.

"Discuss what? I have faith in you, Dr. Fang." Puti's voice quivered a bit. She raised her eyes and looked at Dr. Fang, her look full of unaffected trust.

Fang Zhi coughed slightly and said: "That's good. In that case we are all set. But we still need to have a record of your family members; you need to put them down." Speaking apologetically, he pushed the form toward Puti. It was a form for surgery. On it one item asked for the names of family members.

Puti also coughed slightly, and quickly asked: "Can I sign myself? I don't have any family."

According to professional custom, Dr. Fang would have countered with: "In that case, get your unit to sign." However, he did not speak, but only looked hesitantly and sympathetically at Puti, his gaunt face betraying an almost tragic expression. His eyes, accustomed to looking at blood, scars, and the gleam of knives, seemed to see how Puti had walked a bloodstained path to arrive at the clinic. He said nothing further, but quickly took the surgical list and said simply: "We'll try to do it the day after tomorrow."

Puti stood up, smiling gratefully at Fang Zhi. Fang Zhi, however, looked away. Puti almost rejoiced that she had a serious illness, since in her illness she could depend on the doctor. To fall ill and have a doctor she could trust felt so harmonious, so good. Her shattered and rudderless world of the spirit, centering on the disease, slowly began to right itself.

She went back to the sickroom, took up a pillow, and sat down on the bed. By now both Elder Sister Qi's husband—a wizened little old man—and Cui Zhen's daughter, a blooming young girl, were in the room. Everyone looked on as Puti settled herself, waiting for her report on her time with the doctor. Everyone who saw a doctor had to report on her return: this, it seemed, was the sickroom pattern.

Puti deferred to this custom as a matter of course, although no one told her to do so. Elder Sister Qi spoke up right away:

"Don't be afraid. Surgery doesn't hurt at all. I've been cut into two times. Compared to the drudgery of the temporary work at your school, it's much easier to bear." As she spoke to Puti, her gaze never left her husband. "So it goes! I had to help out with family finances from time to time!" Her husband, smiling good-naturedly, rubbed her temples.

"I'm not afraid of hard work. But our family is always getting sick. The son in the countryside with his grandfather died first. Plenty of money was spent, but there was no cure. The other son got to college after much difficulty. He hadn't been there long when some nervous disease made him deranged." Elder Sister Qi spoke in a tragic tone.

Old Qi explained: "He is still aware, sometimes. Sometimes confused. Has it been several days since Teacher Mei's minor operation?" He changed the subject.

"Then you won't need a minor operation first." Cui Zhen cut Puti off, and rushed to say authoritatively: "Has it been ten days since your minor operation? During that time it's easy for it to spread. Cancer cells are very tenacious, they aren't expelled from where they settle. I've had time to think about it: we need to struggle, we need to be as stubborn as the cancer cells." As she spoke, her daughter sat by her bedside, her young face wearing a timid, anxious look. In those days such a look wasn't often seen on the faces of young people.

"As the cancer cells"—Puti felt a slight psychological shock. When thinking of the cancer cells' fiendish appearance under the microscope, she, too, felt a sense of terror. She closed her eyes, and tried hard to concentrate on the normal cells' appearance, seeking to draw strength from that benign image. Cui Zhen was probably knowledgeable on the subject, but Puti simply did not want to discuss it with her.

Now a Liberation Army soldier of about twenty came into the room, two thermoses in each hand, and placed one at the head of each bed. Cui Zhen, busy reading a tabloid, paid no heed. Old Qi stood up smiling: "You're helping again today."[7] Puti immediately gave her thanks. The older woman said, "Such formality! Let him do." So Puti knew this was her son Xiao Wei.

Elder Sister Qi smiled admiringly. "To have that kind of son would be very reassuring!"

The older woman said "I'm not reassured. Our second son's not on track; he's twenty-odd, still hasn't married—" Perhaps Xiao Wei didn't like listening; he interrupted: "Ma, I'm going to look for the doctor," and went out.

Everyone chatted freely, often interrupting each other with a sentence or two. The atmosphere was very relaxed. This Puti had not expected. She had thought that coming into the hospital, she would be coming into a place shadowed by death. Tormented by the cruel tortures of disease, what could people do but toss about groaning? But here the sun shone brightly, life was full of vitality, the cream-colored silk window curtains fluttered slightly in the spring breeze.

Xiao Wei returned and said that Dr. Xin, in charge of Aunt Wei, still could not be found. This doctor had not shown his face since the day he had first examined the old lady. After supper the family members withdrew, and the room became quiet. Puti stood in front of the window, looking down at the flowers and trees below. In an open space grew several winter jasmine, a kind of lilac. The jasmine were already in bloom, their branches studded with soft yellow blossoms. Next to the open space were the pathology section and the mortuary. The dusk gradually grew more dense; the far-off mountains were hidden in a cloudy mist. Puti felt at peace.

---

7. During the Cultural Revolution, hospital staff refused to do such things and families were requested to be in attendance, whereas formerly this had been discouraged.

"Dr. Fang! You've come!" The other three cried out joyfully, sounding almost in unison.

Puti turned and saw that Dr. Fang had entered the sickroom. In the dimness the outline of the white coat was especially clear, showing his slightly hunched back. He stopped in the doorway and asked: "May I turn on the light?"

"Naturally." "Turn it on." "Who minds light?" came the three replies.

Light dispelled the dusk. Puti saw that Fang Zhi held a rag in his hand. He went straight to Aunt Wei's bed and used the rag to wipe the head of the bed. It turned out that to fight and prevent revisionism and the segregation of medical and nursing groups, each hospital required that doctors participate in cleaning sickrooms and nurses participate in diagnosis and treatment. But doing surgery was a business of real knives and scalpels; not many dared pass themselves off for it. Surgical doctors usually served for a number of hours that could not be reduced. So Fang Zhi in his free time after the evening meal had to come and clean the several rooms assigned to him. Actually, Old Qi, Xiao Wei, and Cui Li already took responsibility for the tidiness of their family members, but the group that included Sister Huo and Dr. Xin considered this a very serious matter having to do with the prevention of revisionism and doctors' personal awareness, and thus requiring management. In point of fact, before the Cultural Revolution, several well-known hospitals had already been run like this.

Fang Zhi wiped tables and mopped with the same speed and precision that characterized his surgery; there was no superfluous motion. As he worked, he answered the patients' questions, usually not really questions but outpourings of woe. Only Cui Zhen of the three was his patient; her condition was fairly good. Elder Sister's head hurt. There was no way to get rid of that; just taking medicine for the pain was not effective. Inwardly, he knew that she was not yet at the most acute stage. Aunt Wei's chest hurt. He thought that according to Aunt Wei's actual age it was still proper to try to perform an operation. Aunt was not older than early fifties. But Dr. Xin looked upon her as though she were over seventy: possibly surgery would not be needed and there was no way of doing it. If Fang said anything, even in ordinary times it would be considered meddling in others' affairs, let alone now with strict divisions between the two factions. When any matter could provoke a mighty uproar, why give a differing medical opinion! Moreover, Xin's voice carried, and his faction had already seized power. Xin was already acting director, a higher authority. "But the sick will suffer," Fang Zhi often thought.

At first Puti wanted to help Fang Zhi sweep the floor. But after Elder Sister Qi pronounced it best not to move, she sat down on the bed. Aunt Wei asked: "You were looking a long time. Did you see if the winter jasmine is in bloom? The day I came I saw buds."

"Looking from a distance, it seems they're open. The peach blossoms are all withered," Puti answered.

"The flowering trees here haven't been cut. In a lot of places they've all been chopped down," Elder Sister Qi said.

Cui Zhen, probably to orient the sickroom's politics, quickly spoke up: "Cutting down a few flowering trees is a necessity. Break the old habits! I don't like flowers. Flowers are basically to continue future plant generations; that's all they're good for."

"Flowers can't carry on the class struggle!" Elder Sister Qi sneered, too.

"But I love flowers," Aunt Wei said earnestly. "There's a flowering crabapple by my front door. I keep thinking about getting home to see the crabapple flowers."

"It says they'll go to Zhong Nan Hai and smoke out Liu Shaoqi."[8] Cui Zhen pointed to a newspaper, and once again changed the subject: "If I weren't sick it would be great, I could go, too! The Great Cultural Revolution is so dynamic and vigorous! Dr. Fang, make me well quickly, so I can join in, march with and support the group in the struggle against capitalist roaders and revisionists." As she spoke, she suddenly remembered Puti's status. Perhaps, after all, the sickroom, without the vigilance of politically charged encounters, had set them apart from daily life. She had consistently treated Puti as just someone who was ill. "I still lack toughening, still lack political sensitivity," Cui Zhen criticized herself internally, as she continued: "Revisionism is all-pervasive; we must always be on guard!" and glanced sideways at Puti.

Puti also looked at Cui Zhen, saw her pale face and serious manner, and thought: "Even in the sickroom, it's hard to get away from the class struggle." There was nothing to say. She only compressed her lips in a half smile.

Fang Zhi, just crossing to mop in front of Puti's bed, took all this in. "The new patient has such a calm attitude," he thought. "She has

---

8. This refers to a leftist (largely student) protest vigil in front of the house of Liu Shaoqi, whose centrist policies were opposed by Mao Zedong's followers. Liu eventually died in prison. Zhong Nan Hai is a section of Beijing where the highest ranking government officials live.

no family. Is this a Three Names, Three Levels person?[9] One can't tell by looking at her. Is it a matter of her past record? Who knows? From the looks of it she hasn't yet experienced a double attack. Of course this situation is unprecedented. Few people have cancer more than once."

He often sympathized with patients. This time he felt deeply concerned; he would have very much liked to seek clarification of her case. However, she was a new patient, even if under his care. He said nothing, but only looked at her, slowly nodding and smiling gently. The smile expressed the surge of his sympathy, rendering his usually kindhearted face even kindlier; it glowed in the lamplight. Puti also suddenly felt a pounding in her heart. Was this not the kindliness of the normal cells? The feeling that the normal cells gave one was like this. Not only Fang Zhi's smiling look, but also Old Qi, Xiao Wei, Aunty, Elder Sister—all seemed to have the spirit of the normal cells. She should have returned Fang Zhi's smile, but instead she quietly looked away.

Now Sister Huo was yelling in the corridor: "The toilets are cleaned every morning, but every evening no one can set foot in them! They're all your rectums, it's really a disaster!" In a while she entered, blustering, yelling at Aunt Wei: "What is your son up to? You've been here several days and he hasn't shown his face! How to manage should be discussed beforehand with family members; he bows out and washes his hands of it!"

Aunt Wei, panic-stricken, stammered: "Really—he's not around? He was here in the afternoon."

Sister Huo wouldn't allow her to get a word in and continued yelling: "Sick beds are in very short supply. Aren't you keeping other people from being treated here? If you don't want treatment, then leave the hospital!"

Aunt Wei looked at her, more panic-stricken than ever, at a loss as to why she was in such a terrible temper. In those days it was in fashion to be hot-tempered. Only wrath could fortify the struggle. One could not show fighting strength with a kind and pleasant countenance!

Elder Sister Qi's head had begun to ache; she availed herself of Sister Huo's pause for breath to cry out quickly: "He was here all afternoon, he looked for Dr. Xin but couldn't find him."

---

9. From 1959 to 1964 conditions in China were very difficult; some people were starving. Liu Shaoqi enunciated a policy of giving special privileges to the three "High Names": famous writers, famous professors, and famous doctors.

Cui Zhen said quickly: "Doctors naturally are busy people; patients must wait for them, not doctors for patients."

Everyone had just been confounded by this reasoning when Fang Zhi, having put away the mop and rag, returned and asked calmly: "When will Dr. Xin have time to meet him?"

Sister Huo was her faction's pathbreaker; when it came to abusiveness, she led the pack. But she was respectful to Fang Zhi. Her tone quieted: "Tomorrow morning."

"Good. I'll go look for him," Fang Zhi said. "Aunt Wei, do you have the address?" Aunt Wei, lips and hands quivering, leaned against the bed to turn the pockets of her clothes inside out, producing a slip of paper. Fang Zhi took it, read it. "I'll go," he said, and left.

Sister Huo was taken aback, then suddenly realized this had been a chance for Fang Zhi to assert himself. She muttered angrily: "You are a bachelor anyway, you have nothing else to concern you. You serve enough. But no matter how hard you serve, it's no use." Without further ado she left.

The room hadn't settled down more than a couple of minutes when Aunt Wei burst out in a spell of violent coughing. She clutched at her chest with all her strength, her face turning purple. Puti hurried from her bed to bring a cup to her. Looking at the cup, tears in her eyes, she shook her head, and coughed some more, suddenly spitting out a mouthful of blood, then another. The cup was soon full. Puti quickly changed to the cup on her own night table, and said in a low voice: "Get the doctor." Cui Zhen and Elder Sister Qi both got up; Cui Zhen went out to find someone.

It was Xiao Ding who returned with her and said with a displeased expression: "Dr. Xin is on duty; he was in the office five minutes, hasn't been seen since." She went over and first gave Aunt Wei an injection to decrease the blood flow, then cleaned up the blood spills and administered a dose of sedative. Another sickroom called her and she rushed out.

The old woman calmed down. Elder Sister Qi's head hurt; she started moaning. Cui Zhen said she was like this every day; there was no use bothering about her. Puti went into the washroom to wash and gargle. Suddenly she saw a thin shadow come up behind her along the corridor. The person swayed slightly in the dim lamplight. Puti simply could not believe her eyes: it was Huiyun!

"How did you get in? Was this afternoon's criticism fierce? You ran this far, you must be tired. If they find out, they'll denounce you more!" Puti grasped Huiyun's hands and pulled her into the washroom.

"I know this hospital well. I know the way. I accompanied foreign guests here, have you forgotten?" She still wore her exhausted smile. "How are you? What day is the operation? If I hadn't made this trip, how could I rest easy?"

Puti talked of the afternoon's events, told about the meeting with the responsible good doctor, told how she wanted Huiyun to rest easy.

"Cui Zhen is your roommate?" A disdainful expression appeared on Huiyun's withered, wrinkled face. "Her nerves are mechanical, how can she have cancer too? . . . After surgery you'll need to have someone with you for a few days. If it's like it was today, if you need me, I'll come. But who knows what tomorrow will bring? Maybe they'll lock me up." Having said this she added quickly: "Being locked up isn't much; it's only that I'm afraid I won't be able to come. In that case, who will stay with you?" She smiled sadly.

Puti only then noticed that Huiyun wore a visored cap picked up who knows where, fastened down with a scarf. She had never seen Huiyun wear a hat before, so she asked: "Is it very windy out?"

"Oh, I must go. I'm really not very easy about you, though."

Huiyun's eyes were circled in red. She quickly lowered her head and looked at the floor, then drew a tea mug from her satchel, pressed it on Puti and, turning, left.

Puti, cupping the tea mug in her hands, stood transfixed, still taking in Huiyun's cap and scarf. Seeing her going, she quickly followed her a few steps and said in a low voice: "Don't worry, Tao Huiyun, I'm not alone." Why she was not alone, she could not say.

Huiyun, reaching the end of the corridor, raised her hand and was gone.

Puti returned to the room and put the mug on the night table. It was packed with spiced tea eggs,[10] the ones she loved. "I am not alone." She felt an inner warmth and comfort. Neighbors on right and left made her feel she was not alone, and then there was Xiao Ding, and Dr. Fang, the calm profound gaze, the gaunt face, the kindhearted spirit that made one think of the normal cells. . . . The normal cells, always numerous, should always be able to triumph over the cancer cells!

Elder Sister Qi was still moaning loudly. Puti, fearing a draft on her, went to close the window. Outside, the moonlight gleamed like

---

10. Eggs cooked in tea-flavored soy sauce.

water, the flowers formed shadows below, a faint scent of trees and grass wafted up. "The winter jasmine is blooming," Puti thought; "other blossoms are in bud." She raised her head to look at the moon, and suddenly realized there was no wind.

Why had Tao Huiyun worn a cap and scarf? As if struck by a heavy fist, Puti sat down suddenly on the bed. She understood. She wanted so much to contain Huiyun's suffering, to wash her wounds with her tears. To tell her that while her hair might have been scattered on the ground, she herself remained upright, an indomitable spirit, to tell her that although she no longer had her hair, she did have Puti and others in the world who still possessed conscience and kindness. . . .

Tears soaked Puti's pillow. All night the moans of illness and the far-off rumble of trains passed in and out of her confused dreams.

# 5

# Under the Knife

THE DAY BEFORE SURGERY, PATIENTS ARE ALWAYS SHAVED AND CLEANED IN the area to be operated on; this is called "preparing the skin." Puti had experienced this previously: she felt just as though she were going to a slaughterhouse.

Xiao Ding's handling was very gentle. While she shaved and washed, she chatted. "Your figure is very good. Afterward you can have a false breast; they have them in Shanghai. You can get one to fit you like the real one, so it doesn't show."

Puti, having endured so much devastation already, was not intensely concerned about a well-proportioned figure, but she still smiled gratefully. When she thought about how she would be disfigured forever, she felt sick at heart. Before, when she had seen a colleague take out dentures to wash them, she always felt very much like laughing. Now she was going to need a plastic false breast. Before, she had had her youth, her parents, a fatherland, a party. Now all were gone, leaving her alone with a body that she could no longer call her own either, destined for the operating table and the mercy of doctors.

"You're lucky." Xiao Ding's tone was gentle; she understood that patients needed comforting. "Tomorrow is Dr. Fang's day to operate. Dr. Fang is still young, but now this surgical department has to rely on the knife in his hand." As she spoke she gave a little sigh. "The old ones are either locked up or relieved of responsibilities, but this operating table is not that easy to stand by."

"The patients all say Dr. Fang is good." Puti smiled slightly.

"Dr. Fang doesn't say much, he has a good reputation," Xiao Ding said. "Even though he can wield a knife, he wouldn't venture to kill a chicken. His temperament is more like an intern's. Some people want to force him out. Letting those guys stand at the operating table would really be dangerous!"

"Did something happen?" Puti asked.

"Of course not." Xiao Ding naturally could not say. She changed the subject: "You're over thirty? Maybe the onset of cancer was earlier."

"That was influenced by morale."

"Exactly. It's all in morale, all in morale!" Xiao Ding said earnestly.

Puti felt that she herself could become a subject for research. Not only rage, but grief, panic, anxiety, resentment, mingled with a complex of other feelings, could clearly have had a direct influence on the development of her cancer, especially breast cancer. She was actually an experimental subject, like a white mouse. With a human being for an experimental subject, if at worst this person died, there were many more Chinese. However, if the whole nation developed cancer . . . To treat cancer it was necessary to diagnose it as soon as possible. When would the nation's cancer be diagnosed?

"Still interested in politics," Puti inwardly reproached herself. "I needn't think of that; I'll think of the cancer in my own body."

It was customary to take a sleeping pill in the evening before an operation and early the next morning to get onto the movable bed. A tranquilizing injection was given, and then you were pushed to the operating room. At this juncture there was an uproar in the sickroom. Elder Sister Qi was disturbed because she did not know why Old Qi had not come the day before. So, early in the morning, supporting herself, she had traveled to the corridor entrance to have a look. Xiao Ding and another nurse were getting medicine for her. The nurse whose duty it was to take the patient to the operating room came in, pulling the movable bed. It wasn't easy to cross smoothly with a broken wheel. And Sister Huo stood resolutely beside it. She suddenly discovered that this routine situation lacked something: the sickroom should be more crowded.

"Your family didn't come? You're going to the operating room by yourself?" Sister Huo's alarm was a little chiding.

"Of course, she has to go by herself. Who can go for her?" So saying, Aunt Wei tottered out of bed, coughing all the way. She went to Puti, stretching out her hand: "Don't worry, Teacher Mei. You'll go and come back!" Her rough feverish hand grasped vigorously. Puti, smiling a little, gave the old woman's hand a firm shake in response.

Rumbling as it went, the movable bed was pushed out. Puti knew that in this kind of surgery there was little chance of an accident on the operating table, even less so with Dr. Fang performing. But thoughts still swept over her uncontrollably. "If I am no longer in the world, flowers will still bloom, the grass will still be green, people can continue to carry on the class struggle. Actually it's the same whoever

ceases to be. Dad's ashes are in Huiyun's care, but how will things go
for Huiyun? Will she go on being labeled an active counterrevolutionary? Go on being criticized, humiliated, having her head
shaved?" When she got home again, that exhausted smiling expression would no longer be of any use to her. Could anything comfort
her in Spoon Court? The oasis in the desert would have vanished
with the departure of Puti.

The movable bed had gone down the corridor and was about to
be pulled through the ward's double doors. Most patients' family
members went as far as this, and waited here for the surgery to be
completed. Xiao Wei was just coming through the doors. Surprised
when he realized Puti was on the movable bed, he said to her shyly in
a low voice: "Come back soon, Teacher Mei."

Puti didn't have her glasses on and could only see the green uniform and red collar insignia in a blur. She knew Xiao Wei had come
yesterday, and that Dr. Xin had again not been there, having gone to
hold a mass meeting of the public health system. Today perhaps Xiao
Wei could arrange a plan of treatment for Aunt Wei. Puti nodded
her head vigorously and thought: "Huiyun can also get ordinary concern from average persons, because the normal cells are more numerous . . . " Her mind suddenly became completely empty and
calm, in a good preoperative state.

The operating room was painted white. On the facing wall were
fresh red characters. Puti, making an effort of will and narrowing her
eyes, made out a quotation: "Be resolute, fear no sacrifice, and sur-
mount every difficulty to win victory!"[1] She felt dizzy and closed her
eyes, the line of fresh characters jumping about before them.

"How do you feel?" The honest voice sounded very kind, very
familiar.

With difficulty Puti managed to open her eyes again. She saw Dr.
Fang bending over to look at her. Like everyone else in the operating room, Dr. Fang had a large gauze mask covering half his face, but
Puti could still make out the profound piercing gleam in the depth
of his eyes.

"Fine," Puti said softly. Now someone gave her a prick on the
foot; an infusion bottle was suspended. Then someone gave her an
anesthetic in her back. Only then was a thick needle used to intubate
a kind of sustained firm coating of a local anesthetic between her
vertebrae. Ice-cold drug fluids flowed into her; she felt a chill set in.

---

1. A quotation from Mao Zedong.

Soon she started to tremble uncontrollably, tremble so that the narrow operating table shook.

"Give her a shot of morphine." It was Dr. Fang's firm voice. The anesthetist immediately complied. Puti's front was covered with a white cloth. She heard Dr. Fang say: "Dr. Xin, are you going ahead today?" Then a harsh dry voice: "No, no. You go on. I'll assist, I'll assist." There was something familiar about this voice. Puti in her dazed condition suddenly recalled this was the voice that had muttered "finished, finished" at the time of her minor surgery. The trembling over, the doctors quickly took their places. Someone pricked her and made sure she felt no pain. The surgery began. They did not seem to look upon her as a human being: the knives, the scissors, were all placed on her body. Puti heard the sound of scissors being placed, the sound of voices, very clearly.

"She's asleep," one voice said.

"This person has a problem," the harsh, dry voice said. "Her unit sent someone to say she—"

"Turn the pincers, turn the pincers!" Dr. Fang raised his voice. Clearly he wanted to cut Dr. Xin off.

"I think, now that Dr. Fang has arranged it, we should do it." Dr. Xin laughed with dry harshness. "I haven't attended in a long time. I should."

"We are medical personnel, we should treat the sick," a voice said.

"At the mass meeting of the public health system they said . . ." It was the harsh, dry voice again. Puti heard every word clearly, but could not comprehend. Gradually the voices grew fainter and she sank into unconsciousness.

The operation was carried out in a very inharmonious atmosphere. Dr. Xin Shengda rambled on while he wielded the scissors. Dr. Fang and his helpers had never been so disgusted as by today's endless chatter. The doctors of the surgical department frequently chatted a little at the operating table, as is customary around the world, but Dr. Xin's monologue really went beyond the limits of "chatting." Dr. Fang felt there simply must be a prohibition, as strictly enforced as the taboo on certain drugs, forbidding chatter during surgery—especially at a partial or radical mastectomy.

Uncovering the armpit demanded the most painstaking technique. Fang skillfully cut open the thin muscle membranes covering the arteries and veins in the armpit, ligated each branch, and cut it, his every movement precise, dexterous, the whole cut neat and tidy, without much blood seepage. While he himself operated, he watched Dr. Xin's cutting, for fear that Dr. Xin might destroy an armpit artery or vein, or either of the two nerves that it was essential not to damage.

This complicated, meticulous job accomplished, he neatly displayed several ribs with a cut in front of the chest, as if waiting to deal with them.

"Dr. Fang, do you plan a radical?" Dr. Xin asked suddenly.

"Yes. Her tumor is on the inside."

"I think that's not necessary, we can finish up. I have a meeting to go to."

Fang Zhi didn't understand the meaning of this. In his ten-year career at the operating table, he had never before encountered a situation like this. "What?" He raised his head to look in Xin's direction.

"I mean that I haven't time. Moreover, for this kind of person, we needn't be that thorough."

Fang Zhi's first reaction was to hastily move his glance toward the other two assistants. "Who can take over?" he thought. Just then the powerful spotlight over the operating table suddenly went out. "The electricity's off," someone muttered.

"How unlucky!" Dr. Xin's voice laughed with harsh astringency. "What can we do? Let's finish, eh?"

Everyone rushed to push open the operating-room windows. Someone turned on a flashlight.

"The patient's blood pressure is dropping," the nurse at the blood pressure gauge reported. These words relieved Fang Zhi's feelings of guilt. He could hesitate no longer. Three words pushed out from between his teeth. "The amputation knife!" He took the long, gleaming knife, and quickly cut the breast, the large chest muscle, and the small chest muscle, as well as the armpit fat, completely off. The blood in the arteries passing through the chest expanse gushed out. Fang Zhi, using a pair of pincers to hold the blood vessels, moved them dexterously with both hands a few times, ligating them completely. The nurse poured a salt solution in the wound, cleansing the blood.

Like her father's surgery, Mei Puti's breast cancer surgery had not been carried out as planned.

While the surgery was in progress, Room 308 had developed into another battlefield. Sometime after ten o'clock Zhang Yongjiang came to the hospital, leading Shi Qingping and others. As if no one else were present, they hurried straight to Puti's bed. Shi Qingping lifted open the neatly made bed and searched everywhere, then opened the cabinet at the head of the bed and took everything out to check it over. There were only the simplest items for ordinary use. When she came to the spiced tea eggs, she curled her lips contemptuously, and with a disdainful expression handed the tea mug to Zhang Yongjiang: "Look! She still has this!"

"Leave it." Zhang Yongjiang could see plainly that there was nothing else and turned to examine the wall at the end of Puti's bed. "Okay to put it up here? At the head or the foot?"

At this point Cui Zhen spoke up: "Aren't you Zhang Yongjiang? What are you doing?"

"Oh, you and Puti are roommates." Zhang Yongjiang gave Cui Zhen an indifferent glance. He knew Cui Zhen was very "Left," but despised her, and addressed only his cohorts: "The head of the bed is better. The poster will be very visible."

Shi Qingping had it: "I think the foot of the bed is better. She'll see it when she opens her eyes. And I don't think it will stick at the head of the bed." She spoke carelessly in Shanghai dialect, as if only she and her husband were present. Zhang Yongjiang nodded and immediately his cohorts began pasting some character posters on the wall opposite Puti's bed. Moving very quickly, in the twinkling of an eye they had put up several, covering most of the wall. Shi Qingping's point had obviously been well taken.

The theme of the big-character posters was startling: "The executioner wants the life of the wicked author of the wicked book, *The Everlasting Rock*, Mei Puti." The three characters "Mei Puti" had been brushed in red.

"What are they doing? What are they putting up?" Aunt Wei gasped to her son beside the bed. She had just finished a violent coughing spell. Xiao Wei naturally had not been able to find Dr. Xin Shengda that morning; he could only keep watch at the bedside. He didn't answer, however.

The big-character posters were ready. Zhang Yongjiang straightened up, and in modulated tones delivered a speech to the patients:

"Mei Puti is our school's class enemy. Recently many persons have unmasked her wicked book, *The Everlasting Rock*, which poisoned the minds of many readers, especially young people." As he spoke he rustled a middle-sized poster. "This is a suicide note written by a student in our department. He says he cannot tell what the meaning of life is, he would rather follow the example of the novel's hero, take his life to seek significance in the next life. He killed himself!"

This dramatic climax sounded out, Shi Qingping and the others immediately raised their arms and shouted: "Down with Mei Puti!" "Mei Puti must pay her blood debt!" The atmosphere in the sickroom was extraordinarily tense, as though it were an execution ground. Aunt Wei, frightened, covered her head with her quilt. Elder Sister Qi, who had not had a headache before that morning, now began to have a splitting one and groaned loudly. Only Cui Zhen listened tensely and with special interest, thinking: "Zhang Yongjiang has real skill! One can learn from him!"

The embattled atmosphere of the sickroom had infected the corridor: there was also a hubbub out there. Two voices reached high pitch: "I have to interfere! How can you denounce people in the sickroom! I never heard of such a thing!" "So you're getting more experience!! Why can't you denounce people in the sickroom? The class struggle must be kept up everywhere!" Shouting, the two entered the sickroom. Xiao Ding in front, red with anger, went straight to Zhang Yongjiang, still swaying in his lecture posture, and shouted at him: "This is a sickroom! Don't you know that? Out with you!" Sister Huo followed right behind, also very red in the face, and yelled loudly: "Keep up the fight! The sickroom is not the Land of Peach Blossoms! Under no circumstances run away from the class struggle!"

"We will not go! We will fight until the class enemy is overthrown!" several people yelled at once. Shi Qingping's tones were especially piercing, sounding out above the noisy medley.

Xiao Wei could not stand it. He stepped forward and said loudly: "You're frightening my old mom terribly! You should remember, there's not just one patient here!"

"The People's Liberation Army should support the Left," Zhang Yongjiang said calmly. "Now I'll read the suicide note of the victim, Qi Yongshou!"

When she heard Qi Yongshou's name, Elder Sister Qi sat up. Her dark gray face turned ghastly pale. She called out: "Who did you say? Who killed himself?" Zhang Yongjiang turned toward her, puzzled. When he understood that this was Qi Yongshou's mother, he felt secretly pleased. This was a lucky coincidence. He was bringing about the struggle of the wrongdoer and the victim in the sickroom! Gravely sounding each character, he read the suicide note into Elder Sister Qi's ear. It was actually the draft of a criticism by Qi Yongshou. In the front of it was: "I think of suicide." Elder Sister Qi listened as she moaned in a loud voice, then simply sobbed out: "The pain is killing me!" She began to roll around all over the bed. Several nurses didn't know what to do. Sister Huo herself muttered: "If we had known the victim's mother was here, they wouldn't have permitted him to come in!" When the suicide note had been read, Zhang Yongjiang and the rest again started to yell slogans; hostility seethed through the room.

The sound of the movable bed rumbled closer and closer. Amid the clamorous sounds Mei Puti was pulled in, lying on the flat bed. She was pale, both eyes quite closed. It seemed all that was left was a body freshly cut into; her soul had already drifted off to a boundless tranquillity.

The tumult in the sickroom quickly subsided. Elder Sister Qi stopped crying. Placing her hand on the bed rail for support, she walked to the front of the flat bed, her eyes on Puti. Xiao Ding was afraid she would fall, or hit out, and rushed forward to support her. She did indeed raise her hand. There were those in the room who enjoyed others' misfortune; others were breathless with anxiety. But she suddenly covered her face with her hands, and began to wail bitterly. Xiao Ding helped her to lie down. She cried again: "The pain is killing me! Really killing me!" Aunt Wei could not keep from weeping, too. Xiao Ding went to fix a sedative injection. Sister Huo went over to Zhang Yongjiang and said a few words to him in a low voice. The gist was that the disturbance had been made; he could wind up. Zhang Yongjiang nodded complacently, still wanting to say a few words to close the curtain, but Sister Huo creased her brow at him and escorted him and his subordinates out of the room.

People helped settle Puti. Xiao Ding had given Elder Sister Qi a shot, and came over to open the drainage tube under the skin on the side of Puti's chest, fit a drainage bottle to it, and arrange it under the bed. When everything was in order she walked over to the wall and reached her hand out to tear down the big-character posters. Just then Sister Huo returned from taking the visitors out and saw her. "Hold it!" she yelled, glaring at Xiao Ding with frowning brow and angry eyes. "Who dares tear up a big-character poster! Big-character posters are permitted by Chairman Mao!"

"Chairman Mao hasn't allowed them in sickrooms!"

The two argued back and forth; they almost seemed about to wrestle. Amid the hubbub Xiao Ding suddenly saw that Fang Zhi had come unnoticed to stand in front of the big-character posters and was looking, horrified, at their captions, apparently unaware of the quarrel in progress beside him.

"Dr. Fang! You say; can big-character posters be put up in sickrooms?" Xiao Ding asked. Sister Huo rushed in with: "You're involving him? What use are Dr. Fang's words?"

"Let's drop it for the moment," Dr. Fang answered unexpectedly, as he walked over to Puti's bed. "I am thinking of a way to change rooms for Bed 3."

Sister Huo looked triumphantly at Xiao Ding. "All right! I've already been humane enough; you, too, should have some principles!" As on entering, the two followed each other to exit.

Puti was slowly awakening. In her half sleep, she had sensed the confusion in the sickroom, but had not had the strength to open her eyes and have a look. She did not even feel strong enough to lie there; her body was really too heavy. After quite a while and a number of attempts, she finally opened her eyes.

The sickroom was very still. She saw Fang Zhi standing beside her, looking at her solicitously. But she could not, however, clearly see his expression, brimming with sympathy, joy, and surprise, could not clearly see his eyes shimmering. Hot tears fell on her hand; she did not feel them. She only felt very much at peace, and closed her eyes again.

# 6

# Fang Zhi

F ANG ZHI DID NOT EVEN KNOW HIMSELF WHY HIS HOT TEARS FELL. THOSE hot teardrops opened the floodgates of memories long since dammed up. Past events surged like great turbulent waves, blurring his cool, calm surgeon's eyes. With difficulty, he gained control of himself and finished his morning tasks as usual. Only when he returned to the dormitory to sit in the small room, admitting just a tea table and a narrow bed, did past events well up in his mind and several clearly defined segments of the past float before his eyes.

He was barefoot, sitting beside Panxi Stream near Chongqing, looking at the flowing of the brook water tumbling along like balls of jade, dashing against rocks large and small, the water spattering snowy spray. He often laughed to himself in happiness, shouting and clapping his hands. Once, trying to catch the spray, he had actually fallen into the water. Drenched through, he had been severely beaten by his father. He had been motherless from a tender age; his father, oppressed by life, had been very harsh with him. So he had made a friend of Panxi Stream. He could amuse himself there for half a day, sitting beside the stream with the water and the rocks, lost in thought. Once he had missed work and his father, upon finding him, had hit him in the face, roaring: "Are you a lad looking for leisure? Look out for yourself. Do you think you were born with a good future?"

His father was a laborer for an art school which had moved from Xiajiang[1] to the vicinity of Panxi Stream. This was a living much better

---

1. On the lower Yangtze River.

59

than the average farmer's. But the debts owed for Fang Zhi's mother's illness and death had become chains around the elder Fang's neck. The teachers at the school often said Fang Zhi had the makings of a scholar and every effort should be made to get him to college. The elder Fang would listen happily, but then always soberly observed: "Studying what at college, eh? I still have debts to pay. To be steady, have a clean record, and be an upright person is good enough."

Fang Zhi often saw the school's teachers and students drawing Panxi Stream. Their dashing stream and huge rocks were very beautiful, but he always felt them to be lifeless. "Water and rocks should live," he said to himself. He collected some waste paper and a pen with which to draw. If he ran into someone, he would hide the paper and pen under a large rock. Once he really felt the water and the rocks come alive. The water flowed roaring over his very body; the rocks resembled those in the great rocky brook exactly, each with a different tale to tell. He placed the drawing on a rock, and stepped back, wanting to view it from a little farther away. Suddenly a hand grabbed his shoulder and shook him ferociously. His father shouted: "You want to learn from these teachers, too! The Eight Characters weren't placed right on your birthday! There's just this way of life!" After a spell of ripping, the water and rocks that had begun to come alive in Fang Zhi's little heart dropped one by one into the stream, swirled against the sides of the rocks, and gradually drifted away with the water's flow.

If it had not been for Liberation, Fang Zhi really did not know whether he could have gone on living. But amazingly the day came when Fang Zhi entered a middle school with an accelerated educational program for workers and peasants. And amazingly the day came when he was admitted to the best medical school in the province.

Among his memories, his father's sickbed was prominent. He sat before the bed on a low stool. His father stroked his shoulder with an emaciated hand, although by this time he was already too old to need this kind of caress. His father, smiling a little, murmured: "My son is a doctor; doctors save lives!—the Communist Party rearranged the Eight Characters! The Communist Party saves lives! Doctors save lives! Effect miraculous cures and bring the dead back to life, to live long and not grow old . . ." The old man, in the midst of these last words, "effect miraculous cures and bring the dead back to life, to live long and not grow old," passed away, quietly and full of satisfaction. Fang Zhi in his grief took comfort in the fact that his father had lived until Liberation and knew the world could be completely changed, knew the sweet taste of the Party's heart-filling warmth, knew his son would not be isolated in bitter loneliness but would have the guidance and support of the Communist Party, far surpassing the abilities of parents.

However, Fang Zhi's entry into the Party did not go smoothly. He was taciturn, unsociable, and eccentric, and after each semester the following was written on his report card: "politically not very active." Only on the eve of graduation was his entry into the Party approved. He wanted wholeheartedly to go to Tibet to bring to more people the great strength that others had given him. When assignments were announced and he heard that he had been assigned to the celebrated hospital in Beijing, he simply could not believe it was real. Beijing! What a glorious, holy word! Could it be that, amazingly, he was going to tread on Beijing soil? Could it be that he was going to see the ancient, red-walled, yellow-tiled buildings, pictures of which he had seen so often, with his own eyes? Chairman Mao lived there! Chairman Mao was living in the hearts of hundreds of millions of Chinese. From 1949 on, the innermost depths of Fang Zhi's youthful heart, filled with beautiful expectations, had been dedicated to Chairman Mao.

Since starting work as a doctor, he had made rapid progress in his profession. His political life, however, had been surprisingly brief. In the summer of 1957, he should have become a full Party member, but at that time the struggle against the Right sweeping the country like a raging fire had brought all normal organizational work to a halt. Every person had to receive a trial, to expedite the process of complete certification. Thus in the winter of 1957, Fang Zhi attended his last membership meeting of the Party branch.

This was the evening of a frigid winter day. The sky was overcast, in anticipation of a heavy snowfall. At this time the membership meeting was discussing the admission of three men to the Party. The position on one was firm: his admission was to be on schedule. Another man's standing was granted with a similar assertion: that his Party standing would begin at the conclusion of their discussion. Last came Fang Zhi. His qualifications for probationary Party membership were expunged. The reason: he sympathized with the Rightists.

Fang Zhi had known before the meeting that this would be the outcome, but it was still hard for him to believe. Just as at first he had not believed he would go to Beijing to work, so he absolutely could not believe that someone such as he could be removed from the Party. As he saw it, his relationship to the Party was like that of a fetus to its mother. He felt himself to be within the mother's belly where there was only security and well-being. He and the mother were one body.

Seeing how many people were labeled criminals, or were re-formed through labor or exiled to the countryside just for express-ing their political opinions, and in his heart feeling this to be insup-portable, he declared his thinking to the branch secretary, Old Wu, allowing further that there were some Rightist ways of thinking that he, too, favored, he had just not bothered to express them. Old Wu was a short man from Shandong. An amazed look spread over his dark face. He tried several times to speak but couldn't. Afterward, he had a few talks with Fang Zhi. In the end he read out the resolution affecting Fang Zhi's whole life.

When Fang Zhi heard the announcement sound out, loud and clear, he saw people raising their hands one after another. He knew that he had neither the right nor the need to remain there any longer. After the branch secretary completed the proceedings, he left the meeting room. Unexpectedly, the branch secretary ran after him, once more wanting to say something, but once more finding himself unable to do so, probably not knowing what to say in con-formity with principle. He repeated several times "You, you—" and after that didn't say anything, only pumped Fang Zhi's hand heartily, and then went back into the meeting. As he went through the door, Fang Zhi glimpsed the thin white smoke in the room; the smell of smoke floated out into the corridor.

The next day just happened to be his time off. He climbed Fra-grant Hills very early. Fragrant Hills in the winter was extremely quiet; the green pine groves in the haze felt remarkably pure and fresh. Without a goal, he crossed back and forth among the groves. It was as though a tumble of tangled objects were being stuffed into his head; the pressure in his chest was hard to bear. ". . . His problem is obviously a question of political stance, in order to uphold the Party's pure and honest character . . ." He seemed to still hear the sound of the resolution against him; the tangled dried twigs were arms expressing approval. He sincerely believed he was wrong. But he also felt that if he encountered the same situation again, he could still sympathize with those "Rightist comrades," could still declare his thoughts, could still make the same mistakes. "To know my mistakes but be unable to correct them—then what?" Fang Zhi thought bit-terly. He usually had a hard time opening his mouth to people and was very much in the habit of talking to himself. Now he could not en-dure facing the desolate mountain, the gaunt trees, and yelled out "Then what?" At the shout, several crows flew up into the dried trees. "Wa!" they replied, as they circled up and flew off into the gloomy sky.

Fang Zhi walked on randomly. He passed the high wall of the Temple of Brilliance. Stepping on dead twigs and withered leaves, he crossed toward a grove of smoke trees. Suddenly he saw a tiny clearing with several piles of cut trees. On one tree stump a book had been placed very neatly, held down by a rock. On the rock, secured with another rock, was a written note: "Great poisonous weeds! Have your celestial burial!"[2]

Seemingly, an item prepared for celestial burial should not be touched, but Fang Zhi unthinkingly picked up the book and turned it over to read the title. The corners of the book were already dog-eared and its pages worn, but its gray-blue two-toned cover was still as bright and clean as new. Obviously the book had originally been wrapped in a jacket. Looking, Fang Zhi saw on the cover a large cliff-like rock drawn with simple lines; beside it were three characters in cursive style: *The Everlasting Rock.*

Fang Zhi rarely read novels; moreover, he didn't know where the book had come from. Without thinking he turned the pages, turned the pages, until, sitting unaware on a broken brick at this celestial burial site, he had read the book from cover to cover.

He was very moved. He wept, he laughed, he felt sprays of sweet spring water flowing over his depressed and aching heart; his senses all opened to the positive. His twisted soul unfolded with the nurturing water. The book was only a story of love, but it told him that no matter what one's inexpressible despair, life was good, people should always have hope. Naturally he did not believe in the richly imbued portrayal of romance, but he shared the deeply held belief that people must never lose hope and faith. People had to be strong.

He very much wanted to take the book with him, but he instinctively reconsidered: the owner was also an ardent lover of the book; perhaps he would repent, return to get it? He hesitated repeatedly, then replaced the book in the position in which he had found it and left.

In his little room, Fang Zhi slowly exerted himself to shut off the sluice gates of memory. "Ah, life is so strange," he thought. Since his never-to-be-expected arrival in Beijing to live beside Chairman Mao, his political life had again quieted. Ten years after the unanticipated opportunity to read *The Everlasting Rock* on Fragrant Hills, he had met the author in the cancer ward, had actually operated on her. Shouldn't she know that she had also operated on him, filling him with renewed hope for living?

---

2. "Poisonous weeds" refers to harmful writings. A "celestial burial" would expose the item buried to birds and beasts of prey.

Let the big-character posters stay, so even more people might know who the author of *The Everlasting Rock* was. But what kind of a person was she after all? She already seemed to be almost an intimate, yet she was also remote, already well known, yet at the same time a stranger. . . .

When Fang Zhi stood up, he saw that it was already several minutes into his time of duty and hurriedly opened the door to leave. Directly in front of him, Xin Shengda was standing, facing the doorway.

"It's good I wasn't talking to myself," thought Fang Zhi, and he began to walk ahead toward the wards.

"Dr. Fang!" Dr. Xin called, rushing forward a few steps. The husky, dry voice had something slick about it. "We have something to talk over, eh?"

Fang Zhi hadn't realized Xin Shengda was seeking him out about something. Since the beginning of the Cultural Revolution, they had divided into two factions, in opposing positions. Actually, their situation was not one of equal opponents: Dr. Xin was one of the ringleaders of the "Red-Tasseled Combat Group." After the takeover he had become an agent for the head of the Surgical Department and was considered quite a personage around the hospital. Fang Zhi, since he couldn't bear the sight of their "dictatorship," inclined toward the other faction's "Five Well Commune." The Five Well Commune, in order to demonstrate its revolutionary spirit, also behaved in a medieval way.[3] Fang Zhi did not agree with this either. He had no alternative but to daily practice surgery, keeping his thoughts to himself. Now Dr. Xin had come to find him, and was asking with a smile: "Is a talk okay?"—meaning to go into Fang Zhi's room.

Fang Zhi silently drew him to the end of the corridor, still not speaking.

"Your words are few but you're a man with brains. So I'm going to 'open the window' and talk plainly." Dr. Xin was a naturally bold person. "I want to ask your help. A student killed himself. You could make out a certificate confirming that it was a suicide, then make a statement at the meeting. It is not just to denounce that woman patient, she's nobody! You'll be denouncing the revisionist black art and health line;[4] someone will write the text. For just this small thing, the reward is our guarantee of your security."

---

3. That is, the Commune was not respectful of personal rights.
4. A term used during the Cultural Revolution to denounce "counter-revolutionary" art and literature.

"Aren't you more effective to handle this sort of thing?" Fang still spoke calmly. He knew that Dr. Xin had already written such certificates many times.

"No. No. Naturally, what you say has force, because in people's minds you are relatively objective. Moreover, you need safeguarding. You need to make a little effort. Otherwise when we try to protect you, the masses won't go along."

Fang Zhi didn't fully understand the meaning of this, but he began to sense that he and Mei Puti were already both caught in a net—a net that had been cast, but not yet drawn tight. Why not find out? He considered a little, then asked: "Where is the corpse? I'll go and take a look."

"It's already been incinerated." Dr. Xin still smiled. "He jumped from the building yesterday."

This was actually quite predictable, but Fang Zhi felt suddenly consumed by rage, his heart almost bursting. This was now indeed a world with executioners running wild! They murdered the person, destroyed the evidence and, further, accused an innocent person on the executioners' behalf! In reality, Mei Puti was also being murdered. The surgery had not been thorough: The lymph nodes in the breast had not been removed. A recurrence might be more extensive. Why gratuitously frame a case against her, plot against her? She had imparted that constant, fine spirit to her readers. Who knew how many there were like her and the student "suicide" whose bones were already ashes?

Fang Zhi's pale face turned red. Slowly the redness left; he glared at Dr. Xin for a moment, said coldly "Excuse me," and turned and walked away.

A cold smile played across Dr. Xin's lips.

Fang Zhi hurried quickly to the outpatient surgical consulting room, where he performed several minor surgeries. He felt extraordinarily tired. Seeing there were two other doctors there, he spoke to the nurse and abruptly left for the ward. He went up the special staircase for hospital employees and through a door, and saw Cui Li coming up to greet him. "I was just waiting for you, Dr. Fang." Cui Li still had that timid look; her long narrow eyelids drooped slightly. "Can Mama leave the hospital? She's very worried, she wants to participate in the movement." She managed a smile; her look was full of apprehension.

"Cui Zhen." Fang Zhi quickly pondered the patient's condition: straightforward rectal carcinoma, cancerous swelling 1 by 2 centimeters twenty days after surgery. Her condition was not bad, but wounds in the perineum were still not completely healed.

"Wait two more days." Fang Zhi answered.

"Will two more be okay?" Cui Li raised her eyes. "Dr. Fang, we all trust you; all day you're involved with suffering, death; you're a good person." Cui Li seemed to be suffering in a way she could not articulate, from a sickness from which doctors could not free her.

Fang Zhi did not understand why she spoke thus; he only looked at her sympathetically and nodded. Now several nurses were asking him things so he sat down at the nurses' desk to handle them one by one.

When he had time to enter Room 308, dinner was already being served. Beside each sickbed was a family member. But beside Mei Puti's, the infusion-bottle holder still maintained its solitary vigil, hanging with no one to check it. Puti, as usual, was lying with closed eyes, looking very tranquil.

Fang Zhi first walked to the front of Elder Sister Qi's bed. Elder Sister Qi was still moaning as she lay. Old Qi, with red-rimmed eyes, sat at her feet, looking as though he had already been trying to cheer her up for quite a while. When Old Qi saw Fang Zhi come over, he rose quickly and grasped his extended hand, saying softly: "If changing rooms is troublesome, it's all right. She doesn't recognize some characters. I remember our child read that book several years ago. He said he liked it enough to shout about it. If it was that book's fault," he nodded toward the wall, "how is it he didn't kill himself a couple of years ago rather than wait for these troubled times? Yesterday I went to their school and didn't see him. He had been hauled off. They didn't wait for the corpse's relatives. . . . It's no use talking about it. . . ." He drew out a dirty handkerchief and wiped his nose.

"Try to cheer your wife up." Fang Zhi couldn't think of anything else to say.

"I still must go and ask their department head; some people say there was fighting and the child was pushed off the building." He seemed to be talking to himself.

Fang Zhi turned to look at Puti. Xiao Wei had reported that she had vomited twice during the afternoon; he had given her gruel and she hadn't taken it. Sure enough, Fang Zhi saw a bowl of gruel by the head of the bed. A warm feeling arose in him. He knew that the infusion bottle was indeed also being monitored.

Unexpectedly, Cui Li also reported: "They also gave her medicine once." Cui Zhen shot her a glance, as though annoyed at her saying too much.

Puti heard everyone's words; she had already opened her eyes. She very much wanted to put her glasses on and have a look at this world she had once dearly loved, but laying hands on her glasses was

easier said than done. She could feel what seemed to be a running
tube in her right chest and liquid flowing haphazardly over her body.
At first, she thought the infusion needle-head was not in the blood
vessel; later she realized the needle-head was bound to her foot. This
sensation of diffuse flowing was probably the lymph fluids. She
turned slightly to the side and the fluids flowed to the left. "If these
fluids carry cancer cells then they'll infect the left side," Puti
thought. "But that's impossible. Besides, the cancer cells no longer
have hiding places."

"Are you all right?" Fang Zhi's deep voice sounded simple and
kind. He touched Puti's wrist lightly, taking her pulse.

"Very good," Puti said unexpectedly, even managing a slight
smile.

"Have you had much pain? We can give you a shot for the pain."

"I haven't had much pain, I don't need a shot. But I'm so tightly
strapped up, it's as though I'm wearing an iron vest." Puti spoke
slowly, with effort. "Wouldn't it be better if the bandages were taken
off?"

"It takes time." Fang Zhi knew it would not be better to take off
the bandages. Only with the wonderful remedy of time would the
wound be properly healed.

"I feel as though a water pipe is running." Puti closed her eyes
again.

"A water pipe?" Fang Zhi couldn't help smiling a little. "I haven't
heard that said before. Your pulse is good. Will you eat a little?"

"No."

"You should eat. It's actually eating to get well." Fang Zhi raised
the head of the bed, picked up the bowl, and turned to look at Cui
Li, hoping she would come over of her own accord to take the bowl.
Cui Li hesitated under Cui Zhen's stern gaze. Cui Zhen immediately
declared that she needed to walk around, and went out, pulling her
daughter with her.

"I'll feed you, okay?" Fang Zhi had to sit simply, on the stool beside the bed. Puti gave Fang Zhi a grateful glance. She didn't have
the heart to go against this good doctor's kindness, and nodded her
head.

Spoonful by spoonful Fang Zhi fed her the gruel. She closed her
eyes and swallowed slowly. Fang Zhi had almost never before looked
carefully at a woman's face, although he had often used the knife on
women's bodies. Women's faces, unless extremely fat or thin, had all
looked more or less alike to him. Now he unconsciously studied the
face before him. It was slightly sharp, but not thin, very full, the skin
not fair, somewhat yellowish, but very fine and smooth, giving one a

feeling of translucence. The brows were fine, the closed eyes cres-
cent-shaped. At the sides of the mouth dimples lingered, adding a bit
of charm to Puti's scholarly-looking face, so that it had, along with
intelligence, a suggestion of delicacy. Although the years had passed,
charm had gone along with learning; experience had deepened the
expression. "Looking at someone like this really isn't polite," Fang
Zhi thought, suddenly coming to. Yet he still could not resist another
look. Just then, Puti opened her eyes and saw him. Her look suggested the stranger as well as the intimate. Where had he seen it?
Fang Zhi felt lost, gripped by a spontaneous feeling of panic.

"Thank you, Dr. Fang." Puti had eaten less than half the gruel;
she shook her head. Fang Zhi hadn't put down the bowl before he
heard Sister Huo yelling:

"So you're here! So you have spare time!" Discovering that Fang
Zhi had been feeding gruel, Sister Huo promptly charged in to take
over. "A patient there is in shock, go quickly!" She snatched up the
bowl of gruel and shoved it at Xiao Wei, standing in front of Aunt
Wei's bed. "He's not busy, let him feed!" She swept Fang Zhi up like
a whirlwind.

Fang Zhi had only enough time to register that Puti was still
looking at him, her expression filled with confusion and sadness.

"There's still Aunt Wei's condition I hadn't asked about. Xiao
Wei is standing here; something must be the matter," Fang Zhi
thought, but he didn't plan on a contest of strength with Sister Huo,
and he quickly followed after her.

"Really. Who'll look after her this evening?" Old Qi spoke with
concern.

The room was silent for quite a while. Xiao Wei said huskily: "I
must take care of my mother. And I'll also look after Teacher Mei."
The roommates knew that Aunt Wei's condition wasn't good. Dr. Xin
had declared that afternoon that he couldn't cure her. He had, indeed, wanted to rush her out of the hospital. Only after piteous entreaties from Xiao Wei had he agreed to observe her for a few more
days.

"What are you worrying about? Who has anybody to depend on!
You yourself are only a solitary spirit, a wandering ghost, without
near ones, without children to depend on in old age!" Elder Sister Qi
started to weep. "What court are you in? That law that lets demons
and ghosts have something to eat! That somehow doesn't look into
how children die! Who are the murderers! My tall, big son is gone
for no reason!" Weeping, she glared ferociously at Puti.

"Take it easy," Old Qi said anxiously. "You rest. You yourself are
so sick—"

"When you're buried up to your shoulders, what are you afraid of?" Elder Sister Qi wanted to continue, but a violent headache suddenly attacked her. Almost with a bang, she fell back on the bed. "Never mind!" she said, afraid of frightening her husband, but then she began to writhe all over the bed. Old Qi's eyes brimmed with tears. He ran quickly out, looking for someone to administer a pain killer. After Xiao Ding had come and given her some medicine, Elder Sister continued to suffer for a while, but she finally quieted down.

Puti was now quite conscious; she had heard Elder Sister Qi's words clearly. She didn't understand what was the matter; it seemed as though Elder Sister Qi had a violent temper, not at all good for recuperating from an illness. Puti had no strength at all; however, she very much wanted to help console and mediate. For a while, she dimly sensed the pair of tear-filled eyes fixed on her. She had no way of seeing the hatred in that gaze; she only felt puzzled and uncomfortable.

At about nine in the evening the thin, weak shadow of a human figure slipped into the sickroom. On her head she wore a cap tied with a scarf, on her body an old loose padded jacket. This was a chilly April, and no one cared about their appearance. Without a sound she walked to the front of Puti's bed and gripped the hand that had no bandage.

When Puti saw her, the thin hint of a smile played across the hollows of her cheeks.

"You don't need to say anything," said Huiyun. "I know you must be terribly tired, feeling very bad. I came to keep you company." She patted Puti's hand, then went to get a basin.

"I can speak." Puti felt her spirits improved several times over. "You've come. Is it okay?"

With an exhausted smile, Huiyun nodded her head and waved her hands. Nodding her head was to say staying to visit wasn't a problem; waving her hands meant Puti had better not talk. She set about nimbly washing Puti's hands and face.

At this moment Cui Li spied Huiyun, and softly said "ya"; the people in the sickroom all looked at her, and at Huiyun, with baffled expressions. Cui Zhen didn't recognize Huiyun, only thought that she looked a little familiar and assumed she was also from Y University. She asked: "What are you to Mei Puti?"

Huiyun and Puti looked at each other. Huiyun answered, "A neighbor," and quickly went to get water.

Old Qi said to Xiao Wei: "What person? A good person! I can tell for sure!"

Cui Zhen thought: "This thing should be reported! Being in the hospital shouldn't make one forget the class struggle!" She quickly wrote a note—for the intellectual, pen and paper are at the ready. She gave the note to her daughter, whispered a few words in her ear, and sent her out.

Cui Li left the hospital. In the light of the doorway she looked at the note. On it was written: "Comrade Zhang Yongjiang, Mei Puti's neighbor has come to visit her. This may need to be investigated." Cui Zhen had signed her name in particularly large letters. Cui Li tore the note up several times and threw it beside the road. The cold wind blew her short hair onto her forehead; her usual apprehensive look appeared even more apprehensive.

Before Fang Zhi returned to the dormitory, he again went to Room 308. In the doorway he happened to run into Xiao Wei coming out. Xiao Wei, seeing that Dr. Fang had no one with him, hurried to tell him his mother's condition and Dr. Xin's response to it, and implored Fang Zhi to think of a way . . .

"There may be no way." Fang Zhi smiled bitterly. He had just availed himself of the time when one nurse remained on duty to look at Aunt Wei's chart: it was a late stage of lung cancer. Dr. Xin's starting point had not been scientific enough, but he had reached the correct conclusion. As far as the cancer was concerned, his prognosis that there was no cure was tragically correct. Truly, in the face of cancer, doctors were so powerless. He thought again of Puti's surgery, and unconsciously gave a deep sigh.

"I looked at your mother's chart." He could still be of a little use and at least console this young man. "If we can just lessen her suffering, that will be good."

"My ma's not afraid of suffering," said Xiao Wei.

Fang Zhi did not answer. When they went into the sickroom, the patients were all asleep; only a wall light was burning. Aunt Wei already looked much weaker than in the morning. She was breathing very heavily, her eyes disinclined to open. But she knew that Dr. Fang listened to her with a stethoscope, and exerted herself to say: "Hasn't Dr. Fang taken a rest yet? As for me, don't worry."

Fang Zhi just wanted to hug the old lady, and admit to her that doctors were all idiots. She was already suffering badly, but said not one word of complaint; it was still "don't worry." A doctor, a doctor working hard at his duty, could only prescribe some medicines to alleviate the symptoms of terminal illness, and utter a few sentences of consolation.

Who was the bony little old lady beside Bed 2? Sitting upright in the dim light, knitting something, clearly she would sit waiting for the dawn.

"You are . . . ?" Fang Zhi asked hesitantly.

"A neighbor." Huiyun answered without wanting to answer. Lifting her eyes, she saw Fang Zhi in his white gown, his pale face gazing calmly, the aura of great goodness and honesty about him, and suddenly she felt that she knew who he was. "You're the good doctor, Dr. Fang."

Fang Zhi, reluctantly, gave a smiling nod.

"She's already taken a sleeping pill and gone to sleep. I'm looking after her, okay?"

"Okay," Fang Zhi said. In his day filled with all kinds of problems, this was the first one to have resolved itself in the ordinary course of events. It looked as though this emaciated old woman's relationship to the patient was out of the ordinary. "The author of *The Everlasting Rock* would naturally have this kind of emotionally rich relationship," Fang Zhi reflected inwardly.

"She may still vomit," he said to Huiyun. But he felt intuitively that he did not need to direct her; this old woman comrade obviously understood much more than unfamiliar doctors.

He quietly left the sickroom.

# 7

# Encounters in the Night

≋

T HE NIGHT DEEPENED. THE RUMBLING SOUND OF TRAINS CAME AND
went. Huiyun often straightened Puti's feet so that the infusion
would flow smoothly. She was extremely weary, but didn't dare close
her eyes. She considered that in addition to her function as nurse,
she also had the responsibility of bodyguard. In the dim light from
the corridor, it was possible to vaguely make out the outline of the
shifts coming into the sickroom. The extreme ferocity of the red
forks on the big-character posters gave the sickroom a disturbed atmosphere, as though they contained some sort of murderous
weapons.

"Old Qi! Old Qi!" Elder Sister Qi suddenly cried. No one answered. Crossing over, Huiyun saw that Old Qi, previously seated at
the foot of Bed 3, had gone off who knew where.

"Old Qi! Old Qi!" Elder Sister Qi called quickly again. Huiyun
immediately had a look at her. She looked at Huiyun. An expression
of loathing appeared on that peculiar face which had suffered so
much.

"I'll go look for him," Huiyun thought. She had just taken a step
when she hesitated. The infusion bottle was hanging quietly. If anyone threw anything toward the bottle the consequences could be dis-
astrous. As chance would have it, Xiao Wei wasn't there either. What
to do? Relying on her habit of always putting others first, she didn't
hesitate for long, but quickly decided: "Elder Sister, please look after
the bottle. I'll go look." Her manner was full of trust. Elder Sister
Qi's tossing and turning suddenly calmed. She looked carefully at
the bottle.

Huiyun hurried from the sickroom. The light at the nurses' desk
was very dim. The duty room was empty. She carefully looked at each
couch in the big hall: there was no one. On the balcony there was

73

only the vast and hazy light of night. "Where did he go?" Huiyun wondered, puzzled. She took a couple of turns up and down the hall. At the very end, in a recess for brooms and like items, she heard someone moaning. Old Qi was squatting, his two hands covering his face, emitting a birdlike sound, a sound so agonized and despairing it clutched Huiyun's heart.

"Old Qi!" Huiyun paused a moment, then quickly went forward. "Are you ill?"

Old Qi raised a face bathed in tears and sobbed.

Huiyun knew what the word "son" could measure. Her great eyes moistened with tears. Compassionately she helped Old Qi up. "Elder Sister Qi wants you." Old Qi's bony frame leaning on Huiyun's arms was indeed heavy. But he stood up right away, quickly rubbed his face with his hands, and slowly followed Huiyun back to the room.

"You're tired, too," Old Qi said softly in a low voice when they were inside.

This was equivalent to a "thank you" and didn't need an answer, but Huiyun answered, in a loud voice: "Because she is a good person." She looked at Puti, still sleeping peacefully, and suddenly became very fearful, reaching out to grasp Puti's wrist. Only when she felt it was normal did she relax.

The next day Mei Puti felt life returning to her body little by little, flowing in like the dripping medicine from the infusion bottle. In the afternoon the infusion ceased. The third day the rubber drainage tube was pulled out. Every time a tube was removed there was a bit more freedom; one could slowly move a little. Lying unable to move had been a fearful experience. The small of her back hurt so, it felt as though it would break; a circle of fire seared her tightly constricted chest. This kind of iron vest and iron belt could be included among hell's implements of torture. However, all in all, things improved day by day.

Early in the morning on the fourth day, Huiyun as usual commenced her activities before the others, thoroughly washing and grooming Puti. She fluffed up her pillow, pulled the quilt even, stood in front of the bed, and was filled with joy to look at Puti and see no objects attached to her.

"Now you and the bed are fresh and clean," she said softly.

"I think I'll put my glasses on." Puti narrowed her eyes, wanting to see Huiyun's expression clearly.

Huiyun hesitated. Wearing her glasses Puti would surely see the big-character posters on the opposite wall; the later she saw these, the better. "Wait another day to put them on. They could strain you."

"They won't strain me. I want to see what's around me, just have a look." Puti was in good spirits. Early on, she had seen the big-character posters stuck up on the wall opposite; she just couldn't make out their meaning. "You must take care. You can't get angry." Huiyun knew the truth would out. "It's only a piece of paper, rubbish not to be taken seriously. There's her, too." She glanced at Elder Sister Qi. "She's really to be pitied, you mustn't mind her." She hesitated and finally handed the glasses to Puti.

With one hand Puti lifted the glasses to her eyes and studied them carefully. Her heart began to brim with warm and strange feelings. Because of these rimless glasses with white gold frames, she had once been stopped on the street and admonished by two Red Guards. "To wear glasses is disgraceful enough, but rimless ones! These are 'four olds';[1] go back and change them!" Puti afterward was infinitely thankful the glasses had not been smashed on the spot. At that time changing a pair of glasses was easier said than done. Puti had to go on wearing hers with her heart in her mouth. She had gone through seeing her father's death, becoming ill herself, seeing the whole nation's cancer growing larger, the pus and blood of defilement everywhere. "So I'll wear you, I'll see the world, but now how will my eyes look at life?" Puti thought. She took the glasses, placed them on her chest, used the quilt and sheet to wipe the lenses, then put the glasses on.

She saw first the exhausted expression on Huiyun's face, the heavy weariness in its deep creases. For three nights Huiyun had not once closed her eyes. Without the slightest cheer for her morale, in a situation severely testing her physical strength, she had only a degree of the Chinese woman's litheness and an extreme tenacity—a special kind of dedication—to support her. She was trying to produce a smiling expression, but failed in the attempt, displaying instead a face full of apprehension. She stood at the foot of the bed, thinking to stand in Puti's line of vision.

Puti quickly saw the big characters wanting her to pay with her life. "There's another!" It occurred to her that Qi Yongshou's tragic ending could forever remain a mystery, and was saddened. As to wanting her to pay with her life, she in fact did not think this out of the ordinary: there had been similar wordings in the public criticism meetings. It was just that then, there had been no specific sacrificial rank, only talk of "spiritually shooting down" and so forth. Puti recollected the many times she had criticized herself: she had now gone

---

1. During the Cultural Revolution, the "four olds" referred to old ideas, old culture, old customs, and old habits.

through several months of the Cultural Revolution. Only with a big-character poster in front of her demanding her life did she realize her own innocence. As to her life, let come what may!

Then she saw Elder Sister Qi's gaze fixed on her with a look at once filled with hate, grief, and confusion. She was obviously the mother of Qi Yongshou. Puti shook from head to foot, her wound paining her as though it were about to split open. She so understood, so had to restrain her own maternal feelings. She wanted to ask: "Do you believe it?" But she did not speak. She thought: "If she believes it, let her attack, let her curse, let her draw blood with a knife from my body! As long as it eases her agony!" Elder Sister Qi in fact made no move, but only glared unblinkingly.

Puti managed to smile a little at Huiyun. Huiyun's small, wrinkled face was full of worry and anxiety. She said, bending over: "Courage!"

"Don't worry, I can manage to feel free and easy." Puti felt a little dizzy. She quickly urged Huiyun to leave and absolutely not to return that evening.

"Step by step you're conquering all, you must keep on," Huiyun exhorted. Naturally she had not stopped worrying, but after three endless nights she had come to feel that the Old Qi couple were not the kind to hurt others.

Cui Li had been sitting in front of Cui Zhen's bed for an indeterminate length of time. She looked steadily over toward Puti's bed, staring especially hard at Huiyun. Since her face wore its look of confusion and timidity, this impolite stare took on the appearance of earnestly hoping for something, of investigating something.

Huiyun felt very uncomfortable: was it possible the girl had some assignment? The best thing was not to approach her.

Waiting until Puti had closed her eyes and gone peacefully to sleep, Huiyun quickly arranged her scarf, picked up her handbag, and quietly left. Cui Li's eyes followed her out the door.

At about ten o'clock, doctors' general rounds were in progress in the ward. Ordinarily rounds were made once a week by the clinic director and the assistant directors, but now each of these persons had some kind of accusation against him. Some were being examined in isolation, some were cleaning toilets, some had arranged other means of subsistence. A real inspection simply could not proceed; inspections had ceased to exist except in name, although there were still a few people going through the motions. This day a cluster of people came into Room 308. Puti suspected that among them were actually several real doctors. Xin commanded the team. Sister Huo and Xiao Ding were both there, with Fang Zhi in the rear.

Xiao Wei hesitantly asked for treatment; Dr. Xin coldly refused to acknowledge him. When Fang Zhi proposed the medicine prescribed during the evening shift, Dr. Xin generously approved it. It so became formally doctor's orders, rather than the special response of the evening shift doctor to a terminal patient. Thus was Aunt Wei's medicine ensured. For several days the old lady had rarely opened her eyes, and her violent coughing was now rare. She did not know that so many people were at her bedside. The inspection for Puti was even more mechanical. As if he had not been present at the operation, Dr. Xin asked a few casual questions, all in the tone of a higher authority. Fang Zhi answered them all conscientiously. Puti wondered inwardly why Xin's voice and the one she had heard twice during surgery were similar.

Elder Sister Qi could not wait for this crowd of pedestrians to reach her bed. She cried out loudly: "Yesterday I was told you were going to operate for the third time. I'm not for you to enjoy slicing up. What is death! I just want to die!"

"You really take things easy!" Sister Huo was smiling.

Dr. Xin turned to inspect the procession: the doctor in charge of neck matters was not there. So he did not respond to Elder Sister Qi, but said to Sister Huo: "Try to persuade her to have surgery. How is Bed 4?"

Cui Zhen was usually not in the room; she was in the habit of going down the corridor to the lounge to sun herself. Dr. Xin did not want to pursue the matter thoroughly. He asked casually: "Should she be discharged?"

"She's running a temperature; she still bears watching," Fang Zhi answered. After her surgery, Cui Zhen had not had a fever; the day after Puti's surgery, for some unknown reason, she had begun to run one, every day at 37.5 degrees.

It wasn't clear whether Dr. Xin heard; he was busy looking at his watch, and murmuring to himself: "Really! I still have a meeting, let's hurry it up a bit." He then drew the group on to another room. Not one person—not even Dr. Xin—had cast a glance at the angry-looking big-character posters displayed on the wall.

They had just left when Cui Zhen returned. She said regretfully: "They all left? I was going to ask Dr. Xin why I still have a temperature."

"Then you trust Dr. Xin?" Elder Sister Qi hadn't spoken much for several days. Now she said provocatively: "If he can tell why you have a temperature, I'll write our 'Qi' character upside down."

"I trust Mao Zedong's thought. I trust the Revolution to solve all problems!" Cui Zhen's deathly pale face flushed with indignation. "In this hospital Dr. Xin is counted the most revolutionary! He's also famous in the health system. If you can't trust him, whom can you trust?"

"I trust Dr. Fang." Elder Sister Qi was unwilling to concede. "Dr. Fang is a good man, honest, decent. You are lucky to have had his surgery. The last time I was in the hospital someone's stomach and intestines ran out after rectal surgery!" As she spoke, she began to weep. "If Dr. Fang certifies our son killed himself, I'll believe it!"

Cui Zhen didn't wait for her to finish. Her face full of disdain, she said: "A good man? Decent? It's bourgeois humanism again." As she spoke, she turned the pages of her book and journal with much rustling.

Puti very much wanted to ask her what she considered, from the viewpoint of biology, to be the differences between men and animals. But she knew that her unfavorable status was not a good background for such conversation. The patients were dividing into two camps; it was so strange. She was really tired: it seemed that what sleep she got still could not overcome her weariness. Still, the more sleep, the better. . . .

After sleeping for several days Puti was already able to walk up and down the hall. On the tenth day, Dr. Fang called her into a treatment room to take out her stitches. Layer by layer, he unwrapped the gauze, until finally the $chi^2$-plus-long brilliant red scar on the front of her chest, and the deep-hollowed pit in her shoulder, came into view. A feeling of sadness enveloped her. She closed her eyes for a moment. Behind her lenses appeared two beautiful arcs. While Fang Zhi dexterously snipped off stitches and removed the ends of the thread, he found some words to say:

"In the future the treatment of cancer should be chemotherapy. Surgery is a method when there is no method."

"That's all right," Puti smiled at him. "The removal was complete."

"You'll still need treatment, cobalt 60 radiation, to kill any cancer cells that have slipped through the net."

"I'll do whatever I should." Puti was still saying this.

Fang Zhi wanted to tell her that he had not taken out the lymph nodes in the breast; he paused without opening his mouth. Puti thought he was uneasy because he had operated and said consolingly: "The surgery was fine. I only have some sentimental feelings—"

"What kind of feelings are sentimental?" Fang Zhi smiled.

"A sentimental feeling is a kind of petty bourgeois feeling, a dull distressed feeling that cannot be shaken off, that makes one want to

---

2. One-third of a meter, or about one foot.

weep, but tears just will not come." Puti still wore a smile, her tone was lighthearted. Fang Zhi's hand, however, trembled. He had to lift the special scissors in the air for a moment.

It was Fang Zhi's custom, each time he removed the stitches after surgery, to explain the surgical situation to the patient or the family members, along with the postsurgical treatment program and other matters needing attention. After he had pulled out the forty-second stitch-head and placed some gauze over the wound, he had still not decided whether to explain to Puti that the surgery had not been thorough.

He asked Puti to sit at the side of the desk, and gave a cough. Puti's expression was calm and sanguine. She looked at Fang Zhi with a smile, as if encouraging him to speak. Fang Zhi coughed again, and finally explained her surgical situation. As to the reason for it, he said only that her blood pressure had dropped suddenly during the surgery. He emphasized that radiation and medicines could exterminate the latent threat. He explained that the cancer of the glands from which she was suffering was a relatively mild kind of cancer.

Puti listened attentively. She wasn't the least bit shocked or frightened. She felt inwardly quite prepared for whatever might follow. Moreover, she had Dr. Fang: he would be able to set everything right. "I trust you, Dr. Fang." She said again: "I leave everything up to you, Dr. Fang."

"Good, good." Dr. Fang, writing on the chart, did not raise his head.

When Puti arrived at the door of the sickroom, she saw the room in temporary confusion: they were just pulling Aunt Wei's bed to a separate room. Xiao Wei and a nurse were pulling it, while Sister Huo was holding up the infusion bottle. When the bed had been pulled to the doorway, Aunt Wei suddenly opened her eyes and gathered the strength to say: "What are you doing? Why are you going to all this trouble? Er Leng,[3] you've taken too much time off—" Xiao Wei softly called his mother's name and rubbed his eyes with the back of his hand. Aunt Wei indistinctly saw Puti standing beside the door and said: "Teacher Mei can walk all over. Good person, good reward. As for me, don't worry about me. . . ." She spoke very slowly. As she was speaking, the bed was pulled out the door and to the other end of the corridor where there was a small separate room, a station on the way to death.

---

3. Aunt Wei's son's name.

Puti heaved a deep sigh. Everyone in the room was going through some kind of fierce life-and-death struggle. She had temporarily triumphed. Aunt Wei, however, was going to depart.

The room was very empty. She stood before the window, casually looking at the flowers and trees below. The winter jasmine was already about to wither; the lilacs were right at their peak, their little white and purple flowers a gaudy array of color. The Chinese flowering crabapple, which Aunt Wei liked, was just in pink bud. The Chinese people[4] loved flowers very much. When Puti was working in the countryside, she had felt this deeply. In front of houses and behind rooms, roses, hollyhock varieties, chrysanthemums, and peonies were invariably interspersed among the eggplant and kidney beans.

People needed the floral hues to bring a little color into their lives of hardship. Flowers were often used as a metaphor for the beauty of the female sex. In reality, though, women, above all Chinese women, and even more Chinese peasant women with their gentle and tenacious virtues of modesty and self-restraint acquired over thousands of years, were quite incomparable to any kind of flower. In every household, when others were already in dreamland, the mother could always be found sewing and mending the family's clothes, shoes, and socks by candlelight; when everyone was still abed she would again be busy about the family meals, including those for pigs, chickens, cats, and dogs. If there wasn't enough to eat, it was always she who first went hungry; if there weren't enough clothes to wear, it was always she who would first feel the pinch of cold. She would fix meals for visiting cadres, stitch army shoes, send her husband off to work or war, and dedicate her sons. It was she who endured astonishing sufferings, always saying with a smile: "Don't worry about me!"

Puti, looking at the buds of the pink flowering crabapple, thought silently: and then among these great and virtuous Chinese women a degenerate had appeared! A degenerate bringing calamity to the country and people!

When Puti thought like this, she would feel an involuntary pang of fear. She quickly looked in Cui Zhen's direction to see if Cui Zhen could read what she was thinking. It so happened Cui Zhen was looking at her, wanting to know if she was having diathermy.

---

4. The Chinese phrase is literally translated as "the old hundred names," meaning average citizens, common people. Here, however, the meaning refers to the Chinese peasant.

"I am."

"Are you having much?"

"I still don't know."

Xiao Ding and a radiologist came in to notify Puti that at 12:30 that night she should go to the outpatient service for radiation. Since the apparatus was in use twenty-four hours a day, outpatients were treated in the daytime, so hospitalized patients had to arrange for the night. The radiologist drew a red line on Puti's chest, to mark the scope of the radiation she would receive. Puti looked at the garish right side of her chest, and could not repress a feeling of loss.

After Xiao Ding and the doctor had left, Cui Zhen said resentfully: "Some things are very strange! For someone like you to receive complete treatment!"

Puti knew Cui Zhen was again talking principles, and only answered slowly: "Someone like me? At the least I am a human being."

Cui Zhen rejoined: "You are only a human being biologically. You know yourself that in reality some people are devils! Whatever is done should be done according to principles!"

Puti gave Cui Zhen a pitying look, and said nothing more. How could there really be people like this in the world who hardened their own hearts to hack and grind, with other people's formulations! Was this proper staunchness, or psychological deficiency? Her so-called principles only profited a minority. Furthermore, Cui Zhen's life was actually a miserable one. Her daughter did not like her "principles" and their relationship was not intimate. No one from the department had come to see her. She did not enjoy as much warmth from others as Puti. Yet she was always proud of her "principles," she was always in a state of self-congratulation, taking pleasure day to day in the level she had attained.

"What produces that state of mind?" Puti said to herself. She could not resist casting a glance at Cui Zhen. During the past few days Cui Zhen had frequently been unable to eat. Her complexion was not only pale, it was also dried up and sickly. Yet she retained her air of self-complacency; to see this was actually surprising. When Cui Zhen realized Puti was not responding, she complacently gave guidance to Elder Sister Qi instead, telling her to have her third surgery the next day, to bravely accept the challenge. Elder Sister Qi sighed in a low voice, saying that it would have been better if she had been sick a few years earlier: at least then she could have had good doctors.

"You say good doctors. You mean pathologists?" Puti purposely asked Elder Sister Qi. Elder Sister Qi, staring at her, turned her head and didn't answer.

Cui Zhen smiled coldly. Xiao Ding came in just in time with a change of subject. "That Dr. Han is an old craftsman. When the Cultural Revolution had just started, he was sent to a mortuary to take care of dead people. Then the pathologists next door were short a man, and called him out."

This referred to the doctor who had let Puti plainly see, before her own eyes, the normal cells and the cancer cells. He was named Han? He was an old doctor? Thinking about it, he did indeed have something familiar about him. However, what? Puti's head started to ache. She slowly lay down and went to sleep.

Because she had to have radiation at 12:30, Puti did not dare to sleep as evening came on: every little while she would look at her watch. With great difficulty she lasted until 12:00, then left the sickroom. The hallway was dim, the rooms on both sides very quiet. From several directions came moaning sounds wafting through the darkness. Patients could not escape their torments at night! She turned her head toward the small room at the end of the corridor: it was silent. How was Aunt Wei? "Tomorrow I'll go and see her," she thought, and started downstairs. She took a few steps, her legs feeling like jelly, and had to lean on the banisters for a bit before going on. Suddenly she saw a dark shadow walking upstairs in the dim light. The two met. Puti's heart gave a leap. The man's complexion was dark; on one-half of his face was drawn a fresh red square. He went right on up. When she reached the second floor another dark shadow came up: his collar was wide open, and on his neck were drawn two red lines. If Puti had believed in ghosts, she really would have believed that she had encountered a decapitated wandering spirit. With great difficulty she proceeded down the stairs, feeling flustered and weak in the legs. At the entrance to the staircase she leaned against a bench to regain her balance and pull herself together.

She heard the rumble of a cart slowly being pushed along. The two sides of a ward door opened. She saw only two people pushing a flat cart. On the cart was something wrapped in a white cloth, and the two people pushing the cart were Fang Zhi and Xiao Wei.

Aunt Wei was dead! Puti understood quickly. She hurried over to grasp Xiao Wei's hand. She bent over to look at Aunt Wei's body, but the layer of white cloth covered her completely. Dead, never again to return, like her mother, her father. Just as the years that had passed would never return.

Fang Zhi looked silently at Puti, and with Xiao Wei pushed the flat cart toward the yard where the lilacs grew, and crossed the yard to the mortuary.

Aunt Wei was over fifty. However, if she had had a healthy body, she could have been said to be in the prime of her life. But after the hardships and suffering that she had endured, she had been forced to leave Er Leng and the flowering crabapple.

That most degenerate specimen of womankind was very possibly Aunt Wei's age. She had not made shoes for the army or fixed meals for cadres, but she was very energetically alive. Casual words from her lips put whole groups of people in danger of their lives. On a path stained with who knows how much red blood and white bones, she had climbed onto the throne, conspiring there with her wicked-looking deputy commander in chief.[5] Was this then the fate of the revolution? How wrong! If Aunt Wei had known this, would she have been able to say, with a smile: "Don't worry!"

"But Aunt Wei, that sort of good heart, simple and unadorned— had she on any account been able to think in this way?" Full of misgivings, Puti sat down outside the door of the radiation section, lost in deep thought. When her turn came it was already 12:40 a.m. A technician beckoned her into a small empty room where there was only a narrow bed, on it a contraption resembling a big hat, shaped like a hairdresser's dryer, though much larger. Puti lay down, and the technician laid a lead apron outside the red lines on her chest, to avoid harming good tissue. She wanted to express her thanks for the technician's working late at night, but this technician's face had a look of displeasure, with no hint of desire to converse.

"Lie still, don't move! It'll be over in a minute!" he said and went out.

It was very quiet all around. It was, after all, deep at night. The round hat-shaped contraption sat on her body like a protruding eyeball wanting to spy on the secrets of patients' hearts. Puti suddenly began to feel afraid. In the operating room, the surgery had been audible, and there had been many people. Here the therapy was invisible: she did not know what kind of thing was penetrating her flesh. Moreover, the walls were especially thick: one could only cope alone. "I must be brave, though, and relax." Puti laughed at herself, worked hard at calming herself down. She was still not completely at ease, however, when the radiation was over.

"So cancer in internal organs is most to be feared, because it can't be seen," Puti thought, walking out to the stairs. From a dis-

---

5. The "degenerate specimen" is Jiang Qing, Mao Zedong's wife; the deputy is Lin Biao, then vice-chairman of the Central Committee of the Chinese Communist Party.

tance, she saw two people sitting on the long bench: the one in green leaning against the back was Xiao Wei; the one in white with bent head was Fang Zhi. Fang Zhi sensed that someone was there and lifted his head. His cool, profound gaze was dulled, his kind-hearted expression seemed frozen. His grief was not less than Xiao Wei's, although from early on he had known what Aunt Wei's fate would be. Xiao Wei was shedding tears, like a son. Fang Zhi was grieving, like a doctor who treated people's ills because he could not cure the hardships of the world.

"Dr. Fang, you should rest a bit," Puti said warmly. "You're very tired."

"Tired, no." Every time he could not cure a patient Fang Zhi felt apologetic and remorseful. Originally he had thought that with the passage of time such feelings of remorse would dissipate: the lives and deaths of patients should concern doctors as professional matters, not as emotional ones; this was the reality. But after advancing in his medical practice from junior hospital doctor to surgeon doctor (even though he had long since ceased to qualify for Party membership), these apologetic moods had remained with him. This year, especially, opportunities to improve the standards of medical treatment were becoming increasingly rare, recently bordering on the verge of exercises in absolute folly. This really pained him. Why proclaim this confused state of affairs to be for the revolution?

At first Puti thought she would go on upstairs. On impulse, however, she sat down next to Fang Zhi. The three sat without speaking.

After a time Fang Zhi said: "Teacher Mei, you go up, the night is cold. I'm thinking about when we can actually cure cancer."

Xiao Wei said consolingly: "The treatment wasn't inadequate, Dr. Fang. If you think about it, lots of people can't even stay in the hospital." He spoke still leaning over the back of the bench.

Puti looked warmly at Fang Zhi, and said thoughtfully: "When my mother died, I wept for quite a few days. My father told me to think often of 'examining the soul,' a kind of game the three of us often played together. 'Examining the soul' means asking whether or not the soul deserves a physical form. I was exhausted from weeping. I felt as though my soul was a line torn by the wind, about to float far away. So I recalled it, set it right. When my father died, my soul felt like disheveled grass; the filth spilled on it was too great; it was difficult to rake. But as I made the effort, I raked it clear. The day I saw the big-character poster in the sickroom, I felt as though my soul were a wisp of white cloud in a blue sky: falsehood so wide of the mark could indeed enable me to realize my innocence."

"I can certify to your power as a writer," Fang Zhi suddenly exclaimed fervently. "Death is not the end, life is boundlessly glorious, I have learned this from experience." Fang Zhi almost wanted to talk about the time on Fragrant Hills, but he was not in the habit of divulging his inmost thoughts. He needed to wait until people asked "Where did you see the book?" Then he could answer. Having uttered two abstract remarks, he felt as though he had said a "thank you" that summed up thousands and thousands of words. Tender feelings throbbed in his chest.

The night was as cold as water. The slightly sweet fragrance of lilacs drifted in from outdoors. Suddenly there was a sound of gongs and drums, people running about everywhere, yelling. Puti thought something must have happened. Xiao Wei stood up, at the ready. Fang Zhi said calmly: "It's probably the newest directive."

Puti returned to the room. She found it in an uproar: the nurses had all come and were running up and down the corridor. The patients were asking one after another: "What's going on?" Cui Zhen held paper and pen, and was sitting on the bed making a great show of earnestness. Her face was so pale it was almost blue. She still wore her "see me, how enthusiastic I am" expression, and was just telling Elder Sister Qi to get up. Elder Sister Qi was not responding. There was a sound of footsteps running down the hall. Xiao Ding rushed in hurriedly and pulled Elder Sister Qi up. Almost immediately several medical students wearing Red Guard armbands charged in and stood about the room like ferocious devils, loudly yelling: "Everyone get paper and pen ready and prepare to take notes!"

Puti hurried to give the paper and pen she already had in hand to Elder Sister Qi. Unexpectedly Elder Sister Qi threw these on the floor, crying: "I'm illiterate, I can't take notes!"

A Red Guard flared up and shouted: "Not taking notes is counterrevolutionary!" He raised the belt in his hand and moved to hit Elder Sister Qi. Puti instinctively bent over to shield her. Elder Sister Qi, taken aback, clung to her. The two women's tears flowed together.

# 8

# Spoon Court

MEI PUTI HAD BEEN GONE FROM THE HOSPITAL FOR OVER A WEEK. DURing that week Fang Zhi felt that life lacked something; he was even morose. Every day early in the morning, he put on his long white gown, attended a morning meeting, and passed Room 308. He could never refrain from turning his head to look at the door. Elder Sister Qi was the only old patient left behind, firmly refusing a third surgery. She was doomed to leave the world before long. When he was on duty, he often thought of asking about Bed 2's blood tests and appearance, but then remembered in a flash that she had already left the hospital. She had completed a period of treatment; after the treatment her white blood cell count was only three thousand, platelets dropped from fifty thousand. There was nothing for it but to suspend treatment and let her go, keeping her under observation outside the hospital. As a resident doctor at Z Hospital, his responsibilities had ceased. Unfinished cases were an outside responsibility; following the practice of years, a matter for the "follow-up" group. However, he was a friend; their relationship had not terminated. He often thought of her little book that had so heartened him, thought of her "examining the soul" words of the bench. Even though her soul itself was like a white cloud in a blue sky, how could this woman, disfigured by disease, go on living?

It was already the beginning of May. Spring had come late to Beijing; the blossoms were still not over. "The struggle to take power" had been going on for some months. Since the end of April the Beijing municipality had established revolutionary committee members' meetings. The *People's Daily* published an editorial about this, with the theme "The Unvanquished Thought of Mao Zedong—a New Song of Triumph." Those who were to assume power had already assumed it. They naturally still needed organization, so for special

87

expansion they added three combinations of leaders to cope with struggle-criticism-transformation.[1] The "May First" editorial used black-bodied characters to set forth Chairman Mao's teachings: "We must take care to unite with all those with whom we can unite"; "it is necessary to implement the teachings of Marx: 'Only when all humanity is liberated can the proletariat itself be liberated.'" The editorial further stated that not only was "courage needed to attack a handful," but "daring to liberate a large segment." In reality the two groups' estrangement became increasingly profound, as each set itself on its own course of revolution, on resistance to the opposite faction. At heart each felt an angry sense of injustice, and an oppression of the spirit that prompted them to struggle to the death. For those who were not "big target" "monsters and demons," times improved somewhat; some people even met with kindness, permitting them to resume their lives among the masses conducting the revolution.

It was a Saturday afternoon. Fang Zhi was on duty in the ward. He was leafing through a small notebook in which were written some plans for surgeries, simple case histories, some addresses, telephone numbers. Alone on the last page was written "Spoon Garden, Y University, Number 1." He had already more than once stared blankly at the paper on this page. He had also more than once gone to a patient's home, to ease the sufferings of critically ill patients, to arrange treatments for patients with relapses. He had more than once made life-and-death decisions regarding the treatment of patients. But facing this page, he could not decide whether to call on this patient about whom he was especially concerned. There was nothing for it but to put down the notebook, and casually turn over the mail on the office desk. Suddenly he saw a letter with the words "Dr. Fang Zhi, personal."

The letter was from Tao Huiyun. It asked very simply about the efficacy of currently popular anticancer tablets, asked whether Puti could make use of them, asked whether Fang Zhi could act as the purchasing agent for some. Since the professional duty to produce good results was without question a bad effect of bourgeois or revisionist thought, new products were necessarily not produced professionally. The result had been the emergence of all sorts of unorthodox therapeutic methods. Numerous mimeographed materials touted

---

1. For the Great Proletarian Cultural Revolution, this was the ideal three-step formula for reform; however, the ideal was seldom realized in the confusion of reality.

magical anticancer remedies and devious body-building long-life come-ons. Fang Zhi had never believed in anticancer tablets, but presently he was indeed thankful that there was talk of anticancer tablets in the world, so that Teacher Tao had written the letter. He need no longer turn the matter over hesitantly in his mind, need no longer endlessly, senselessly worry himself. By five o'clock in the afternoon he was standing before the entrance to Spoon Court with anticancer tablets in hand.

The vase-shaped little gateway faced obliquely on the reed pond. The new reeds were green and lush, not very thick, and the mud exposed their roots. To the right and left of the little entrance, two large heaps of garbage had been piled up and long since neglected; someone was just emptying on one. The day would inevitably come when the little gateway would be impassable. . . . What was the scene inside the little entrance? He carefully read the number on the doorplate beside the gate, the paint of which was peeling off, feeling that if he did not knock at once, he would arouse suspicion. He put out his hand to knock, and with the knock discovered the gate was unlatched, so he pushed it lightly and went in.

The first thing he saw was the strange rock in the middle of the court. A wild climbing plant embellished it with a few branches and leaves, the green shades on the upright prominence softening it considerably. "This then is the Everlasting Rock," Fang Zhi thought. Beside the rock were two little rooms. He hesitated a moment, then asked: "Is Teacher Mei at home?"

"Who is it?" The fine, soft voice floated out from behind the pale cotton-print curtains.

"It's Fang Zhi."

"Oh! Fang Zhi?" The voice was full of astonishment. The door opened. Mei Puti stood beside it, still utterly graceful and comely. However, looking carefully, one could sense that she was definitely one-sided, her whole person askew. "Dr. Fang!" she smiled and put out her hand. "Please come in."

"Is it a surprise?" Fang Zhi came in, and sat down on an old chair beside the door: there was no space in the room for him to walk further.

"I expected you. You are a conscientious doctor—everyone knows that. I thought you would come—perhaps it was a kind of longing. I'm concerned: how is Elder Sister Qi?" Puti continued to smile as she spoke. She pulled open the curtain and sat herself down in front of the table on an old rattan chair.

The room brightened considerably. Fang Zhi saw that Puti was no longer sallow, that her spirits were good. He felt very comforted.

He spoke briefly of Elder Sister Qi's condition: she probably could only drag on one or two months more. Puti sighed deeply. He asked about Puti's health; he knew it had been completely normal after the second diathermy. He still needed to examine the incision. He thought it best to have a third person present, so he asked: "Is your good neighbor—Teacher Tao—at home?"

"Saturday is the day for cleaning the toilets. Huiyun is matchless, a good person. I was really lucky to have her when I became ill—even luckier to have you, Dr. Fang." Puti leaned to look out the window. From this aspect one could see her eyelids quivering slightly.

Fang Zhi said quickly: "Don't think I am a particularly conscientious doctor. I don't treat all patients equally."

Puti turned to look at him. "I don't believe that. You just about do that, to the best of your ability." She thought of Aunt Wei, wrapped in the white cloth. "However, if you see me in a special light, naturally I'm all the more grateful." She smiled broadly as she spoke.

"If you want to speak of gratitude, that's of course all right, too." Fang Zhi hesitated. "What I mean is that I'm really not some kind of good person. Sometimes I'm really disgusted with myself. I'm a long way from being a real doctor. We all are."

"If you can consider yourself a long way from it, you're pretty close to being a good person."

"When I was young I once thought of being an artist. If Liberation hadn't come, I wouldn't have succeeded at anything. The year of Liberation—I was fifteen—I caught the disease kala-azar. A Liberation Army doctor saved me. So I wanted to become a doctor and save people. Only when I put on a long white gown and took up the surgeon's knife did I realize how hard it is to be a real doctor." Surprisingly, Fang Zhi had not waited for any questions but had said all this in one breath.

"I also wanted to study medicine at one time." Puti suddenly thought dejectedly of the bygone days of her girlhood. "But I loved literature even more. Who would have thought that literature could have brought this kind of suffering?"

"Successful doctors are reactionary authorities, too. It's hard for anyone to escape." Fang Zhi paused, and, turning to look out of the window, couldn't refrain from saying: "I saw the Everlasting Rock as soon as I came in."

"You call it the Everlasting Rock seeing it for the first time?" Puti was surprised.

"Isn't it? Although I don't often read novels, your book was so beautiful, I couldn't not read it, and upon reading it, I couldn't help weeping." He, then, without pausing for breath, told Puti of his encounter with the book on Fragrant Hills. But he did not tell her about his reason for going to Fragrant Hills.

Puti was both surprised and moved. "This is actually a little like the novel."

"So I'm really thankful to your school's rebels; otherwise I would have gone my whole life without ever coming to know the author of *The Everlasting Rock*. When I read nonmedical books, I usually never pay any attention to who the author is."

Puti knew that the pen name that she used made paying attention rather pointless. "You didn't believe those critical articles? And the big-character posters demanding my life?"

"Previously there were some critical articles I believed." He still believed he himself had taken a mistaken position. "Afterwards—afterwards, I don't quite know how, I stopped believing them. It was not necessarily just because of your book."

There was a sound from the neighboring door. Puti got up and knocked on the wall. In a little while Huiyun entered. She cried out with pleasure and surprise: "Dr. Fang! I knew you'd come. I can't shake your hand: I've just been cleaning toilets." She still wore the protective green scarf; even her forehead was covered. Wreathed in smiles, her expression was completely unlike the time he had seen her in the hospital. One could sense, however, that she was extraordinarily tired.

Fang Zhi immediately took Huiyun's hand, and shook it firmly. "I'm going to ask your help. I need to inspect Teacher Mei's incision."

The two women immediately understood Fang Zhi's motive, that he didn't want to do the inspection alone. They smiled at each other, and both looked solemnly at Fang Zhi.

Puti's incision was doing very well. Fang Zhi carefully and gently pressed a finger on two slightly raised places beside the crucial spot: "leftover fatty tissue." "It's all right," he said, relaxing. "You can check it often yourself, the other side as well. For a few years, there's always a chance." They understood he didn't actually want to say the word "recurrence."

"As time goes on, it gets safer and safer, doesn't it?" Huiyun asked.

"You could say that."

They chatted casually. Fang Zhi could never have imagined that in this broken-down old courtyard, in the company of two women long since past their springtime, he could feel such peace of mind and contentment. Only when he was ready to take his leave did he remember the anti-cancer tablets that had amounted to his invitation card. He pulled them out and placed them on the table, saying to Huiyun: "These are the anti-cancer tablets Teacher Tao wanted—"

Huiyun, laughing, quickly said: "Oh, Dr. Fang, are they of any use?"

"You asked for them?" Puti looked at Huiyun, then suddenly saw the light.

"I don't believe they're of any use. This medicine is arsenic, actually white arsenic. There's no other component."

"White arsenic?" Huiyun and Puti asked simultaneously.

"White arsenic. Perhaps someone thought that poison attacks poison. But the matter isn't that simple. I brought the medicine with me, however. Teacher Mei absolutely does not need to take it."

Such was Fang Zhi's advice. Puti nodded with a smile. Huiyun said, grinning craftily: "I'll use them to take care of mice. There're too many mice here."

As Fang Zhi was on the point of leaving, Huiyun solicitously asked him to come again the next week. He hesitated, then agreed. Only when he went out of the courtyard gate and turned to look back did he become aware of a tall willow tree beside the gate. He felt the courtyard behind the tree to be utterly beautiful, overlaid with an atmosphere of romance. Yet, in reality, he had only seen two people and a rock.

After a week, as expected, Fang Zhi revisited Spoon Court. During the course of the week he had twice come to Y University to have a look at the big-character posters, each time lingering for a while before returning home. He himself was unaware that he was lingering on the school grounds in the hope of running into Puti, although he knew that she surely would not come out. Upon reentering Spoon Court, he noticed several plants with large gaily-colored flowers under the eaves of the little room, their petals like soft yellow and lavender gauze. Puti, glimpsing him from the window, opened the door and welcomed him in. Seeing him looking at the flowers, she explained: "These are *yulan* magnolia. Tao Hui found them on the garbage heap after she moved here. We didn't think they could still bloom." Fang Zhi felt surprised that he had not noticed them on the previous occasion.

He again took a single step before sitting down on the chair and, looking casually around, observed that the room, although small, was pleasantly clean and tidy. A board was tacked to the west wall; a bed was placed against the east wall facing a quotation from Chairman Mao, a sentence he had written: "Since this is so, it's better to accept it."[2] Puti sat at the table. On the table she had a thick china bowl half-filled with dark fluid, a copybook, and sheets of paper originally intended for writing big characters.

"You were practicing calligraphy?" Fang Zhi smiled.

"I've heard that practicing calligraphy can calm your nerves. If my nerves are transmitting normal information, then they probably won't allow cancer to start."

"Right—you've read a lot of medical books. Can I see?" Fang Zhi picked up a sheet of characters. The characters were remarkably graceful—looking at them, one knew they were a woman's strokes. "I can't read without punctuation." He continued to hold the characters up admiringly.

"This is Sun Guoting's calligraphy manual"—Puti handed over the copybook—"remnants of writings that have been carefully patched up and pasted on newsprint. I picked it up on the garbage heap. We have both profited from finding odds and ends." Puti laughed nonchalantly. "These can be very useful to me, with no books to read; nor can I knit wool—I have no way of managing the struggle with the yarn. Writing characters, on the other hand, can exercise my arm."

"Maybe we should provide character writing in the hospital to build patients up."

Puti did not answer, but passed over several rough sketches, all of bamboo. Some were uninhibited and dark, some interestingly pale and sparse. "Last time you said you liked to paint?"

"But that was an emotional exercise. I can't really paint anything. From early childhood I grew up beside Panxi Stream. I only painted the rocks and stream. These bamboo are very good; I also like bamboo."

"You are a Sichuan man, I knew it the first time I saw you. I lived in Chongqing. Dad taught there during the War of Resistance."[3]

"Have you been to Panxi Stream?" He thought of Panxi Stream with its rocks, some large, some small, some weirdly shaped, some glittering and translucent.

"I've been." She thought of saying something, but swallowed.

An emaciated, unprepossessing little tabby cat squeezed in from the space between the door and frame and rubbed itself back and

---

2. This sentence was from a letter from Chairman Mao to a cadre friend who was ill. It became a commonly used saying for the sick. Its use here is not intended to be ironic, but comforting.

3. That is, against Japan.

forth against Puti's feet. "This is from the garbage heap, too," Puti introduced. "It wants something to eat." As she spoke she opened the door and went out, the little cat following quickly at her feet.

Fang Zhi, trying to dispel the memory of the rocks, turned over the paintings before him. He saw that on one was written: "Without leaving the ground, the bamboo already has joints; when it reaches the sky, it is without pretension."[4] Waiting until Puti returned, he said: "These two phrases beautifully express the nature of bamboo. This could be the making of the upright person, too. But at present I simply don't know where the joint is."

Puti casually added a bamboo stem to the painting of bamboo. "I don't know either. We are permanently in the midst of being remolded. We want to believe in the Party, to believe in the system, to reform ourselves, criticize ourselves. But if we can't believe in ourselves, how can one find the 'joint'?"

"I still believe in doing good surgery."

"If I had studied medicine, I could at least trust my stethoscope. But now, according to Party theory, I have been wrong. All wrong. And yet, I can only believe in this 'wrong.'"

"Only a few people are 'right'!" Fang Zhi blurted out.

"In reality it's a few people usurping one person's power, grabbing hold of the destinies of hundreds of millions." Puti still smiled offhandedly.

"Why does he allow it?" Fang Zhi asked poignantly.

Neither could answer. As they spoke, the two instinctively looked at each other in surprise. Many people were thinking similarly, but exceedingly few dared to speak out, or even talk to themselves. Everyone's heart had a locked door behind which no one, not even the person himself, dared to peep. Words such as those just uttered by Fang Zhi and Puti could quite simply put a person's life in danger. Such was the situation in the year 1967. Several years later, when two people came together casually, each could express his or her gloomy personal views, and having spoken thus, could say half jokingly: "If you expose me, I'll just say you said it!"

After a pause Puti said: "When I first entered the Party, I really cherished the ideal of dedication to the cause of Communism, an ideal that seemed very real to me then, even though its outlines were

---

4. "Joint" here refers to moral integrity at a critical juncture. The poem's meaning is that even after a person has acquired high status, he retains his moral integrity.

somewhat vague. I believed that each person would have the right to live as a human being. The meaning of 'The White-Haired Girl'[5] stood for this. The old society had turned people into ghosts; the new society would transform ghosts into people. If we, in our turn, turn many innocent people into ghosts, what kind of 'new society' will it become! But so often, one has to be wrongly attacked oneself before one can truly understand the misfortunes of others."

"There are times when I still don't understand." Fang Zhi then told Puti about his encounter with "anti-Rightism." "Others said I was muddleheaded. Why did I want to give an account of my thinking, lose my Party membership? I thought that if the Party didn't want someone who thought the way I did, then I definitely didn't want to join it under false colors."

Puti fixed her gaze on Fang Zhi, on that gaunt face with its famished look. Even though they had only known each other a little over a month, she had come to know Fang Zhi would have behaved like that.

"Although at that time I suffered, because I had never imagined the Party would reject me, I accepted the decision without complaint. I still felt unalterably a part of the Party. At that time I had not seen others' misfortune. I always believed the Party could do no wrong."

Words gushed from the depths of their hearts like spring water, cleansing their souls of the dirt and blood smeared on them both by their opponents—and by themselves. Without their being aware of it, the last rays of the setting sun disappeared from the Everlasting Rock. Puti said firmly: "Agreed, I'll go and cook some porridge; you eat here with us." Huiyun did not want to let Puti perform such tasks, but Puti would not listen to her.

"Is it convenient?" Fang Zhi was somewhat at a loss. Turning suddenly to the question of eating, they had dropped from the gentle and soft world of emotions down to earth. But for Fang Zhi the down-to-earth of Spoon Court was still very warm and gentle. "If you need anything done, I'll do it. You're a patient, you direct. I'll do it." He followed Puti in and out, helping her wash rice and pick vegetables.

Huiyun came in the door just then, pushing her bicycle, and happily greeted Fang Zhi. Seeing Puti working in the court, she gave a "Hi" and, balancing her bicycle with one hand, deftly seized the vegetables in Puti's hand with the other.

---

5. A favorite story of the Chinese Revolution, about a peasant girl whose hair turned white from her hardships. Liberation saved her.

"This is the director," Puti smiled at Fang Zhi. "We'll both take orders from her."

So under Huiyun's direction the three ate a simple evening meal, seating themselves casually in the court. Huiyun as usual sat on her little blue stool. Placing a large enamel cup and a chipped china dish—her ashtray—on the ground in front of her, she interspersed raising and lowering her cigarette with drinks of water. Puti sat on the old rattan chair, Fang Zhi on a brick fragment beside the large rock facing the willow tree outside the court. The sky was not very dark; light came from buildings in the distance, and the stars shone dimly. They could hear the frequent sound of heavy footsteps passing by outside the courtyard.

Spoon Court, the little green oasis in the desert, had acquired one more wandering traveler. Henceforth, Fang Zhi came every two or three days. Each time he came he felt, afterwards, as though he had taken some soothing medicine that both cleansed and nourished his spirit. And each time he came, he contributed to Puti's strength to go on living, and raised Huiyun's hopes.

One evening, an unexpected guest arrived suddenly in Spoon Court. Puti saw her standing in the courtyard, a perplexed and fearful expression on her plump round face, and quickly recognized Cui Li. She had come to find Huiyun. It was then almost eight o'clock; Huiyun had still not come home. Puti invited the girl into her room to sit down.

Cui Li seemed very uneasy. She sat for a while without saying a word, and then, bending over the table, began to weep. Puti was astonished.

"What is it? Calm down a bit. How is your mother, anyway?"

Puti's second question brought up Cui Zhen's illness. "Her? She's not going to die," Cui Li said with a sob. "I—I—"

Puti poured her some water and patted her shoulders encouragingly.

"I—I and Qin Ge—" Cui Li couldn't speak for sobbing: "We were friends at first, then he suddenly said he didn't want me anymore. I think he has someone else—" Cui Li, having struggled to say that much, suddenly began to weep uncontrollably.

So it was that kind of thing, Puti thought. That explained why Cui Li had paid so much attention to Huiyun at the hospital. "Where is Qin Ge now?" she asked eagerly. She knew this was Huiyun's greatest concern.

"He stays in the basement in the main building at the college. He's living there. I used to live there, too." A smile flickered over Cui Li's tearful face.

"He's never come home. He completely cut off his relationship with his mother." Puti looked Cui Li up and down and spoke slowly.

"I—know." Cui Li gradually calmed down, lifted the cup of water, and drained it, as though she had not drunk water for a long time. "At first we could be compared on every point. My father had killed himself; his mother was a counterrevolutionary. My mother was one of the revolutionary masses, his father was Kuomintang. He wasn't even as good as me. But now he resents me, ignores me. There's got to be someone else."

"Perhaps he's just absorbed in carrying on the revolution," Puti said comfortingly.

"We never affected the revolution, either." Cui Li paused, then said: "He criticized his family, criticized it thoroughly. But I always felt he worried about his mom. He certainly didn't talk about that. When I saw Tao Huiyun in the hospital, I always wanted to talk with her. I even let Mom stay a few days later at the hospital, but afterwards I didn't see Tao Huiyun." She didn't feel it at all unnatural to speak of Tao Huiyun directly.[6]

"How did you 'let' Mom stay a few days later in the hospital? Wasn't she running a high fever?" Puti was rather surprised.

"That was my 'letting' the thermometer go up." Cui Li was a little proud of herself: "I put the mercury head in the hot water bottle, for not too long. I wanted to talk with Qin Ge's mother. I was awfully depressed." As she spoke she suddenly seemed to think of something, and asked: "For Heaven's sake, how's your illness?"

"It's okay." Puti smiled. Recently she had been feeling chronically unwell, though not in the same way as at the onset of her illness. Her strength, restored to a certain level, seemed difficult to increase.

"I raided your house. What was your house, in the bamboo grove. You didn't notice me: when I came in I hid toward the back. I don't have a lot of nerve, my fighting spirit isn't strong. It's very hard to change." Cui Li spoke almost apologetically. It was unclear whether she was apologizing for raiding Puti's house or for her lack of fighting spirit. She paused a bit and said: "That evening, we came on that big, fat Zhang Yongjiang's orders. Six people went from our school, following the college student cadre. Now one is already dead. In some violence he was knifed in the pit of the stomach; he died on the spot. One is still in prison: he raided houses everywhere, confiscated

---

6. During the Cultural Revolution, such untraditional direct references to older people became common.

thousands of yuan; he got caught. Then there were two who actually escaped, I don't know where to. I felt we were like grains of sand blown all over the sky by a big wind, only to drift to earth who knew where. Aunt"—somehow Cui Li suddenly reverted to this polite form of address—"I actually envy you your cancer a little: you can be peaceful for a while." Cui Li's voice quavered: she spoke from her heart.

"You can take good care of your mother. You don't have to go out and run around. You can be peaceful, too."

"Her!" Cui Li's lips curled. "She's always complaining because people aren't revolutionary enough, because she herself isn't revolutionary enough. I really don't understand how my dad could have married such a wife!"

Puti, contemplating Cui Li, was at a loss. She felt extraordinarily tired. But Huiyun had still not come home.

Cui Li stayed on a while, then, seeing that Puti had a very weary look about her, said she must be going. As she was about to leave, she said: "I'll come again later."

"Does your mother know you've come? She wouldn't approve?" Puti asked.

"Her! She doesn't know. I won't let her know!" Cui Li curled her lips again—her long, narrow eyes held the hint of a smile—and strode out. Already she seemed to have shed most of her worries in Spoon Court, seeming far less agitated than when she had first come.

That evening, as it happened, Huiyun came home late. Puti sat alone under the lamp, waiting to tell her the news of her son. She felt confused, unable to sort things out, and tired, as though she had run for several blocks. She walked back and forth across the room, then leaned, dazed and sleepy, against the bed.

In the hazy moonlight she recalled the first time her house had been raided. Was Cui Li there? She didn't remember. She thought back to the first sound of running steps, then the terrible clamor of the slogan: "Down with Mei Lian!" before they had rushed in. The leader had been a handsome, fair-skinned, pink-cheeked young man. Coming into the living room, they had first thrown to the floor all the precious, antique chinaware, which had been arranged in a cabinet. When a pair of Ming dynasty vases would not break against the floor, they had used another pair of square-mouthed dragon-headed copper vases to pound them. With just one burst of tumultuous sound, the whole room lay in broken fragments. This had been the overture. They had then flung a reluctant Mei Lian, already asleep in his quilt, into the living room, pushing his head down and bending him over at the waist to arrange his stance. Then they had begun the revolutionary operation of book-burning. Because there were many books, they had asked the old man which his favorites were: "They would try to think of a way to ensure these were left in the book cabinets." Trembling, the old man had spoken of a genuine set of Zhuang Zi from the Song dynasty;[7] only a few such sets existed in the entire world. He also possessed a set of Zhuang Zi that he had read in his youth; on these there were three-colored marks of black, red, and blue, recording what he had learned. Shaking, he had poured out words, hoping to save *The Four Books*.[8] When they had finished questioning him, they took a big flower pot, carried it into the courtyard, opened the living room door, and cried out harshly: "Mei Lian! Look!" Sneering, they had taken the fine books Mei Lian had just named and torn them up. In an instant they had lit a fire pan, with flames leaping so high they turned the courtyard wall completely red. Some people had thrown books on the fire, others had gone into the two bedrooms to rummage through chests and cupboards, cutting up sheets and clothes with scissors. On Puti's little dressing table had been a perfume bottle brought from France by her aunt in the 1950s. Puti had never used this, always putting it aside. The smart pink-and-white-faced young man had lifted up the bottle and fulminated: "You bourgeois, you really enjoy a life of ease, vampire!" So saying, he had broken the bottle. The perfume had run out all over the floor, its fragrance permeating the atmosphere and filling the room. Several people, breathing deeply, had said: "It's still really a good smell." Rummaging here and there, they had next brought out the Mei family's photo album. On it were two pictures of Aunt's family, one on the bank of the Seine River in Paris in front of the Notre Dame, the other at their Paris home. A Red Guard had cried out loudly: "Look! A foreign get-up! That man's a foreigner! This house is really fancy! You have illicit relations with a foreign country, huh? You old bastard!" With one hand he had lifted the photo, with the other had given several smart slaps at the old man's head. After ascertaining that the picture was of the old man's younger sister, they had ordered him to tear the pictures into pieces and throw these in the fire pan to be burned along with the books. The poor old man,

---

7. Zhuang Zi, a philosopher of the Warring States period (475–221 B.C.E.), advocated Taoism.

8. *The Four Books* was a comprehensive collection of Chinese classics published by the Commercial Press, Shanghai, in the 1920s.

throughout his whole lifetime in an earnest relationship of older brother to younger sister, had often worried about the younger sister's drifting about overseas. Now he had to tear up these pictures. He reached out his hand, then shrank back, then reached out again, still not touching the pictures. His gaze was on the fire, burning the paper fragments and remnants of pages. Suddenly he began to sob with a great wailing sound. Puti had snatched the pictures being held up in front of her, torn them up, and dropped them into the fire. The pink-and-white young man had immediately burst into a towering rage, yelling: "Who told you to tear them up for him! You schemer!" He had pushed Puti hard, pushed her until she staggered and pulled away, to sit down abruptly on a sofa covered with fragments of china. She had only heard a word of the tongue-lashing when her pants ripped and brightly-colored drops of blood gushed forth.

"Hidden weapons! Hidden weapons!" Several people had shouted again, carrying in some ancient weapons: a two-edged sword, a *fang tian hua* halberd,[9] some bows, some varieties of arrows. These weapons were mostly gifts from friends. Lian had never used them as anything but decorations. Now suddenly on a random day in the 1960s he was being charged as a criminal. Puti had explained these had been weapons in ancient times, but were now historical relics. The Red Guards absolutely would not listen. One had begun to dance with the *fang tian hua* halberd, and with several bangs had completely smashed the large lampshade and the wall lamp in the living room. Luckily, by this time weariness had set in, revolutionary sentiments were not as vigorous as on arrival, and the fruits of battle were already splendid. Some people gave orders to stick paper strips everywhere they could be stuck up. Then they began to withdraw. The handsome pink-and-white-complexioned young man had walked proudly up to Puti with a triumphant look, in his hand a leather purse inlaid with red and blue pearls. The father and daughter's meager living money and a modest rainy-day fund were inside. Puti had chased after them for a couple of steps, calling out sternly: "We still need to eat!" A jeering voice had come back: "You're unreasonable! Throw her a couple of dimes!" Silence had followed, broken by the old man's sobs. Wreckage spattered with dark red bloodstains covered the floor knee-deep. The smell of burnt paper blended with delicate perfume.

---

9. A halberd carried by a mythical deity.

She remembered, too, the ceaseless flow of visitors coming and going through the now completely destroyed "home." Some casually jumped in through the windows. There had also been people in ordered lines, conscientiously attending this lesson. Like an animal, Mei Lian was ordered out for exhibition on demand. Sometimes he had to answer questions, and was insulted if he did not do so satisfactorily. To visit the home of a "reactionary authority" was a "special show" program. "Can you see the real privilege?!" she had once thought, laughing grimly to herself. Now, thinking of it, she again laughed grimly. Gradually the faces of the floods of people and the destruction on the floor blurred together. As though she were in a trance, she witnessed these scenes as though they were terrifying waves in a great sea. On the sea a battered boat jolted. It had run aground and was being bumped about at random by the wind and waves, in the process of breaking up. "Insane!" Puti herself seemed to be observing from a place far from the sea. "Where is the pilot? Is he drunk?" All that could be seen was a whirlwind sweeping up endless sand and rocks from the boat. The grains of sand became little people: there was Xiao Ding, there was Zheng Liming, Zhang Yongjiang, Shi Qingping, and there was Cui Li—she held onto a handsome young man and would not let go. Screaming together, they all tumbled into the great sea, now hidden, now visible in the great waves. Not a few of the little people wore the tall paper hats of humiliation. On one tall hat was written: "Reactionary academic authority Mei Lian's daughter, the counterrevolutionary, wicked author of *The Everlasting Rock,* Mei Puti." Puti simultaneously felt that she was floating in the sea as well. Her fear of drowning made her giddy and dizzy. She wanted to cry out, but no cry would come. Suddenly a shining dagger appeared overhead and Fang Zhi's deep, wholesome voice sounded out: "Grab it! Grab it!"

"How can I grab the dagger?" Puti thought. "Where is Huiyun?"

She probably grabbed the dagger. She only felt intense pain right to the depths of her heart. She awoke from her half sleep, drenched in a cold sweat, and realized the pain was actually in her right chest and right upper arm. She heard the sound of the neighboring door, and the sound of Huiyun's light footsteps.

"I'll tell her tomorrow, I'll let her go to sleep without bothering her—it's late." Actually Puti did not have the strength to get up. "I'll have a good sleep, too. . . ."

However, she did not once that night fall into deep sleep. When she awoke the next day she was still very tired. She heard the sound of Huiyun's gentle steps beginning the day's bustle. She hurried to get up and push open the door. The little courtyard was heavy with smoke. Huiyun was standing under the west wall struggling with the honeycomb briquette stove.

"Did it go out again?"

"No. I added charcoal cakes." Huiyun turned around to sit down in exhaustion on the little blue stool. She had placed the big enamel cup and the chipped plate—already full of ashes—on the ground. She was not wearing her scarf: her gray hair had already grown three inches. She often humorously referred to her "fashionable man's hairstyle."

From the dilapidated kitchen cupboard Puti took out pickled vegetables to slice and said: "Cui Li came last night." She wanted to see Huiyun's expression, but Huiyun lowered her head and looked at the ashtray without speaking.

"She said she knew where Qin Ge is living," Puti probed.

Huiyun raised her head and looked at Puti. Her large but lifeless eyes assumed an even more melancholy expression. She said slowly: "I know. Someone in our group delivered bricks there and saw him. I've been there." Her tone was apathetic.

"You've been there?" Puti was shocked.

"I've been. A Red Guard was on duty at the building, and wouldn't let me in. I said I was Qin Ge's mother. The Guard said that he'd heard Qin Ge's mother was a counterrevolutionary; he said, 'You old woman, you're still at large, running about everywhere.' While he was talking, Qin Ge came out of the building."

"He came out?"

"He came out. When I saw him come over with those big manly strides, I couldn't help thinking of when he was little and his fat little legs had just learned how to walk. He saw me, too, and pulled me over to a fruit tree close by. I even thought he was going to hit me. I didn't expect him to perversely call me 'Ma.' I really felt so bad I couldn't bear it." Huiyun gazed into the distance. "How is he still like my son? His head is completely swelled up; his attitude isn't human. I told him not to fight. He said everyone fought like that, he wanted to be in the revolution, too. He also said that he knew I lived at Spoon Court; if he had a chance he'd come to see me. While we were still talking some confused yells came from the building. What they were yelling was 'Get going,' and someone called, 'Qin Ge.' My son wanted to leave. I pulled him. He pushed me hard. I stepped on a rock and lost my footing." Frowning, Huiyun stretched out her left foot. The foot had swollen so much that the shoelace couldn't be tied.

"You! You shouldn't have gone!" Puti put down the knife and walked over. "He can always come back by himself." She looked the badly swollen foot over and quickly went into the room to fetch some alcohol, moistened some cotton with it, and rubbed the foot.

"He's obsessed. . . ." Huiyun muttered. "But after all, I did see him. He still calls me 'Ma'—actually, if he had ignored me it would have been better."

"Cui Li said they were good friends."

"Really!" Huiyun's melancholy eyes glittered for a moment. "What do they say a daughter-in-law is?"

"Qin Ge cast her aside, too."

"Oh. Cast her aside." Huiyun was again gazing at the ashtray with her head lowered.

Puti rubbed the foot, swollen like a steamed bun, worked hard at fitting on the shoe and sock, and stood up. She saw that the cigarette in Huiyun's hand was almost burnt down, and the ember was scorching the yellowed finger. Huiyun, however, made no move. "*Tao Hui!* It's burning your hand!" Puti carefully tapped the finger, knocking off the cigarette butt.

Huiyun lifted her head. Her eyes stared ahead panic-stricken, yet focused on nothing. Her right hand was still raised in the posture of holding a cigarette.

"What's the matter? *Tao Hui!*" Puti felt her own head exploding. Was this mental derangement? But what to do? She gently shook Huiyun's shoulder. "*Tao Hui!* What's the matter? I'm here! Puti is here!"

"Really?" Huiyun shivered, her whole body in spasm. She drew back from looking at some unknown distant world, pulled herself together to look at Puti, and said with an effort: "I'm a little muddle-headed . . . what's the matter with me? I have to go to work!" She took a big step toward the courtyard gate. After two steps, however, she swayed, about to fall. Puti rushed to steady her: "Today ask for leave. You need to rest."

"Ask for leave? Is that okay?" Her voice was very feeble, almost as though it could not come out.

"When people are ill, they have to rest." Puti choked back sobs and, helping her into her room, settled her down. Thinking that Huiyun had perhaps not had anything to eat since the previous evening, she set about fixing her a cup of sweetened water.

Huiyun opened her great eyes, but saw nothing. She managed with some effort to move her lips. Puti could make out that she was talking about asking for leave, so she said: "I can go. You drink the water first." Huiyun lifted herself up so as to obediently drink the water, but didn't stop trying to talk. "Quickly, quickly!" she mouthed.

Puti ran into her own room to look at the clock: it was already ten before eight. She hurried to push the old bicycle. When she reached the courtyard gate she lifted the bicycle's handlebars with her right hand, as had been her custom. Suddenly there was a pain in her right chest; the right half of her body seemed to contract in a spasm. She stopped walking and leaned on the bike for a bit, then changed her position so as to take the handlebars with her left hand, only mounting once she had pushed the bicycle out of the courtyard. Hoping not to meet anyone, she took a little road that crossed over a lotus field. Going over a slope, she had another spasm of pain, and had to dismount and bend over the bicycle. Someone grabbed the bicycle seat: "Mei Puti! How is it you're out?"

Raising her head, Puti saw it was Zheng Liming. Now when he talked, he did not look right and left; his manner was much calmer. When he learned that Tao Huiyun was ill, he said he would put in a word for her to those in charge, since his way went past the Foreign Language Department; Puti didn't need to go. He said, too, that the situation was now much improved; many people opposed Zhang Yongjiang. Thinking a bit, he said he would come to visit Puti.

This news seemed pretty good, but Puti's greatest concern now was Huiyun's sickness. Was she losing her mind? This was more to be feared than death. She quickly hurried home. Huiyun's great lifeless eyes were still staring up at the ceiling, while she moaned, anxiously and incessantly moving her head from left to right. Puti's eyeglasses misted over. She knew that the sufferings that Huiyun's body and spirit had endured had been overwhelming: she was on the edge of collapse. Puti wiped her eyes and glasses at the door and walked lightly to the side of the bed: "I asked for your leave. You can rest and relax. You're very tired."

Huiyun's eyes continued to stare blankly at the ceiling; she did not stop rolling her head. Her lips had turned pale, but the deep lines in her face were suffused with a purplish color. Puti gave her a sleeping pill, and put a hot water bottle wrapped in a woolen cloth on her foot. Gradually, she quieted and turned to look at Puti, her expression a baby's look of utter dependency and complete unawareness.

Only when Huiyun had fallen asleep did Puti return to her own room. She knew there was no remedy for this kind of sickness; she need not hurry to find a doctor. But among the ten thousand doctors, there was one she longed for. She often looked out of her window at the court gate, to see if he had unexpectedly come through it, so that they could together help Huiyun, together cope with life's sufferings. He could wipe away her tears and soothe the wounds in her heart. She had not known before that she could yearn and hope so achingly. But should she involve him . . . ? He was so young, so kindhearted, so good.

A breeze stirred, and the aroma of lotus drifted in the air. The green leaves on the Everlasting Rock glistened brilliantly in the summer sunshine.

# 9

# An Alliance of Alarm

⇌

T HE SUNSET COLORS ARRIVED, AND THE GREEN LEAVES ON THE EVER-
lasting Rock grew dimmer and dimmer. The courtyard gate
creaked and Fang Zhi appeared at the vase-shaped entrance. Puti, almost dashing to his side, said in a low voice: "Tao Hui is ill," and told
him about her sick condition.

"Don't worry." Fang Zhi looked carefully at Puti's face, which suddenly appeared thin and pallid, and instinctively grasped her hand.

Puti felt a warm current of emotion washing over her lonely
heart: "You've come, so it's all right now."

They went into Huiyun's room and saw her peacefully sunk on
the camp cot, her face ashen. She opened her eyes, and a consoling
smile crossed her face.

"Have you had anything to eat?" Fang Zhi spoke casually, partly
to test her. Further questions inquired where she was from, how old
she was, and so on.

"Is it possible you thought that I was mentally ill?" Huiyun suddenly grew angry. Covering her head with her quilt, she said: "You
two can go. I want to sleep."

Fang Zhi said thoughtfully: "You should have a good sleep," and
withdrew first. In a little while Puti also came out. Gently pulling the
door to, she said in a low voice: "How is she?" They went to sit in
Puti's room. Still pondering, Fang Zhi said: "It looks as though the
trauma she has undergone has indeed been very great; her nerves
are delicate; it's hard to tell how it will go."

"Who can protect her from trauma? It's just like looking on helplessly while others force her to take poison."

"Yes, it's quite clearly taking a knife and twisting it inside someone, but there's no means of protection. Nowadays people's lives
aren't worth as much as ants'. How can human beings sink so low? . . .

You were right to give her a sleeping pill." Fang Zhi changed the subject. "Most of the important medicines for treating different categories of mental illness are either sedatives for the nervous system, or tranquilizers for nervous excitement. Naturally, she's not yet at that stage."

"Using tranquilizers on the one hand, while disturbing her in various ways on the other. Who could endure it?" Puti sighed, gazing at some black bamboo stems on the white paper lampshade.

Fang Zhi looked at her anxiously, and said nothing. He was visualizing Puti against the solitary lamp, left all alone in the little room. She was using a handicapped body to take on two sick people's adversity. Could she sustain this? How could she go on? Fang Zhi was silent for a while, then said suddenly: "Shall we go out for a walk?" This was actually not at all what he had planned to say.

"The room is stuffy, isn't it?" The room was undersized and damp, already oppressive although it was not yet midsummer. She got up, as she did so picking up a thin bed quilt to give to Huiyun. Returning, she said with a smile: "She's sleeping nicely." She and Fang Zhi went out of the courtyard gate, locking it carefully.

A new moon hung in the top of the willow tree. Over the deep, dark stretch of the reed pond, the air was filled with the faint aroma of lotuses. Spots of lamplight from nearby houses seemed lonely and bleak. "The people who live here all feel disappointed, cut off from the bustle and excitement of life," Puti sighed. "Contented people have already long since moved to better places." They went out the entrance to the campus grounds and were soon walking on the little road between fields, with lotus tracts on either side. The pale moonlight hovered over the lotus leaves; the flower buds stood up straight and stiff, as if poking their heads up to look at something.

Each of the two had a thousand words to say, but neither spoke. Both seemed to be appreciating the pale moonlight, the faint perfume of lotus, the vast stillness. Fang Zhi felt that the sick woman at his side made that whole scene incomparably beautiful and gentle. This peaceful night stirred his heart and shook his soul far more than the most shocking events of the past year's turmoil and chaos. He very much wanted to express his sentiments, but he felt that any words used to convey them might seem frivolous. He finally said earnestly:

"Are you tired, Comrade Mei Puti?"

Puti was just then immersed in the long-unfamiliar vastness of the natural landscape. Fang Zhi at her side gave her a feeling of calmness, of well-being. His earnest form of address surprised her a little. He had always previously used the address "Teacher Mei."

"I'm not tired. I've been used to walking since childhood."

"That's very good." Fang Zhi's manner was stiff. He coughed softly and turned to look at Puti. Instinctively, Puti halted. "I think you should get married."

Puti blinked, lowered her eyes, seemed to smile a little. When she opened her eyes again, they had a sorrowful expression, but in the pale moonlight this was not apparent.

"Naturally," she said in frustration.

"Then marry. Breast cancer patients should marry. The reasons for this are complex. In your present unfavorable circumstances, too, you should get married; then you would have legitimate care and attention—" Fang Zhi said in one breath.

Puti very much wanted to say: "Dr. Fang, thank you very much for your advice, but just whom do you propose I should marry?" But feeling that this kind of teasing, bordering on the absurd, was really not an answer, she continued to walk slowly ahead.

Before long, a little brook flowed across their path. The water flowed gently. In the water were several white rocks. Under the moonlight they looked dazzling. Fang Zhi asked suddenly: "Do you want an Everlasting Rock?" As he spoke, he jumped down to the brook, took up a rock, and stood before Puti.

The two were transfixed, as though by the rumble of thunder, or by an electric charge. A scene from twenty years earlier rose up in two hearts.

That year Puti had been eighteen. The whole family had been preparing to leave Chongqing and return to Beijing. She and several fellow students had gone on a tour to Panxi Stream. The waters of the stream had flowed sometimes slowly and unhurriedly, sometimes furled in waves. Coming upon a little waterfall, with everyone in high spirits, they had all run to touch this curtain of water. In the midst of the dashing spray had stood a rock, about the size of a book, lovely, sparkling, and crystal clear. Puti had called to her companions: "This rock is so pretty! It would be great if I could pick it up." Suddenly an emaciated eleven- or twelve-year-old child had jumped down, picked up the rock, and stood in front of Puti. His childish, colorless face had worn a kind of yearning, respectful, yet stubborn expression . . .

Now, once again, the water held the sound of tinkling jade, as if Panxi Stream had flowed on, through times gone by, arriving at this little nameless brook in the perfumed, mysterious emptiness of the moonlight and lotus, to quietly laugh, perhaps quietly weep, at this finalization of an unconscious pledge, carried forward through time to this far-distant place.

"Is it you?" Fang Zhi asked softly. "I have looked for you for twenty years."

"Is it you?" Puti asked in return. If she had still been eighteen, she, too, might have exclaimed, as she threw herself into his arms: "I've waited for you twenty years." But twenty years had passed, and she was already a middle-aged woman of thirty-eight. She could only look at him, deeply moved, and cover her face with her hands, her tears flowing down over her wrists.

Puti could not sleep at all that night. She was tensed to catch the sound of Huiyun's movements, while with wide-open eyes she examined her heart. Her aching, always pulsating heart was now deeply immersed in a kind of warm and gentle sadness. The once-blurred past now unfolded before her clearly and smoothly: that emaciated country child willfully raised his head to look at her. The dripping rock sparkled slightly. She patted his head, thanking him. He persisted in holding the rock, running after them all the way down the mountain, placing the rock in her hands, without looking at her again, then running back up the mountain. When the whole household left Chongqing for the north, she had naturally not been able to take a rock along; it was abandoned in some unknown spot. The child had grown into a man: Fang Zhi! Unlikely as it had been that the two of them would be lucky enough to meet each other again, they had come upon each other once more in a hospital, becoming acquainted by virtue of the surgeon's knife. Once again he had suddenly held up a rock and stood before her, wanting to give her all the treasures of his soul. Could they really help each other in the mire of life? Perhaps underfoot lay deep ditches, perilous abysses, and overhead, lightning and thunder! And she, what could she give in return?

There is not a young girl who does not weave her own rosy dreams. Puti's dream-net had in the very beginning fallen over a neighbor's relative. This had happened after the family's return to Beijing. The young man had already entered a research institute; in his leisure time he played the violin, casting a tall and slender silhouette on the window curtain, the melodious sound of the violin drifting gently, slowly melting Puti's heart. This kind of feeling is usually without result. Nor had Puti even thought of any result that she wanted. She merely wove her net quietly, for her own pleasure, to the tune of the violin, feeling that her dream-net, too, held that kind of beauty and mystery.

After that, the net had fallen on a young mathematician. This had been a relationship agreeable to everyone, with a successful conclusion possible. But in the warm tide of the revolution, Puti had felt the mathematician to be detached and dull, and she herself to be urgently in need of thought remolding: such things as dream-nets and tenderness all amounted to just so much petty bourgeois sentimentalism. Constantly bent on reform, her contacts with him naturally came to an end. Following this, she had gradually contracted the contagious disease of soul-hardening, making cool-headed judgments when her relatives or friends introduced particular "friends" to her. Such introductions actually followed a pattern: the two parties were weighed for equality, to avoid one side's getting a bad deal. Since everyone naturally hopes that the traveling bag of life, when carried together, will be filled with pearls and precious treasures, Puti had rejected many men in this way, and was in turn rejected by many. Such encounters had all been experienced in her "hardened" condition, without giving rise to any emotion or regret.

All the same, these had all arisen with illusions of "moonlight and roses," and it was only when they ended without a trace that she realized there had never actually been anything there to begin with. Only Fang Zhi was real. He wanted to begin carrying the traveling bag of life with her. Even though now, in everyone else's eyes, not even "rocks" were inside, but only garbage, narcotics, and other such proof of her guilt! Couldn't this perhaps destroy him? He was still young, a doctor with a future. He should have happiness, a satisfying family life; his wife should be warm and gentle and competent, not a person weakened and mutilated by disease as she was, without her hardened spirit, not a "criminal killer"! Really, if Fang Zhi were her own younger brother, what opinion would she give him? She would surely admonish him, try to dissuade him: he should not want Puti; she—she was only going to die.

Reaching this point in her thinking, Puti was startled. How could she leave him? This was the person she had waited for, for many years. Hadn't she turned her life over to him the first time she had seen him in the examining room? That evening beside Aunt Wei's corpse, they had each glimpsed the other's soul, and in the days in Spoon Court since, they had penetrated each other's spirits and put down roots. If she rejected Fang Zhi now, it would be like blocking the fountainhead of a freshwater spring in the desert. . . . Perhaps she would not have a recurrence of the cancer, but her hardened heart would never be cured. She would die of thirst. "That way I would indeed die!" said Puti to herself. "But I want to live." Want to live! Wasn't this a matter of unswerving principle? People were born to live, not to die, to love, not to hate. Puti felt that her lonely heart, isolated and cut off from love for so many years, had been ground into fine powder by the dripping rock that Fang Zhi had embraced since his childhood. She really did not know what to do.

At one o'clock she went to check on Huiyun and saw that she was still sleeping peacefully. At four o'clock she again went to have a look. Huiyun had awakened and was staring at the pale rays of daybreak with wide-open eyes. Hearing the sound of footsteps, she turned to look at Puti. She still wore an exhausted smile on her face.

"I'm much better," she said. "You needn't have gotten up." In the dim lamplight she quickly made out Puti's disturbed appearance. "You're very tired."

"I'm not tired. My mind is just very confused." Puti actually hadn't planned to speak, but she knew that nothing could be hidden from that pair of caring eyes.

"What's the matter? Tell me."

"I'll discuss it with you later. You should go on sleeping for now—"

"I've slept a lot. If I sleep any more I'll get dementia." She seemed clear-headed, her attack a thing of the past.

"You'll be happy. Fang Zhi—he proposed."

Huiyun, dumbfounded, said: "He said he wanted to marry you?"

"You could say that."

"What did you answer?"

"I said I'd think it over."

"My!" Huiyun gave a cry and sat up with a whirl. "Think of what? Marry him today!"

Puti was flustered: "I still have to think for him. I have cancer. I'm six years older than he. Politically stained. He's still young; he has skill. I think I'm not the kind of person he needs."

"He's also not a little boy. He knows what he needs." Huiyun spoke resolutely and decisively: "I'm going to look for him and tell him you're agreeable!" With this she got out of bed—fully clothed.

"I said I'd reply in a week. You still need to get a good rest." Puti's tone was warm and gentle. "Don't worry about a thing!"

"You know, this is the only matter I don't feel relaxed about. I just want to see that a good man like Fang Zhi will keep you company for the rest of your life and I'll die happy." As Huiyun spoke, her sad eyes sparkled, glistening with tears. "As for Qin Ge, I can't bother about him too much."

Puti's eyes were also moist. With Huiyun's friendship and Fang Zhi's love, she would have all that she needed from life. She believed that Huiyun would someday be reunited with her son, once these insane times were over. But that day was perhaps still a long way off. She felt that for the time being, she had better not mention Qin Ge's name. "You should know I'm not so stupid as to push happiness away. I probably should respond."

"Why probably? You're really not being straightforward." Huiyun smiled quickly through her tears.

Puti, knowing that Fang Zhi might still be coming to see Huiyun that day, tried every possible way to get her to promise that she wouldn't bring the matter up, that she would wait for Puti to raise it herself. Huiyun sat for a while. She felt very dizzy once again, and lay down, urging Puti not to worry about her.

Puti stared blankly at the Everlasting Rock, the first rays of the morning sun playing on the colors of the Rock and its green leaves. She seemed to see Fang Zhi standing calmly beside the great rock, intending to move it. "Do you want the Everlasting Rock?" he asked. The simple, deep, and honest voice, that calm profound gaze, and that kindhearted and stubborn expression moved Puti to give thanks for the immense happiness that had come to her. She felt that she simply couldn't bear it a moment longer.

"Fang Zhi! I'll marry you!" her heart cried out. "Fang Zhi! I'll marry you!" She spoke the words out loud. She had made the decision. She found it surprising even to herself that she should have wanted to ponder it, to "think it over." This was her fated marriage, it was meant to be, the eternal union for this life and the world to come.

# 10

# The East Window

≈

A T THE SAME TIME THAT FANG ZHI AND PUTI WERE REKINDLING A twenty-year-old relationship in the lotus field, Zhang Yongjiang, Shi Qingping, and Xin Shengda were together behind the closed doors of a third-floor apartment at Y University. Since this apartment had been instrumental in driving out the reactionary gang of monsters, it had taken on an authentic rebel character; hence it was termed the "Revolution" apartment. The two men were analyzing the situation surrounding the struggle between the two factions. Shi Qingping was crocheting a white cotton tablecloth, frequently interjecting one or two emotional sentences.

Zhang Yongjiang, Shi Qingping, and Dr. Xin were all from the faction in power at Y University and Z Hospital. For this "power" they had to work their hearts out and rack their brains for schemes. More and more people opposed them: in order to maintain power, they had to continuously and desperately plan and devise new strategies. They could never relax their vigil. The stew of class struggle was not easy to swallow—this could be seen from Dr. Xin's simultaneously puffing on two cigarettes. Zhang Yongjiang, on the other hand, had never acquired the habit of smoking; besides tea, he and Shi Qingping only drank coffee.

"We have here the recently founded June First Commune. In the name of liberating the masses, they want to speak well of some demons and monsters." Zhang held a cup of coffee and pursed his lips to sip. "The demons and monsters are already dead men; they wouldn't dare to do much. Truthfully speaking, they have a lot of power; otherwise how could they be favored by the black line?"[1]

---

1. The "black line" or "black gang" refers to capitalist-roaders, revisionists, and counterrevolutionaries.

"Mei Puti's lucky," the voice like a scraping fingernail said. "She got ill and had time off. She hasn't been denounced since the time the big-character posters were put up in the sickroom."

"Really!" Dr. Xin threw in. "It would have been better if we had taken advantage of Qi Yongshou's death to wrap up that criticism meeting. If she has three or four sessions of denunciations, she'll qualify! There's no big interest in taking up small infractions."

"It's very strange. Qi Yongshou's mother hasn't sought her out to square accounts. His father, on the other hand, has often called on us to make trouble; he came again today. He insisted that someone had pushed his son from the building. When we suggested he go and look for Mei Puti, he said that only real guns and real knives could kill people; a book couldn't kill anyone. A Red Guard in the department said he was opposing Mao's quotation[2] and trussed him up. After that the District Court had a man come and lead him away." There was a hint of weariness from Zhang Yongjiang, who was trying hard to unfold his body, which was deeply ensconced in the sofa. That sofa was a piece from Tao Huiyun's father's study.

"What insanity! Crazy! I think someone must have told the real truth to her." The voice like a rasping fingernail was very indignant. At the words "real truth" all three started. As far as the real truth went, Qi Yongshou had in fact not killed himself. The rebels had been beating someone, he had suddenly demurred, and had begun to wrestle with Zhang Yongjiang and others. In the ensuing confusion someone had pushed him out of the window. Investigating the matter was hardly possible. Although all three were seasoned rebels, when it came to a matter of life and death, they were beset by some misgivings.

"If we had wrapped up that criticism meeting and put forward as fact the accusation that Mei Puti's evil book had been responsible for the deaths of some people, we would not have had this trouble." The husky, astringent voice sounded deeply regretful. "The one named Fang at our hospital is too detestable."

Zhang Yongjiang spoke: "Actually it doesn't matter if he doesn't sign the certificate. You can still get it signed. Some legal medical experts will sign what the unit tells them. A fall from a building is always open to question. Right now we are just too busy. We must tackle that faction."

---

2. Mao Zedong said that books could kill, that they were "soft knives."

"You don't know. Fang Zhi could influence patients. They trust him. Originally I wanted to win him over."

"If he won't be won, attack him!" Zhang Yongjiang said sternly, putting the cup heavily down on the little tea table. "We need to take the initiative!"

"Getting a hold on Fang Zhi will be easy." Dr. Xin's husky, astringent voice rose. "He's a Rightist who slipped through the net. Several of us have discussed it. We want to attack the Five Well Commune, so we have to get at their people. We have a handle on Fang Zhi and can attack him. He and that faction's people don't have much contact; there won't be anyone to protect him."

"He's walking the white and expert road," Zhang Yongjiang pondered, suddenly remembering that a few years earlier he himself had been bent on being an expert. Now his life's goal had changed. If somebody was still bent on his profession, he was indeed a fool. "That kind of man is easy to deal with."

Someone knocked at the door, and Sister Huo entered. "I— thought you'd be here! Today you're on duty, my doctor!" She looked around the room and said to Shi Qingping: "You're getting fancier and fancier in here. This little red dressing table is really tasteful, and you've fixed it up nicely!" Shi Qingping didn't like hearing praise for other people's furniture, but the last phrase left her feeling quite comfortable.

Only after Sister Huo had lit a cigarette and seated herself cozily did she state her reason for coming. She told them that she could not find Qi Yongshou's mother anywhere, simultaneously watching Zhang Yongjiang and Shi Qingping for their response.

"She can't get out of bed, where can she have gone?" Dr. Xin was astonished. Zhang and Shi yawned simultaneously. Both were bored through with the Qi Yongshou affair.

"You said it. Patients suit their own convenience. Especially Elder Sister Qi. One word and she's flushed and pale with anger, having a falling-out with you. In any case she won't live many more days. It's just that I'm afraid she's gone out to stir up trouble."

"Did her man go to the hospital in the afternoon?" Zhang Yongjiang asked.

"I heard he went; the two talked and clucked for quite a while, wiping away tears the whole time, most probably missing their darling son."

Zhang Yongjiang's interest was aroused: was it possible that she had gone to look for Mei Puti to square accounts? That could work out fine. But Sister Huo objected to this: "The Qis didn't have anything against the one named Mei. They didn't believe the book Mei wrote could kill someone." After she spoke she suddenly exclaimed: "To be sure! I mean, there is someone who often goes to see Teacher Mei."

"Who?" the three asked, curiosity aroused.

"Fang Zhi, Fang Zhi!"

"Good! We were just wanting to attack him. That way, you needn't find any other weapon with which to wound Mei Puti. Attacking Fang Zhi will certainly strike a big blow to her spirit." Dr. Xin was full of enthusiasm, seeing the advantage of taking this initiative.

Shi Qingping put aside her handiwork and stood up, her body looking emaciated and rigid: "I've never seen such a target! She rests, then looks for a doctor sweetheart! We should lock Mei Puti up to examine her!" she shouted, facing Zhang Yongjiang.

"This is class struggle! Maybe we should squeeze her as the opportunity arises." Zhang Yongjiang pondered, then observed: "We still have to debate with the June First Commune tomorrow. There are many pressing matters."

"I'll write a big-character poster, to bring to light her looseness even with illness!"

"Hey, that won't do," Sister Huo said quickly, her plump face trembling. "We are fighting a political struggle. No way can we get into that kind of meanness. Dr. Fang has always been a respectable person." Sister Huo seemed a little regretful as she offered this information. "It's all right to have two factions, but not abandon personal ethics."

"Respectability can't compete with public opinion; public opinion can be created. Understand? This is called 'discrediting,' 'painting black.' Teacher Zhang knows this kind of thing has often happened in the course of history." Dr. Xin still spoke full of the mood to enjoy such a smear campaign.

"Say, Dr. Xin, shall we see the patients? You're on duty this evening!" Sister Huo got up to go. Zhang and Shi quickly proffered enthusiastic farewells, repeating that friends made since the Great Cultural Revolution were so valuable; they hoped there would be many such contacts. After they had left, Shi Qingping took a watermelon out of the cupboard and cut it in two. The two started eating with little spoons, the knife remaining on the table.

Dr. Xin left on his bicycle. When Sister Huo went out Y University gate, she heard a moaning sound from behind a tree in the shadow of the wall. She could make out someone squatting on the ground. From instincts developed over many years of nursing, she wanted to go over and have a look. She thought better of it, however: a person in such dire straits was very likely to be a counterrevolutionary, one of

the five elements from reactionary gangs or whatever;[3] associating
with such a person would be inviting trouble. The bus came and she
hurried to get on. She turned to look back at Y University gate from
the bus, recollecting that the Zhang household's furniture really
wasn't at all bad!

In the evening, the period between bus trips is long; all was stillness. The dark shadow at the base of the wall slowly got up and
quickly sat down again; then, leaning with one hand against the wall,
moved with great difficulty, step by step. When it had moved out
from the shade of the tree and the shadow of the wall, a woman
wearing patient's clothing came into view at the school entrance, her
hair in disarray, her eyes staring. It was indeed Elder Sister Qi! She
took a couple of steps toward the school gate, then drew back a few
steps to look in the direction of Spoon Court. She moaned unceasingly, the sound not loud but embodying hopeless suffering, a sound
to make one's blood run cold.

Elder Sister Qi's mind was clear. She realized that she wouldn't
live long. Before leaving the chaotic world of men, she wished to
know only one thing: how her son had died. Old Qi had come many
times to Y University, and still had not received an answer. Elder Sister Qi could recognize no more than a few characters; Old Qi wasn't
at a much higher level, but normal clear-headed reasoning was quite
enough for them to differentiate right from wrong. She wanted to
ask Zhang Yongjiang who indeed had harmed her young son!

A few people passed this strange figure. None, however, bothered about a matter that didn't concern them. So Elder Sister Qi
dragged along undisturbed, step by step through the schoolyard. She
had often been to the school on temporary jobs; she knew the way.
The "Revolution" apartment was very close to the school entrance.
She almost used up what strength she had left opening the building
door. She bent over for a long time at the entrance to the stairs, then
climbed on all fours up to the third floor, coming to a halt outside
Zhang Yongjiang's door.

Zhang and Shi, husband and wife, had already eaten the watermelon. The skin and the knife still lay on the table. The man was
preparing for a debate; the woman was working on the most deroga-
tory phraseology to vilify Mei Puti. Without warning, the door opened

---

3. The five elements, the major targets of the Cultural Revolution, were
landlords, rich peasants, counterrevolutionaries, evildoers or bad elements,
and Rightists.

and Qi Yongshou's mother entered. Both gasped involuntarily at her clothes, her appearance. Elder Sister Qi looked at them, they looked at Elder Sister Qi, all momentarily dumbstruck.

It was Zhang Yongjiang who first regained his composure. Taking a step forward he shouted: "What are you doing here? Go away!"

Elder Sister Qi had already reached the side of the table. She slid down a table leg to the floor and sat down. "Teacher Zhang," she said breathlessly, "be merciful, tell me how my son died." Her face was devoid of color, her lips were trembling; she clutched the table leg with one hand to keep from falling over.

"Who knows how your son died!" Shi Qingping started yelling. "What right do you have to come to us here! It is ridiculous!" She moved over to pull the sick woman up and push her out of the door.

Zhang Yongjiang signaled Shi not to do this. Controlling his voice as much as he could, he said: "Your old man already came this morning. Comrade Qi Yongshou killed himself. He was a good comrade; he was just poisoned by an evil book's poison—"

"It's no use deceiving people. Have mercy. Tell me the truth: nothing else will do. We are old, we are ill, can we seek vengeance?" Elder Sister Qi spoke in gasps, beads of perspiration running down her cheeks. Her whole body pained her, as if hacked to pieces by an ax; her eyes closing, she still stared desperately.

"How should we know!" Shi Qingping began to shout again. "You can't just come barging in here! There are many dead men; should everyone come to ask us about them?"

"If I could, I would certainly ask the authorities!" Elder Sister Qi clung with both hands to the table leg, exerting all her strength in an effort to stand. "Why can't I come to your place? Is this the grounds of the imperial palace?" She almost exploded with resentful grief and indignation. "I'm not only barging in on you here, I'm also going to die here in your 'Revolution' apartment!" She looked at the knife on the table. In less than a second she had grasped it and thrust it against her neck. Fresh blood spurted out like spring water. A great red streak colored the table. Shi Qingping screamed in fright. As she screamed, Elder Sister Qi fell over heavily. Shi Qingping, too, fell in a faint against Zhang Yongjiang's arm.

"How could such a thing happen! How could such a thing happen!" Zhang Yongjiang, taking in the streak of blood in front of him, felt somewhat dizzy. He first hurried to support Shi Qingping into an inner room. The neighbor across the way, having heard the noise, came in and was also astonished.

Zhang Yongjiang talked with his Leftist neighbor awhile, then sought out some intimates who were also Leftists to help him. Some went to fetch a legal medical expert, some stayed inside to give each other courage. He himself telephoned right away in search of Xin Shengda, rejoicing inwardly that the comrade of the rebel faction on telephone duty had placed the telephone at the doorway to the inner room. Placed on the dining table, it would have now been steeped in a pool of blood. Sister Huo answered. Hearing it was Zhang Yongjiang, she said: "Didn't he just come from your place? And you want him again!" Fortunately, for once, Xin Shengda was, surprisingly, actually on ward duty. Hearing what had happened, he almost dropped the phone in amazement.

"I'll come." He put down the phone. Looking to see that there was no one to the left or to the right, he told Sister Huo of the direction Elder Sister Qi had taken. The birthmark on Sister Huo's forehead turned scarlet. She said quickly: "I've never heard of such a thing, I've never heard of such a thing!"

When Xin Shengda arrived at the "Revolution" apartment, Elder Sister Qi was still lying on the floor. The legal medical expert was on call elsewhere. Xin stood awhile beside the corpse and saw that Elder Sister Qi's head was skewed to one side; half her face was immersed in a pool of blood, but her eyes were closed. The facing side appeared exceedingly peaceful, without a trace of her usual agonized expression. Xin Shengda, who was used to illness and death, remained imperturbable. Nevertheless, he was now baffled. "This year of revolution, what it has brought!" he thought, as he made the usual examination and quickly wrote out the death certificate. Everyone confusedly rearranged things and agreed it was best to take the corpse to the school hospital mortuary for temporary keeping. Tomorrow, Old Qi would be sought out to arrange for its disposal.[4]

When the two invited legal medical experts went for a stretcher, Zhang Yongjiang asked Xin Shengda to have a seat in the inner room. The two men were silent. By now Shi Qingping was sitting on the side of the bed, wrapped in the bedclothes, distancing herself from the corpse.

"I would never have believed she could have come here to you." Dr. Xin's uneasy mood had still not dissipated.

"Now where she goes is not up to her." Zhang Yongjiang was by now quite calm. Lowering his voice he said something to Dr. Xin. Listening,

---

4. Old Qi, however, had not been given the body of his son.

Dr. Xin's mood brightened, and from time to time he interjected an opinion.

"You have something confidential to say?" Shi Qingping asked. "Can we still go on living in this apartment? I want to move."

The two men paid no attention to her. Before long the stretcher arrived. Zhang Yongjiang led several men downstairs carrying the corpse. They in fact did not go to the school hospital but out of the school gates. They followed along the lotus fields, moving quickly in the sweet aroma of the flowers.

Elder Sister Qi's life had ended, but she was still being ordered about.

# 11

# The Recurrence

A T SIX O'CLOCK, PUTI OPENED THE COAL STOVE, REJOICING TO HERSELF: "It's still okay, it hasn't gone out." She put the kettle on the stove and sought out the only egg to prepare a bowl of egg soup for Huiyun. She wanted to make it as good as if Huiyun had made it herself. "Afterward I also want to cook for Fang Zhi. His color could be better." Puti cherished warm and gentle thoughts. The water still hadn't boiled. She lightly sprinkled and swept the little courtyard, straightening up often to take the measure of the "Everlasting Rock," bending from the waist again to nimbly carry on, feeling lively in body and spirit.

She put the sweepings in a dustpan to carry to the court gate. Before opening the gate, she put the dustpan down. Only after looking around at Huiyun's window, to check that she was sleeping nicely, did she open the gate easy in her mind.

She pulled back the bar. The gate opened inward of itself. There was something leaning on it; the thing dropped at her feet. As it fell she only saw a disheveled head. "Someone has fainted." She moved the body over to lean against the gate frame. When she went to step out of the gate, she focused her glance, and felt her heart suddenly miss a beat, her soul floating away, wisplike, from the crown of her head. Her legs began to shake uncontrollably. She wanted to run away from this frightful thing, run far away, escape forever from such a terrible world. But she could not take a step; she seemed nailed to the ground. Her body swayed, but she didn't fall.

When she could think clearly, the first thing she thought was that it was lucky it hadn't been Tao Huiyun who had opened the gate. "Tao Hui would have gone crazy right away. I can take it." She felt a piercing pain at her waist that almost made her bend over. She nevertheless exerted all her strength, telling herself: "I can take it, I can

123

cope." People were coming one after another to dump garbage beside the garbage heap. She said loudly: "Come quickly! Come quickly!" Thank heavens that the garbage heap was beside the gate!

One by one several people came over and looked, stupefied. "Who is it?" someone asked. Poor Puti, she still did not know who it was. She studied the face, half purplish red, half mottled with bloodstains. The face was peaceful; there was no trace of a struggle or suffering. "Elder Sister Qi!" Puti cried. "How did you come to be here?" Someone saw that beside the gate there were a couple of sheets of paper and took them down to read: "Wanting Mei Puti's life! *The Everlasting Rock* killed my son, Qi Yongshou!" and smiled coldly: "This was her reason!" Puti turned her head slowly to look at the black characters on the white paper. That her life was wanted was not surprising, but how was it Elder Sister Qi came to want it? She and Old Qi were both sensible people. Perhaps she really would have to pay with her life? How would Huiyun get along? And there was Fang Zhi, Fang Zhi, for whom she had waited so many years, she really was letting him down! But she still had to think of what to do at this moment. Who knew what the next moment would bring! She gradually regained her composure, walked to the front of the gate, and straightened up the corpse, leaving it still leaning on the gate.

"You are not allowed to change the scene of the crime!" someone yelled hatefully. There were already quite a few onlookers.

"It was like this when I opened the gate," Puti explained. She was afraid Hui Yun would come out and be frightened. "I'll go and report to the police station."

"You needn't take the trouble." Zhang Yongjiang emerged from the crowd. His plump square face had slackened considerably during the night; his cheeks drooped. "Comrades of the Revolution!" He turned to face the crowd of onlookers, some residents of Spoon Court, some students on special assignment. "The evil book of Mei Puti, a counterrevolutionary in our department, has spread poison far and wide, poisoning many young people. Our department's student, Qi Yongshou, is an outstanding example. He jumped from a building and killed himself. Now Qi Yongshou's mother, demanding a life for her son's, has cut her throat with a kitchen knife." As he spoke he picked up a knife that no one had noticed lying beside the stone steps. "Doesn't this truth, written in blood, fill us with loathing, grief, and indignation! Chairman Mao teaches us: some people kill with guns, some kill with pens. I know from experience that using pens to kill is even more insidious and diabolical! Now we will begin to criticize and denounce Mei Puti. Comrade Qi Yongshou and his mother, too, will not have shed their blood in vain!"

The young students in the crowd were filled with moral indignation. A Red Guard leader shouted a slogan: "Debts of blood must be paid in blood!" "Down with murderer Mei Puti!" "Don't let the June First Commune shield a murderer!"

Two men came up and pushed Puti onto her knees. "Confess your crime to Mama Qi!" With a great roar, they pressed her head down until it touched the ground. Her two hands were twisted hard behind her, as though they were twisting two strands of hemp.

"She is ill." "She has cancer." "She has just had surgery." Some people in the crowd spoke kindly. Some old women from Spoon Court could not bear it and brought out handkerchiefs.

From the vase-shaped entrance a drumming began like the patter of rain; Huiyun shouted out from inside: "What's going on? What's happened? Puti! Where are you? Let me out!"

"Let her out to keep her company!" Zhang Yongjiang said calmly.

Puti suddenly summoned all her remaining strength to cry out loudly: "Tao Hui, don't worry. There was a dead person outside the gate. Elder Sister Qi has killed herself!" Her breath blew the dirt on the ground in front of her into her throat. She choked and began a coughing fit. The Red Guard pulled her head up and stuffed her mouth with a dirty cloth picked up from the trash pile.

The gate opened. Huiyun appeared at the vase-shaped entrance. Puti's words had already been enough to calm her. Looking neither to the left or right, Huiyun walked straight to Puti's side, knelt down, and leaned against her at the Red Guard's feet, bowing her short hair to the ground, too. If Puti was about to be beheaded, she would suffer the knife with her.

A sob swept over the crowd. Then the denunciation began. But people were in no mood to listen. Some people felt that the living were even more deserving of sympathy than the dead, while some others felt that bullying and humiliating these two sick women was not enough: they proposed taking Mei Puti to a public security bureau. This was revolutionary moral indignation: it soon won the upper hand. For a while the sound of slogans filled the little space beside the garbage heaps. Before the gates of Spoon Court, people were aroused. The Red Guards bumped Tao's and Mei's heads hard on the ground several times. Puti's glasses fell off and were kicked far away by a young militant. "Curse you! Elitist!"

Zhang Yongjiang realized by now that this case could not withstand deliberation. He wanted to wind up now that the showdown had been made. But now the "revolutionary fire" burned ever brighter: he could not dash cold water on it. Already some people had pulled Mei Puti, intending to tie her up, when suddenly a skinny little old man squeezed out from the midst of the crowd, declaring as he walked: "I am the owner of the corpse, I am the owner of the corpse." Coming to Spoon Court gate, he looked for a long time at his dead wife, turned and raised his head to the sky and cried out: "I, the owner of the corpse, do not accuse Teacher Mei."

Again a stir swept over the crowd. The young militants were somewhat disheartened. Zhang Yongjiang quickly availed himself of the opportunity to withdraw, announcing: "It's a fact that Mei Puti has killed a man, but settlement must wait until a later stage of the movement. The Cultural Revolution must go deeper, and continue to expose and criticize. Hopefully it will win larger victories and facilitate the exposure of new crimes." When he had finished speaking, he walked over to the old man to discuss the removal of the corpse.

One after another, people left the scene. Even the young militants guarding Puti walked off quietly without any further show of force. Puti's whole body ached unbearably. No one was twisting her arms any more, and in the absence of this support she simply fell over on the ground. Huiyun hurriedly jumped up, slowly lifted her up, fished out the dirty cloth from her mouth, and let her lean against her. Neither shed any tears. All emotion—sadness, dread, anger—had long since vanished. There was only the matter of the moment.

Puti's sole thought at that moment was to find her glasses. Huiyun helped her over to sit under the willow tree and quickly found the glasses in the dirt and debris nearby. Amazingly, the two very thin pieces of glass were still intact, giving Puti a feeling of satisfaction. Using the edge of her clothing, she wiped the lenses clean and put the glasses back on. The sun was already high, casting shadows between the willow branches. There were still people beside the reed pond looking around wonderingly at Spoon Court. A three-wheeled cart came and went. Several people walked past her; only Old Qi gave her a wordless glance.

Puti very much wanted to run after Old Qi and take his hand to tell him that it surely was not she, Mei Puti, who had killed his wife and son. If there had been even the slightest indication of this, she would certainly have been willing to pay with her life. He could go and ask Fang Zhi, go and ask anyone who had read the book. She knew Old Qi was a reasonable person, they were all reasonable people, but indeed someone, in the name of Elder Sister Qi, had written the characters asking for her life, and more astonishingly still, Elder Sister Qi had herself committed suicide at her gate! What reasonable discussion could there be in a world such as this!

Huiyun had already cleaned up the entrance and called Puti to come back in. She again wore her exhausted smiling expression, but her head had renewed its shaking.

They went in, fastening the gate latch. Now it was Puti's turn to take care of Huiyun. Huiyun was clearly on the verge of losing consciousness: she could no longer support herself. She lay down and took a sleeping pill. Puti stood beside her bed, thinking at that moment that she wanted to do three things: rinse her mouth out as hard as she could, lie down, and then fix a bowl of egg soup.

The news that Qi Yongshou's mother had killed herself in front of Mei Puti's gate, demanding Puti's life, quickly circulated around Y University and Z Hospital. Fang Zhi did two surgeries in the morning; lunchtime passed; in the afternoon he substituted for another doctor in the outpatient clinic right up until dinnertime; only in the dining hall did he hear the talk. He wanted desperately to fly at once to Spoon Court to see Puti. Outside the hall, Xiao Ding hailed him, telling him: "Dr. Xin told us to notify Old Qi to go to Teacher Mei's house. But Elder Sister Qi didn't generally believe all the wild talk on the big-character posters; actually she said she wanted to go and ask Zhang Yongjiang. Old Qi said this was perhaps a case of moving the body."

"In that case the people who did it will have to take the legal consequences."

"But, where is the law now?" Xiao Ding continued. "So long as revolutionary placards are held up to fabricate charges against 'monsters and demons,' the legal case doesn't matter. Old Qi says: 'The law court serves less good than closing the door.'" She also wanted to warn Fang Zhi to watch out for his own safety, but, seeing that he was in a hurry to go out, she said nothing more.

Fang Zhi pushed the Spoon Court gate; the latch held firmly. Only after he had knocked lightly a number of times did he hear Puti's trembling voice: "Who is it?" "Fang Zhi." The gate opened. Puti looked up at him. In the dim twilight he could see that she was on the verge of tears. She quickly lowered her head, motioning Fang Zhi to go in.

"Just where you're standing," Puti said in a low voice. "The main thing was that I hadn't the slightest inkling beforehand. I was overcome with fear."

"I wasn't there to protect you." Fang Zhi resented himself.

"I am fine. At this time who can protect anyone? It's only that Huiyun can't stand it. She was getting better. After this morning's troubles, her head shaking's come back. Now she's a bit better."

"The medicine's effect on her isn't very great," Fang Zhi observed with some frustration. "What a doctor can do is very little."

"You are helpful to her, because she cares about me." Puti lowered her voice so that it was almost inaudible. They stood in the middle of the court. Above their heads, in the corner of the sky revealed by the little court, the dark canopy of the heavens seemed very soft. Outside the wall, at the tips of the willow branches, a pair of bright stars seemed very close. Puti wanted so much to weep in his arms, to let tears wash away the brutal smears, the wounds, but when her eyes moved from the two bright stars back to Fang Zhi, her expression remained calm and she stood upright even as she seemed to incline her body.

"We are really unfortunate to have been born in this era." She sighed gently. Her gaze stroked Fang Zhi's face, as if saying: "I have only you, I have only you . . ." She closed her eyes for a moment, displaying those curving arcs. She was thinking about what kind of involvement she, a "murderer," a person suffering from cancer, could lead him into.

Fang Zhi only wanted to hold her close, to do every tiny trivial thing for her, so that her whole body and mind could relax and rest. But he felt that this idea might simply be "taking advantage of a precarious position," and would thus be unforgivable. So, he stepped back a little and said: "I, too, feel we are very unfortunate. Everyone involved in these times is unfortunate. Can it be that Zhang Yongjiang and Dr. Xin are happy? It cannot be."

"They? Those who scheme to hurt other people can never be happy."

"Actually, they are manipulated by invisible forces," Fang Zhi said. "As a matter of fact, I feel it's only because fate brought this tempest about that I met you." As he spoke he took a step backward.

"Also because of invisible forces?" So saying, Puti smiled impulsively and invited him to sit in the room.

They analyzed the Elder Sister Qi matter meticulously. They believed Old Qi spoke the truth: there would not be a serious aftermath. But in Puti's position, since she did not have the right to speak out, she could only wait. When it was time for Fang Zhi to depart, he was very worried about Puti. Today's events outside the courtyard only added to his concern. Maybe she would be very afraid, maybe she would have nightmares. He hesitated and hesitated, and finally asked: "Are you afraid? I'm thinking of spending the night in the courtyard, to keep watch over you, okay?"

Puti was astonished, then gave a warm and gentle smile, saying: "That's not necessary. If I needed you to stay, I'd have you stay in the house." She walked him out, shutting the gate behind him with lightning speed.

For several days afterward, Huiyun and Puti lived in a constant state of alert. The sound of unexpected footsteps outside the wall alerted them to long observations of the courtyard gate. No one, however, returned to make trouble. The weather had suddenly turned blazing hot. The little rooms off Spoon Court were low-ceilinged and suffocatingly humid. The courtyard, small and enclosed, did not admit a breeze. Huiyun and Puti both doused themselves with water several times a day and also doused the courtyard, although there still wasn't much hint of coolness. "It's as though we were in Guangdong; we need to hang wet cloths over our shoulders," Huiyun observed.

This was the day on which it had been agreed that Puti would announce her decision. At last the momentous and happy day arrived in the little courtyard enveloped in shadows. Huiyun was very happy, her spirits much improved. From early in the morning, she had been playing the part of one who can cook without rice, "supercook," preparing the evening meal for Fang Zhi. At noon, while Puti was in the house washing herself down, Huiyun was chopping something up under the eaves.

"Oh!" Puti let out a little cry.

"What 'oh'?" Huiyun stopped chopping and came in to see.

Puti was undressed and sitting on the bed. At the end of her shoulder blades, on the wound over her right chest, was a node about the size of a *meng* bean; within her left breast toward the side was another node. Huiyun, gazing fixedly at her, felt her heart pounding: "A relapse! A relapse!" Puti closed her eyes for a moment, a careless smile playing at the corners of her mouth. She had been aware that the roving enemies within her body had not necessarily retreated, that very possibly they had found a new base and settled down. The two looked at each other a moment. Puti said suddenly: "Tao Hui, you must promise me something."

"Anything," Huiyun said, choked with sobs.

"Promise me you will never again get sick, for my sake."

Huiyun lowered her head, then lifted her great spiritless eyes: "I will try my hardest." For the remainder of that day, their mood of anticipation changed completely. If "happiness" had in fact come to Spoon Court, it would have been highly inappropriate. They were now faced only with suffering compounded upon suffering; the shadow of death had moved from the front gate to Puti's body itself.

The little court, however, was completely tidy; the faint perfume of lotus wafted in the summer heat. Fang Zhi came earlier than usual. As soon as he entered the gate he sensed the uneasy atmosphere. Huiyun was again sitting on the little wooden stool; at her feet were her teacup and the cracked china bowl, overflowing with cigarette ashes. Puti, half turned to the side, was pacing up and down. She darted a glance filled with worry and grief at the guest, and went on with her pacing. Fang Zhi was very apprehensive.

"The doctor has come! We were waiting for you!" Huiyun rose and said anxiously: "Have a look at her."

"What is it?" Fang Zhi very quickly had a look at the two nodes. Pressed upon, they felt very hard. The one at the side of the wound was very possibly an odd piece of thread; naturally it could also be a tumorous growth from cancer cells left behind by the surgeon's knife. The one in the left breast was even more likely to be a cancerous growth. Very possibly there had been a recurrence in the left breast, transmitted from the breast lymphs on the right side.

Huiyun's gaze never left Fang Zhi; she carefully observed his expression. Puti, on the other hand, was trying hard not to look at him, and lowered her eyes. Fang Zhi, who normally always analyzed clearly and spoke plainly, now stammered, at a loss for words. He was plainly alarmed and bewildered.

"So how is it?" Huiyun still fixed her gaze on him. "Say!"

Fang Zhi was silent for a time, then spoke. "Possibly it's only a little fatty tumor. However, we can't determine what it is from what's to be seen on the surface. That requires the microscope." He did not deem it necessary to mention that there were times when the microscope was not clear either.

"Will another surgery be needed?" Huiyun asked, looking hard at him.

Fang Zhi made no sound. Puti smiled: "That's minor surgery. It doesn't scare me a bit. Whatever kind of test is required for treatment, that's the kind of test I'll have." With an encouraging smile, she looked inquiringly at Fang Zhi.

Fang Zhi rose suddenly, saying: "I'll go and ask Han Lao. Tomorrow you go and see him at the pathology section."

Huiyun restrained him: "Sit for a while—I'm going to write a self-criticism." She gave Puti a meaningful look and went out.

Fang Zhi immediately took Puti's hands in his own. "Puti!" This was the first time he had called her that. His pale face reddened a little. "What—what did you decide?"

Hadn't she already decided that evening? She had cried out to herself: "Fang Zhi! I'll marry you!" But now within a week the situation had changed. Withdrawing her hands, she gently stroked Fang Zhi's like a big sister, and still smiling said: "I'm asking for a postponement. Let's wait and see. If time is already short, why should I disturb your life?" With lowered head, she spoke with great objectivity and calmness.

Fang Zhi wanted to lift her head, to look directly into her soul, but he could only grip her hands hard and say anxiously: "I know this isn't what you were thinking originally. What you have seen is not a recurrence for sure, and that apart, we can certainly overcome illness together. . . ."

Puti was silent, her head still lowered. Fang Zhi, panicking momentarily, released Puti's hands and ran from the room, at the court gate turning back halfway to tell her that he could perhaps urge Dr. Han to come that same evening: if there was a knocking at the gate they should not feel afraid.

Upon his arrival, Fang Zhi had been in a particularly joyous mood. He had had a wonderful feeling of expectancy and unperturbed happiness, believing that this evening he would receive his beloved's pledge, that from thenceforth his small ship, tossing about on the ocean of mankind, could moor on the Everlasting Rock forever. If Fang Zhi had discussed his secret with kith and kin, no one would have approved his choice. But he had no family, no relatives, no friends with whom he was willing to discuss his feelings. He had relied only upon his own heart, that passionate heart which had not contracted the "disease of soul-hardening," to guide him to Spoon Court.

Now as he left he was in a particularly unhappy and fearful frame of mind. Cancer cells indeed permitted no lapse in vigilance! The possibility that cells had been transmitted during surgery was not great; each time he performed surgery he was extremely careful about changing knives. At the start of the movement the previous year, there had been a big-character poster saying that he changed knives frequently in order to appear awe-inspiring. However, cells remaining in the lymph nodes of the breast were potentially dangerous, and when to these were added traumatic life experiences—most recently the terrorism of the moved corpse—they were enough to defeat the normal systemic defenses against cancer. Nevertheless, he had faith in Puti's basic physical strength, her staunchness—and detachment—and, above all, her ardent love of life. He also believed in his own love, in a love greater than life itself. If he could not keep his beloved in the world, what then was the meaning of life and love?

He looked for Han Lao in the pathology department next to the mortuary. There were two large vats placed against the doors of the room; they held formalin for soaking human limbs and trunks. A hand extended from the fluid. Han Lao was sorting laboratory test reports under the lamp. When he heard why Fang Zhi had come, he pondered a bit, then said: "For her to come here isn't convenient. We'll go there. So let's go." As he spoke, he put away pieces of paper and glass slides one by one. "Actually I wanted to warn you: you need to watch out for your own safety."

"I?" Fang Zhi was stupefied. In truth, owing to his busy routines, and owing to the fact that he was unaccustomed to doing so, he rarely thought about himself. But now he responded: "Han Lao, if something happens to me, I'm asking you to look after Mei Puti, okay?"

"Provided I can. It's strange how up to now I'm still at liberty." Han Lao turned to look at Fang Zhi, yet did not look at him. He immediately turned back to put away the things in his hand. This done, he promptly locked the door. They quickly exited from the rear of the hospital, a part of the building that few people frequented.

Han Lao and Puti immediately recognized that they were old acquaintances. Doctors and politicians alike are skilled at recognizing and remembering people. "The last time with those cancer cells, I thought they were your mother's." The old man spoke in a relaxed manner, then began the examination.

"You let me compare the cancer cells with the normal cells," Puti said. "There are so many normal cells, how can they possibly fail to overcome the small number of cancer cells? I really don't understand."

"When the higher nervous system is out of balance, the cancer cells become very powerful in a very short space of time, and then they're hard to check. However, the normal cells should always be able to win out." Han Lao made a diagnosis identical to Fang Zhi's: the node in the left breast should certainly be operated on. They stayed only a quarter of an hour, then left.

The following day Fang Zhi came to tell Puti that he had already made an appointment for surgery that afternoon at three o'clock in the outpatient department. He would come to get her.

That day it began to rain heavily at noon. Huiyun had not returned. The rain was torrential; in no time at all Spoon Court was over a foot deep in water. Several rills of water flowed zigzag along the wall and down. Before long the roofs of both rooms were letting in the rain. Puti, listening to the pitter-patter of the rain, placed what basins and jars she could find on the bed, the table, and along the wall.

At one-thirty Fang Zhi had not come. At two, he still had not. The incessant heavy rain should not have delayed him. Puti stood before the table, looking toward the court gate, through the white sheet of the heavy rain. She felt a nameless anxiety rising steadily within her heart. A strong wind blew the court gate open with a bang, but no one came in. After a long while, the rain gradually subsided, the sound of raindrops from within the room now all the more audible.

Three o'clock. Fang Zhi still had not come.

# 12

# The Fall

═══

THAT MORNING FANG ZHI ONLY PERFORMED ONE OPERATION; AT A LITTLE
after ten he was off. Afraid that if he went to the dining room for
lunch at noon someone would seek him out, he thought of going a
bit earlier. Taking off his watch in the washroom, he carefully washed
his hands up to the arms. Each time he left the operating room to return to the dormitory, he washed like this; it was a kind of addiction
to cleanliness. Afterward, he rested a little while in his small room
containing only a table and a narrow bed, as he murmured: "Wait,
wait." His soliloquy was originally addressed to himself, but later it
was addressed strictly to Puti. "You certainly don't like this habit," he
suddenly said without thinking. Just when he was about to go out,
the door opened softly, and a head reached in. It was Sister Huo.

"Dr. Fang, come." Sister Huo wore a smiling expression and
spoke calmly. "Dr. Xin wants to discuss a few patients' cases with you,
at the rear of the building." The rear of the building, which faced
north, had originally been the surgeons' study and conference room.

There were indeed several plans for patient surgeries to talk
over. Fang Zhi had planned to talk later on, in the ward, but thought
that to talk now was also all right, since it might avert unexpected
problems arising later on in the afternoon. He followed Sister Huo
to the rear of the building facing north and went in. Sister Huo
locked the door from the outside. In the room sat three men: Xin
Shengda, a pharmacist, and an electrician. "They're here for no
good. I absolutely must not allow them to delay my going to fetch
Puti," Fang Zhi thought, glancing behind him at the locked door.

"Fang Zhi! Listen well." Dr. Xin spoke very sedately. After a year,
activities, "admonitory talks," and "bringing people to trial" were, for
the most part, not as clamorous as they had been at the start of the
Great Cultural Revolution, and had much more finesse. "We are

going to examine you. We will examine the question of whether or not you are a Rightist who has slipped through the net! Nowadays, we do not plan to allow those who slipped through the net to escape again! You must believe in the Party, believe in the masses, honestly confess your wrongdoing!"

Fang Zhi took the measure of the three men one by one, calculating that if it came to a fight he would be the loser. He then observed: "My affairs are public knowledge for the whole hospital. A probationary suspension is not punishment. If there is anything that is not clear, I can provide more information." As he spoke he sat down.

"Provide more information? What you say is very convenient!" The pharmacist smiled coldly.

"Now, we have three questions for you to answer." Xin Shengda spoke without emotion. "First, with respect to the views which you aired in 1957, and your statements and deeds during the anti-Rightist campaign. . . . We want to know the truth about how you slipped through the net as a Rightist. Who covered for you? Second, your relationship with the reactionary authority Han Liwen.[1] How have you covered for him? Third, some people report that you have been going out a lot lately. What contacts have you had? Write it all out clearly, then we'll discuss it!" Xin Shengda pointed to paper and pen on the table, and then the three men stood up. Sister Huo now came in again, threw two steamed buns on the table, and the four swept out as though blown by a wind. Fang Zhi rushed to squeeze out with them, exclaiming loudly: "I can come back to write. I have patients to care for. You cannot detain me!" Two of the men twisted his arms to push him to the middle of the room; he heard the sound of the door locking, of retreating footsteps, then only silence.

This was a scene not atypical during that era's revolutionary situation. "Man" is not a sublime word. Man is but a living organism: any man needs only to have the armed might to subdue and control others and he can manipulate them at whim. This was just as things had been in history's dark ages; in truth, at times, worse. Then the "primitive" struggle had at least been fairer: it had been a struggle of life pitted against life, without the domination of body and mind, without conspiracies, without political frame-ups. But at this very moment, on the soil of our wretched motherland, how many were being

---

1. Han Lao's name; "Lao" is a respectful term for middle-aged and older persons.

subjected to the lash, to humiliation, to execution, to burial alive! Theoretical concepts were used to legitimate all sorts of cruel torture. Was this then our beloved socialist motherland? The very same, which had permitted Fang Zhi's old father to die peacefully, with mind at ease, which had trained Fang Zhi to become a doctor, which had saved thousands upon thousands of lives, yet was now banishing thousands upon thousands to the depths of hell. "How have we sunk so low?" Fang Zhi mused bitterly. "How could the land that we labored so hard to build have degenerated to such a pass?"

He sat at the table, staring blankly at the paper and pen. He wanted to write simply in big characters, special characters, "I am not a Rightist who has slipped through the net! Han Liwen does not need protection! My movements are those of a free person!" But he smiled bitterly and wrote nothing. He rose and paced up and down. Hearing steps he pounded on the door with his fist and called loudly: "I am Fang Zhi! I want to get out!" He hoped there might be Five Well Commune people passing. But each time he heard sounds of someone approaching, they died away again. No one heeded him.

He stood at the window for a while, pondering bitterly how to deal with the situation. Outside the window the sky darkened; inside the room it was suffocatingly hot. He stretched out his hand to push open the window, thinking it was perhaps already nailed shut. But it unexpectedly opened with one push. A cool wind blew in. It was apparently already raining; large raindrops were falling. As the rain fell it grew heavier; fine drops of water sprayed him. It occurred to him that this room was on the second floor, not high above the ground. In the blink of an eye, the curtain of rain changed into one vast expanse of whiteness; he could no longer see clearly below.

How was Puti? What time was it? Was she just then anxiously looking toward the vase-shaped entrance expecting him? She would now have yet another worry. What to do? Fang Zhi carefully inspected the room's wall inch by inch but could not make out any way of escape. He recollected that it was in this same room that he had once read aloud a paper about a famous English doctor's surgery for an acute illness that he had studied enthusiastically; in this room he had discussed Marxism, Chairman Mao's work, and all sorts of Party policies with his surgical colleagues. More than once he had confessed himself to have departed from the correct stand in the anti-Rightist struggle, and more than once he had discussed surgical plans. This was all gone; he could not now even give shape to any systematic recollection. His mind wanted to leave such thoughts behind, and concentrate on how to escape from those four walls and go to Puti, even if only to tell her that she should not wait any longer:

that she must go by herself for her examination and to arrange for any further treatment.

But how was he to tell her? How could he go? Fang Zhi paced up and down again for quite a while. The rain gradually diminished, the sky brightened. He stood before the window for a long time, sizing things up. He discovered he was only at the height of approximately two men above the ground. "I'll jump out of the window!" He was suddenly seized by the idea. With this in mind, he quickly surveyed the terrain. Underneath the window was an asphalt road; the strip of earth against the building was very narrow, and overhead were many electricity cables. The ground on the far side of the road was now uncultivated; originally it had been planted with several different kinds of flowers and trees, but now there was only a confusion of wild grasses. "It would be better to jump a little far out and land in the grass." He deliberated for an instant, then made up his mind to jump from the window.

Before arriving at this decision he had repeatedly told himself that once he had made up his mind he should not hesitate—such had been Fang Zhi's practice during many years of medical practice. He jumped up on the window sill, checking to see that no one was walking below. Rays from the rainwater sparkled on the road. Stillness lay all about. . . . "You cannot keep me! Cannot lock me up," he silently exclaimed. This mood of intense defiance and his longing to see Puti were sufficient to send him flying through space to land, without mishap, in Spoon Court. He leaped! Instantaneously a voice screamed out, cutting the stillness like a sharp knife. He had fallen on the grass, but on his buttocks. His back felt as though it had been broken at the waist, and an excruciating pain had caused him to scream out uncontrollably. Like a dying fish, he writhed this way and that on the grass.

"What's happened to me? What's happened to me?" Fang Zhi heard his own howl, felt himself turning over, then realized in a flash that it was pointless to cry out and that he couldn't move. All the same, he couldn't hold back several more loud cries, after which he quickly lost consciousness.

At Spoon Court Puti stared blankly at the vase-shaped entrance, turning often to look at the clock. Time went past by the second, by the minute, but still she did not see the man for whom she waited. "What has happened to him?" She knew Fang Zhi was as good as his word; if he had by now not come, she could almost certainly conclude that he had met with a mishap. In this uneasy state of mind she picked up her blue holdall, hesitated an instant in front of the door, then abruptly went out of the house.

At a quarter to four Puti arrived at Z Hospital. She looked attentively at each white-clad person, but did not inquire about Fang Zhi's whereabouts. They hurried by; no one paid any attention to her. She walked slowly toward the door of the consulting room for surgery. There were not many people there. A nurse was arranging something at the desk in the corridor. Her figure very much resembled Xiao Ding's. Standing in front of the desk, Puti could see that a list of names for surgery was lying on it, and that beside the three o'clock there were the three characters: "Mei Puti." "Shall I do it or not?" Puti thought uneasily. It was very minor surgery; it would not be a problem for her to go home by herself. But what had happened to Fang Zhi?

The nurse raised her head. It was, as expected, Xiao Ding. They looked at each other and smiled. Xiao Ding said: "You've come very late. Dr. Fang gave you a three o'clock appointment."

"Dr. Fang"—Puti was grateful Xiao Ding had mentioned him first—"where is he?"

"On the ward. He isn't booked in here this afternoon."

"Are there critically ill people on the ward?" Puti smiled casually.

"Today there's nothing," Xiao Ding answered absently, as she put out her hand. "The surgical list?"

Puti handed it to her mechanically, and mechanically followed her into the surgery room. She heard her say a few words to the doctor who was washing his hands. The doctor glanced at Puti impatiently and motioned her to lie down. Puti lay down on an empty surgical bed; there was another one in the room with a surgery in progress.

The doctor came over to examine the areas with the nodes, quickly antisepticized them, and was about to give an anesthetic, when Puti suddenly heard a terrible cry. It seemed to shake the whole roof. She shuddered instinctively.

"Don't move! I'm just about to give the shot. Who'll be responsible if it goes in at the wrong place?" the doctor said.

Right after this Puti again heard a scream, a piercing cry as if from a person undergoing unbearable torture; her heart was almost torn apart. She turned her head to look at the patient on the other bed. That person was lying quietly, covered with a surgical sheet. "It isn't he," Puti thought, then sought an explanation from the doctor: "Did you hear that scream?"

"What scream? There was no scream," the doctor said uncomprehendingly, and looked uncertainly at Puti. He stood up impatiently. "Do you want it done or not?"

Puti did not speak again, and tried her best to calm herself. The surgery was of short duration. The cuts in the flesh had no particular sensation. She was, nevertheless, in excruciating pain. The tortured scream wound around her ears; invisible axes seemed to chop at her joints so that she felt an agonizing sensation right in the marrow of her being.

When she sat up she felt dizzy. She left the operating room and sat down in the corridor. At this time those about to go off duty had about an hour to go; people wearing long white coats were already few. In the entrance hall there were several very sick-looking people crowded on the only long bench. On the floor, scraps of torn paper and gobs of sputum lay everywhere.

Puti found herself standing in the hospital entrance once again. She felt her heart pounding, calling out: "Where is he? Where is he?" How she wanted to cry out in a loud voice, to let Fang Zhi know she was looking for him. Should she go home? Could it be that she was to return without result? Leaving what? But how could she find him? She turned this way through the hospital doors, then suddenly grasped the holdall and walked quickly in the direction of the ward.

Yet she simultaneously knew Fang Zhi would surely not be on the ward. If things had been as normal as that for him, how was it he had not come to Spoon Court as arranged? How was it he had not come to the outpatients' service to see her? She stopped in front of the stairs where she had met Fang Zhi and Xiao Wei. She thought of Han Lao. There weren't many people in the pathology department now; Han Lao would not have left work early. She turned and went out of the door. Coming quickly to the doors of the pathology department, she suddenly heard voices from a confusion of people behind the building; some people were running about. She seemed to hear among the voices: "Someone jumped from the building." "These days good men don't jump from buildings!" She saw some men in white gowns go by. The words "Fang Zhi jumped from the building" assailed Puti clearly.

Puti wanted to walk to the rear of the building. Voices now drew closer. Several men came toward her carrying a stretcher. Was it possible they were going into the mortuary? Darkness enveloped her; she felt the muddy ground rise straight up in front of her, forcing her backward. She had not taken a step. Already leaning against the door, she sat down and promptly fainted.

When she came to, she found herself lying on some kind of bed. A white-haired old man sat beside the bed in front of a little table. He was just taking her pulse. It was Han Lao! Puti did not speak; her tears welled up first, dripping onto the pillow. Han Lao released her hand and said: "Fang Zhi is alive, you can rest easy."

Puti still could not say a word. Han Lao continued: "You can relax. He jumped from the building. It looks as if it's a broken lumbar vertebra; they have already taken a picture of it. He will need to lie in bed for a couple of months. I have been to the x-ray department. He's probably already lying in the dormitory. Don't worry." He paused, then said loudly: "If you need to weep, weep. No one can hear you here." Those attended to in that room were not living, but dead bodies, so naturally there was no one to hear.

"You cannot see him, he is under surveillance." Han Lao continued his monologue. "There's no need; it would only be asking for trouble. We can take care of him. Aren't there always more normal cells in the world?" His tousled hair—long untouched by any comb—hung down in locks around his face, adding to his appearance the slight suggestion of a beast of prey that had lived for a long time in a cave. "However, if you can get up, you can write him a note." He knew that Puti's "bed" was ice-cold and hard; he didn't want her lying there any longer.

Puti herself had indeed not noticed that she was lying on a small dissecting table. She got up. She felt dizzy and her incision hurt, but she felt quite strong enough to take care of herself. It was only that the tears welled up uncontrollably; she could not check them. Her handkerchief was already soaked; she used her sleeve to wipe her eyes again and again. Finally, with great difficulty, she spelled out the words "Everlasting Rock" on a pathology report form.

Puti left by the back door of the hospital, her tears still falling. Seated on the bus, she still wept. Both sleeves were now wet: she had to hold up the cuffs of her jacket to wipe away her tears. She was aware that the people nearby were looking at her, but she could not stop. Tears from the cuffs of her jacket seeped down, soaking her long pants. A stranger pressed against her ear and said in a low voice: "Don't weep. It can cause trouble. People suspect those who weep!" After this speech Puti was, surprisingly, even less able to brace herself and simply wept out loud, her sobs growing louder and louder as she wept. The people sitting directly in front of and behind her started weeping too—the one in front was a middle-aged woman, while the one to the back was a husky fellow. For a while the noise of weeping and the vehicle's rumbling were the only sounds to be heard on the bus.

# 13

# Detention

FANG ZHI DID NOT KNOW HOW LONG HE HAD BEEN UNCONSCIOUS. ALL he could remember was jumping straight out from the building and landing on the grass. Now his eyes were looking up at a round window at the top of the building. Beside him stood many people, all gazing silently down at him, no one speaking out loud. "Did a patient named Mei Puti come for surgery?" he wanted to ask them, as he leaned on his hand to get up. But his body would not listen to his commands; he could not speak, and his arms had no energy. He felt only the ice-cold slipperiness of the smooth ground. He was in fact lying on the wet asphalt road. "What's happened!" He didn't understand. When he again tried hard to move, an intense pain shot from the middle of his back right through his body; nothing existed in the world but the reality of that pain.

When he regained consciousness again, he found that he was lying in his own bed. Yes, he had hurt himself falling. People had carried him on a stretcher to have an x ray taken; what the results were, he did not know. It seemed that he was only required to lie there. How had Puti managed? Had she finally had the surgery or not? These four walls cut him off from her, from life; moreover, he could not move! At this stage in his musings Fang Zhi realized it was pointless worrying. Having thought this far, he felt much clearer in his mind.

However, he also felt bewildered, because he suddenly heard the sound of sobbing. The sound was so remote that it came and went, then came close enough to linger in his ears. For a time Fang Zhi thought it was he, himself, weeping. But when he listened again carefully, he could make out that it was Puti. The sobbing was uncontrolled, yet it had a kind of gentle delicacy. Nevertheless, it struck Fang Zhi's heart with incomparable force, producing an agonizing sensation ten thousand times worse than the breaking of any bones.

"Puti! Where are you weeping? Puti!" He could not keep from yelling out loud.

The door opened; someone stood in the doorway. Fang Zhi could not see clearly who it was; he could only make out the scarlet armband. The person shouted: "Are you still acting up? You behave yourself!" and closed the door with a bang. Fang wanted to ask if there was someone weeping outside, but he didn't have time.

The bang of the door cut short the dimly discernible sound of weeping. Fang Zhi inclined his head and listened attentively, but now there was only the hum of the cicadas outside the window. Having taken a rest after the big rain, they were beginning to chirp vigorously again, more in evidence than ever, surrounded on all sides by the stillness.

So there were still people guarding him. He really was in a prison. Actually, what need was there for them to set up a cage for him again? This lone body of his could not move; it had a natural black rope.[1] Fang Zhi was not a philosopher, nor had he read many books on the subject. If he had, he would have known that in the view of some philosophies in the world, the ten thousand things—his own body, even—were in effect already imprisoned in this world. Such knowledge and understanding would undoubtedly have calmed his mood and made his soul more peaceful.

For a time, he would be in a daze of suffering, then for a time, he would be clear-headed. When he was clear-headed again, he instinctively picked up the watch on the table. It said 7:45. The sky was hazy; he mistakenly thought it was still morning. "It's late!" He almost sat up; of course another stabbing pain followed. Only when he realized that it was already evening did he also realize that he had not seen his patients for eight or nine hours. How were they all? The one he had operated on for stomach cancer just that morning was extremely weak; he could not even go to have a look at him—and he did not know when he would be able to see him again, indeed, *if* he would be able to see him again! They certainly should use dextran glucoside in his infusion bottle. This was a blood plasma substitute now not readily given to patients. When Fang Zhi evaluated how special was a particular patient's case, he could only consider the patient's condition, not whether the patient had power or influence. When he had first prescribed this medicine, he had worried about whether it would actually enter the patient's body. There was also a

---

1. A black rope was used to detain criminals in ancient China.

rectal cancer patient who, three days before, had run a fever after surgery; his antibiotic dosage must on no account be reduced. And there was a man with intestinal cancer, whose condition was very good; he should be switched to a semifluid diet. . . . He worried about everything in the hospital. A doctor unable to treat his patients, who had himself become bed-ridden, perhaps crippled for life, who was now unable to continue with his medical responsibilities—if it was to be like this, what meaning would there be in life?

The door opened again and Sister Huo entered. Her fat face looked lifeless, the red birthmark on the left side of her forehead standing out plainly. She carried a cup of milk in one hand; in the other, a large paper bag.

"How is the infusion situation in Bed 18? He should certainly have some plasma substitute." Upon seeing Sister Huo, Fang Zhi poured out all his concerns in one breath. He knew that Sister Huo and her partner, Xin Shengda, were not entirely alike; her heart was not really evil. That afternoon's search for a stretcher and the other matters had all been organized by her. Even in his dazed condition, this fact had clearly imprinted itself on Fang Zhi's mind.

"You really are a miserable wretch, to have smashed yourself up like this, yet still be thinking of your patients," Sister Huo said to herself, while she quietly committed Fang Zhi's medical advice to memory. She took out a card and handed it to Fang Zhi, saying as she did so: "Look at your own card. They say you'll be two months in bed at the very least."

Fang Zhi understood that this "they" referred to the bone department. The bone department consisted almost entirely of Five Well Commune people. But "they" were very cool toward Fang Zhi; some had even proposed tossing him out. Surprisingly, he had jumped out himself. The card was very definite, for the diagnosis was written: "the fourth and fifth lumbar vertebrae compressed and fractured." Fang Zhi slowly lifted his two legs. He could move both: the nerves were not crushed, and it seemed as though he would not suffer sequelae. "So I'll lie here. Thank you."

"We have arranged for some men to look after you." She mentioned several names. The majority were "out of power"; among them was Han Liwen.

"The manpower being expended on me is too great," Fang Zhi said. "They've even posted a 'sentry guard' at the door. Why? I cannot move."

Sister Huo thought that it would have been better if he had been able to move, since the sickrooms were in a mess. What came out of her mouth, however, was: "Don't bother yourself about the man at the door! Recuperate from your injury!" So saying, she made a move to leave, then turned and paused at the door as if wanting to speak. Fang Zhi availed himself of this opportunity to put in a few words about the next day's surgery. Sister Huo nodded, said nothing, then opened the door and went out.

Fang Zhi drank the milk with a siphon. Summer days are long, but by now it had turned dark. The sound of the cicadas quieted for a while, then their chirping started up again. He knew that the pain would pass, but that people who have experienced very severe pain are never the same as before. He recalled how, when he had started working at Z Hospital, he had first seen a patient die. It had been a chest surgery. The intern's responsibility had been to pull on the ribs with a hook, exposing the internal organs, a completely manual exercise. The arm doing the pulling had ached to the point of numbness. But he still could not relax; he had to hold out until the surgery was over. After the operation he had been responsible for taking care of the patient. The patient had been very calm; the liquid in the infusion tube had dripped away, drop by drop. Fang Zhi had alternated with the nurses, now taking blood pressure, now checking the pulse. Everything had seemed normal. After midnight, he had gone to have another look. As he entered the room, he had had a peculiar feeling. When his vision adjusted to the dim light, he had only been able to make out that the patient's eyes were tightly shut, and that he was sweating profusely, already in a state of shock. Fang Zhi had quickly called the nurse to fetch the doctor in charge. The patient had opened his eyes for the last time, looked imploringly at Fang Zhi as if begging for help, then closed his eyes again. In his distress Fang Zhi had jumped on the bed to give artificial respiration. But there had been no response. He had been pulling the patient's arm vigorously when the head of the surgical department, Han Lao, had come in. Han Lao had rolled back the patient's eyelids and looked at him; then, while laying him out, had pronounced: "He's already dead, there's no use." The nurses had come and covered the corpse with a white cloth. Fang Zhi had stood up dumbstruck, feeling an inexplicable grief, and had almost begun to weep out loud. Controlling himself for as long as he could, he had gone alone to sit in the stairwell. A flood of tears had come as though breaching a dike. Like a child he had simply wailed and wept, wailed and wept.

"Dr. Fang, what's the matter? It wasn't your mistake, and it wasn't anything wrong in the surgery. You needn't take it to heart so. You'll gradually get used to it." Han Lao had come over to console him and he had quickly got to his feet. He recalled the stairwell's dim light and that Han Lao's hair, at that time, had been jet-black.

However, Fang Zhi never grew completely accustomed to death. Right up to Aunt Wei's passing away two months before, he continued to feel the same kind of regret, the same kind of impact. It was just that there were no longer tears.

He thought of the number of times in the past ten years he had looked into beseeching eyes, the number of times he had witnessed death that could not be averted, feeling each time at a loss, powerless. He suffered each time when, in the struggle between life and death, life was defeated and death prevailed; whenever, in the struggle between medicine and cancer, medicine lost and cancer proved victorious. As a doctor he had the duty to treat cancer, but often he had been unable to fulfill his duty, to save people's lives. He knew that Han Lao was not aloof and indifferent either. In fate's reckoning of life and death, medicine and cancer, responsibility and inevitability, such tragedies were constantly being repeated.

He had never ceased believing that tragedy was not without an end. But now, as he lay in his sickbed, he wondered where it would all end. Z Hospital and the whole nation existed in a state of turbulent upheaval. Both high and low, the whole country was caught up in the struggle against revisionism.[2] Resonating in the hospital, this struggle meant confusion, filth, accidents, and death! Standards of medical treatment had fallen so low as to be irreparable. Cancer was again advancing on fronts previously under control. Repeatedly, doctors had to withdraw, defeated. This was not only helplessness in the face of one patient, but in the face of the whole nation, the whole society! What impotence! Fang Zhi, meditating thus about himself, about Puti, about his patients, about the nation, about the common people, wanted to pound the bed and weep bitterly.

He was engulfed by this emotional turmoil when someone came in. He could vaguely discern in the dimness that it was none other than Han Lao. How could Han Lao comfort him in his present pain? He slowly went over to the front of the bed and turned on the table lamp, rotating it so that the lamplight would not shine in Fang Zhi's eyes.

"Did she come?" Fang Zhi asked with effort.

"She came. It was done. She wrote this for you." Han Lao handed him the pathology report sheet. Across a table of columns were written the words "the everlasting rock" in graceful characters.

---

2. The struggle against revisionism in the early 1960s referred strictly to the struggle against Soviet socialism. After the Cultural Revolution, the term was used in a vaguer, more general sense.

This was the promise of life, this was solace for the soul. The characters expressed the normal cells' capacity to defeat the cancer cells, expressed the conviction that life could defeat death. Fang Zhi could feel his emotional turmoil abating.

"Her slide?" he asked carefully.

"It still hasn't been delivered." Han Lao sat wearily in the lone chair. "Just now the chiefs called me in for a talking-to. They talked for a long time. I only understood a little. Someone wanted me to do surgery. I am being transferred from the pathology department."

"If your surgical knife can be used, that's after all a good thing. But where? Who wanted you?" Fang Zhi looked with concern at Han Lao's whitening head.

"Who knows? I'll still go to the department to look at the slide. If there are results, I'll tell you." As he spoke, he brought out pen and paper and a piece of cardboard, following the practice of doctors preparing carefully pondered items. "Write. I'll deliver." He respectfully turned to face the door. Fang Zhi wanted him to sit down. "I have things to attend to," he answered.

Fang Zhi wrote very slowly. Lying down, it wasn't easy to move his hand. Nor did he want Puti to see crooked handwriting. He still had not finished writing when Han Lao suddenly rushed over and abruptly seized the writing materials. Quick as a flash, he had stuffed them—who knows where. The door opened; the guard came in, blustering and truculent, and said to Han Lao: "Haven't you finished yet? What are you dawdling over?" Han Lao did not answer, occupying himself with a few trivial matters. Then he nodded to Fang Zhi and left.

That night Fang Zhi and Puti could both feel the trains rumbling, in and out of awareness. The sound, accompanied by the cicadas, completely filled the boundless darkness of night. Combined with his pain, they crowded in on Fang Zhi, so that he could find no relief.

The next day the "sentry guard" was not quite so energetic. When, by almost noontime, the next shift had not arrived, the first shift left of his own accord. Only the name list posted on the door remained to watch over Fang Zhi. Xiao Ding came to see him and saw that above the list was written: "No one may enter other than listed persons!" She took it upon herself to stroll in. People from the Red-Speared Combat Group,[3] passing in the corridor, pretended not to see her.

---

3. A specific Cultural Revolution militia group.

On the previous day Xiao Ding hadn't waited to go off duty before she slipped home. So it was only today that she had learned about Fang Zhi's leap from the building. When Puti had come to the outpatient surgery room that morning to inquire about Fang Zhi's condition, she had left behind her a letter and roll of paper. Xiao Ding now handed these two items to Fang Zhi, remarking: "Teacher Mei is very brave."

Fang Zhi took the letter and the roll of paper. For the moment he didn't open them, but first asked about his patients' conditions. Luckily, Xiao Ding had had a turn on the ward. She answered, leaving Fang Zhi feeling satisfied for the time being. A wisp of a smile appeared on his pale, thin face. Xiao Ding sighed: "Dr. Fang, you are really a good person; nowadays the good person is not rewarded. In surgery this morning the patient was out of luck: it was Dr. Xin again."

"If only he wouldn't worry so much about holding meetings for this and that." Fang Zhi rejoiced a bit that Sister Huo had come the day before; perhaps Dr. Xin would have listened to what Sister Huo had relayed.

Xiao Ding thought a bit and said: "Before the surgery I heard Sister Huo and Dr. Xin jabbering away in the duty room. They didn't know I was in there; I'd gone to get something. It seems they were talking about how Elder Sister Qi had killed herself at Zhang Yongjiang's house; the corpse really was moved. In any case, Sister Huo knows about the matter."

"There is a witness," Fang Zhi said thoughtfully. "However, Sister Huo is quite loyal. She wouldn't turn against those she has wrongly sided with."

"They have their times of dog-eat-dog!" Xiao Ding was angry, her fair complexion reddened. Seeing that Fang Zhi wasn't opening the letter, she made a move to leave, then voiced a sudden recollection: "It's being passed around that they're going to send a group to Gansu Province. It's surmised it will be a 6.26 medical team;[4] people with power and influence for sure won't go." Then she said: "Tomorrow afternoon I've been assigned to serve as a doctor in the outpatient clinic. I don't plan to go and I haven't studied."

---

4. 6.26 refers to June 26; during the Cultural Revolution Mao gave "highest instruction" one June 26 that doctors and nurses should go out to serve poor and lower-middle-class peasants in rural areas. Many medical teams were sent out under this instruction. They were known as "6.26" teams.

"If it were me, I wouldn't either," Fang Zhi agreed.

Xiao Ding left silently.

When Fang Zhi saw the door had closed, he quickly opened the letter. It was brief. She had written: "I came for surgery at the appointed time. Your recovery will comfort me most. Don't worry. Isn't it clear that I know why you jumped from the building?" The roll of paper was Puti's calligraphy and painting. One she had slipped in was from the previous evening when she hadn't been able to fall asleep. These were words from Zhuang Zi's *Great Master of Learning:*

> Break your body, dismiss your intelligence
> Forget your shape and consciousness
> Let yourself become just like objects of the world.

Then there was a quotation from the fourteenth of Elizabeth Barrett Browning's *Sonnets from the Portuguese:*

> . . . Nevermore
> Upon the threshold of my door
> Of individual life, shall I command
> The uses of my soul . . .
> And when I sue
> God for myself, He hears the name of thine
> And sees within my eyes the tears of two.

Fang Zhi understood Puti's intention in writing these verses, yet his mind was soon filled with thoughts of that morning's surgical patients, patients who had no choice but to accept the diagnoses of nurses rather than of a doctor, and he wanted to change the last words to: "And sees within my tear-filled eyes the people's sorrow." The new verse didn't rhyme, but that didn't matter.

From the several sheets, Fang Zhi picked out a wash painting of bamboo and rock. In the middle of the painting was the great Rock of Spoon Court. Puti had not painted the Rock very skillfully, yet Fang Zhi felt that the "Everlasting Rock" of his heart could not be otherwise. Next to the Rock, several bamboo stood out sparse and plain, expressing the spirit of the words: "Without leaving the ground, the bamboo already has joints; when it reaches the sky, it is without pretension."[5] It seemed to be Puti standing beside the Rock, her eyelids lowered, the curved arcs of these lines giving one the feeling of a smile. From this sheet great waves of tenderness radiated forth, lifting him from his hard bed, embracing him, rocking him,

---

5. See above, page 94.

soothing him. Although his body was doubly imprisoned, he felt an intimate and vibrant relationship with life.

Fang Zhi spent the whole day looking at the paintings. He thought a great deal. Originally he had imagined that he could ensure Puti's happiness. Now the situation had changed. He might completely recover, but he might always have a sore waist and aching middle back, which could affect his work. His political future was not great: the "hat" of a Rightist, who had escaped unpunished, awaited him. And from now on, the future prospect of the average doctor was to hurry about barefooted in remote, thickly forested mountain regions. The list for this first medical team, if he hadn't been hurt in his fall, would surely have included his name. To serve the people had been his earliest wish, but how could Puti's body withstand the hardships and uncertainties of that life? Although she was the woman he most desired to be with, perhaps he no longer had the right to cherish the trust that had begun with those rock-giving years so long ago.

A long, slow day passed. He meditated. The moon shone bright and clear through the window. He continued to meditate. As his anxiety-laden dreams unfolded in the moonlight, he still pondered achingly how best he could ensure Puti's happiness; how he could restore his patient's health.

# 14

# A Bright Moon

---

A T THE SAME TIME, THE BRIGHT AND CLEAR MOONLIGHT WAS SHINING ON
Spoon Court.

The night that Fang Zhi jumped from the building, Puti did not
sleep at all. She wept on the bus. Back at Spoon Court, her tears were
exhausted, her mind a blank. She felt only confusion and heartache.
Several times she forced herself to lie down, but always got up again.
Huiyun, hearing her tossing about, threw on some clothes and came
over, opened the ink slab, ground the ink stick, and said: "There's no
use your trying to sleep. Write. Write Zhuang Zi. Write Chan Sect
quotations. Write 'Puti is no tree; the bright mirror also lacks a
stand.'[1] You know so much by heart. Paint rocks, paint bamboo. Just
don't let your imagination run wild." Her exhausted smile was
slightly plaintive.

Taking the ink stick, Puti said: "You go back to sleep, don't worry
about me." As she spoke she ground the stick a few times and then
indeed grasped the brush to write. Resting her cheeks in her hands,
Huiyun looked at the ink traces on the page, saying to herself: "Is it
really true that 'blessings never come in pairs, misfortunes never
come singly'?" Unconsciously, she gave a deep sigh.

"You go back to sleep," Puti urged again. "I'm much better. You
still have to work tomorrow." Huiyun stood up. Puti continued: "At
work time, remember to loaf on the job." She often gave this warning,

---

1. The word "puti" in Chinese signifies a kind of tree. It was under a
bodhi tree that Buddha is traditionally believed to have attained perfect
knowledge, so the word also means "supreme wisdom," or the enlightenment
necessary to achieve a higher state of being in Buddhism.

but it was actually very difficult for Huiyun to do this. Huiyun also gave some advice: "Just as soon as you're calmer, you should lie down and rest. After all, you've just had surgery." So saying, she pulled the door shut.

Puti stroked at random for a while, feeling hot and muggy, then turned out the light. The moonlight poured in through the window. Suddenly a faint coolness enveloped the room. She thought of the words "Puti is no tree." If, indeed, she could see through the vanity of the world, believe that life was after all an illusion, that she herself did not exist, then what suffering could one speak of? When her father had chosen her name, most probably he already knew that she would endure unbearable suffering in her life and prepared an anesthetic for her. She turned her head to look at the pot with her father's ashes; in the moonlight the brown earthen pot looked a somber black. She thought of simply calling him out loud, calling her mother, calling Fang Zhi, but instead she grasped a handkerchief firmly, turned on the light, and wrote characters as the hot tears flowed. In this way she spent the night: thinking, writing, weeping, and lying down. The moonlight grew dimmer, and the sky gradually brightened.

Puti went to the hospital after getting up. She knew that going there put her in danger of being publicly denounced, but she didn't much care. Since her life had been forced into so many "didn't much care" situations, she now had a "didn't much care" spirit. Although she would not be able to see Fang Zhi, she thought of how much just looking at her calligraphy could comfort him.

That day was a long one at Spoon Court, too. In the evening the moonlight again painted the top of the Everlasting Rock a pale white. Only then did Huiyun come home. When she opened the door she held a letter in her hand. "This letter was thrown in at the yard gate." She handed it to Puti as she spoke. At that time letters were not delivered to houses; each residential area had one box, and sometimes letters were thrown on the ground. Looking at the writing, Puti knew it was Fang Zhi's. She ripped at it twice with her right hand but couldn't tear it open. She thought of fetching some scissors. Then she felt that would take too long, so she tore with her left hand. By the light of the moon and the street lamp, she read. The letter said:

> Puti, please excuse me. I am resting. There are people caring for me. Everything is all right. You can rest easy by all means. Han Lao has left the pathology department. You can come on schedule to the outpatient clinic to get the results; typically it takes about a

week. I know staunchness and calmness are Puti's special qualities. Looking at the words "Everlasting Rock," I look forward to whatever life may bring. I am resting . . .

The letter wasn't finished. The calligraphy strokes were still neat, only slightly slanted. Obviously they had been written in bed. The letter had been mailed out when he had had the chance. Puti hugged the letter to her breast and fixed her gaze on the two not-very-bright stars at the top of the willow tree.

"What is it? Is he all right?" Huiyun fretted.

Puti handed her the letter. After reading it she sighed gently: "You see, he's all right, you should relax. In answer we can send Cui Li with something for him to eat. I just saw Cui Li at the school entrance. She came over and said she'd come in a couple of days." Huiyun paused and said: "She probably has news of Qin Ge. Ai! I'd really love to hear."

A couple of days later Cui Li came as expected. She was much thinner. She looked wan and sallow, her face projecting even more of a bewildered yet disapproving expression than usual. Her life had taken on a very irregular pattern, with great fluctuations in her energy level. As she came in the door she pursed her lips, looking as though she were full of grievances, as though she were about to cry.

Huiyun and Puti both asked about Cui Zhen's illness; Cui Li replied as usual: "Her? She can't die." She repeated some gossip, then said to Huiyun: "Aunt Tao, I've come to tell you: Qin Ge wants to go to the Great Northern Wilderness[2] to construct a frontier region." She felt that she received much more warmth and affection from Huiyun than from Cui Zhen, although she hadn't actually talked with Huiyun very much.

Huiyun opened her great, dull, lifeless eyes wide: "Are you going?"

"I don't know. I don't have to go. But I want to go, too."[3] The reason for her wanting to go was quite plain.

"Construct the frontier region," Huiyun said to herself. She knew that this was close to Qin Ge's heart. In his second year of senior high school, because of his outstanding academic record, the school had given him permission to take his college entrance examinations early. But he hadn't taken them: he had wanted to go to a farm vil-

---

2. In northeast China.

3. If there were several children in a family, at least one and sometimes more were required to go and work in the provinces.

lage, go to the frontier regions. "That's how he was brought up. Perhaps he has to go. When is he going?" Huiyun seemed to be asking herself.

"It's said sometime in September. There's lots of time. He has just applied." Cui Li looked curiously at Huiyun.

"I must fix something for him, bedding, and so on." Huiyun stood up as she spoke. She looked as though she were about to put her hand to it right then and there, but in her little room there was nothing but mugginess. "What's to be done? The Great Northern Wilderness is very cold."

Puti said they should get Zhang Yongjiang to return some things through the department's Cultural Revolution office. If that failed, she could give Qin Ge the bedding her father had used in his time on earth. As she spoke, she opened the old box at the foot of her bed and let Huiyun have a look. Cui Li came into the house, too. She asked: "Aunt Tao, do you approve of his going?"

"He's not going to ask whether I approve or not." Huiyun smiled bitterly. "But we should consider whether or not he'll accept the things we get ready for him."

"He might need them because he has nothing," Cui Li said with a sigh. "But should I go too, or not? They filled out their applications quite a few days ago."

The two adults looked at each other; they suggested Cui Li should talk to her mother. Perhaps she should stay and take care of her mother.

"Her!" As usual Cui Li said this first. After a pause she observed: "She's very obsessed with not being revolutionary enough. She's forever sharpening her wits to be an activist. She could push me to go. I'm actually not very interested. If it wasn't that—"

"Qin Ge is similarly 'obsessed,'" said Huiyun.

"He's sincere, he's a sincere revolutionary." Cui Li defended him ardently. Suddenly she turned to Puti: "Aunt Mei, I really envy you and Dr. Fang. You've had so many twists and turns, but you're still happy. Our generation doesn't share that kind of emotion. We're too realistic, and too ruthless."

In truth, beside the generation that had been swept up by this windstorm, to come down again they knew not where, perhaps her own bitter experiences were nothing: Puti's heart brimmed with sympathy. She had no idea, however, how best to comfort Cui Li.

"It's very painful," Cui Li muttered. She turned and went out the door. Huiyun and Puti thought she was going into the courtyard, but they heard the sound of the courtyard gate. She had gone.

After this, Puti's days revolved around letters. Daily, a letter would come from Fang Zhi telling her of his condition, comforting her and encouraging her. Although he never mentioned how much he missed her, how much he wanted to know her news, his frame of mind was, nevertheless, unintentionally revealed between the lines, distressing Puti all the more.

The eve of the day of the test verdict, the bright moon overhead was already waning. Since the courtyard was small, the four walls all seemed to reflect the moonlight, making the little yard very bright. Huiyun, having finished her account of that day's thoughts,[4] was sitting in the courtyard with one hand holding the little wooden stool, the other raising the teacup. That cup had not seen a tea leaf in several days. To improve Puti's nutritional intake so that she could cope better with who knew what cruel treatment still lay ahead, Huiyun economized to the point of almost saving every scrap. Puti firmly opposed her not even drinking tea, but Huiyun would say, her face wreathed in smiles: "The tea flavor in this cup is quite enough. That's an advantage of not washing the cup." Puti, at this time, was feeding the little tabby cat under the eaves; the cat stretched itself, emitting a loud cry.

From the courtyard gate came the sound of gentle tapping, as though someone feared to alarm the household. The two householders and the little cat all glanced lynx-eyed toward the gate. A voice said: "Teacher Mei is at home?" and an old man entered. In the moonlight, his full head of white hair shone like silver filaments.

"Han Lao!" Puti put down the cat's bowl, and went forward happily to greet him. Huiyun also stood up.

"Please sit down, please sit down," Han Lao said politely. "I've come to announce a piece of good news. Teacher Mei is well and doesn't have anything." As he spoke he took out the pathology report form and with a flashlight showed it to Huiyun and Puti.

Written on the pathology report form was: "Did not see cancerous changes."

Huiyun let out a long breath and said: "Now my heart can return to normal."

Puti was very relieved as well. However, at the same time, she felt that in order to really feel free of onerous burdens, she would need

---

4. A person with Huiyun's suspect political status during the Cultural Revolution had to write a daily account of his or her thoughts.

to see other conditions met. She smiled casually and asked: "And Fang Zhi? How is he?"

"Completely normal." Han Lao was all grins. "Did you get his letter?"

"I got it. And you? How is it you're no longer in the pathology section?"

"It's said there are people who want me to do surgery." Han Lao's smiling expression disappeared. "Naturally it must be a senior officer. Otherwise they wouldn't let me go. These past few days it's been studying the rules and writing essays, and I've had to write down my thoughts, talk about my reflections. I can't go out in the evening. This is not a good sign."[5]

Puti suddenly thought of an affair in ancient times when an empress was dying of smallpox and the imperial doctor was about to be executed. She looked with concern at Han Lao's ashy old countenance, its deep creases showing plainly in the moonlight, and said slowly: "I wish we could all transform danger into safety."

"There is another incidental matter, also good news." Han Lao then told of Sister Huo's knowing about the corpse's being moved.

"Saying that, I will no longer be accused of being a 'murderer.' This frame-up is actually very rich in romantic overtones." Puti sighed. "It's only that Elder Sister Qi—the whole family is really—"

"We should tell Zheng Liming, let him ask Sister Huo." Huiyun's eyes opened wide.

"Luckily Han Lao came to tell us," Puti said thankfully.

Han Lao said: "Fang Zhi told me to pass that on. He was anxious to know Teacher Mei's results. When I went to find out about them, I myself saw the slide. Tomorrow when you go yourself, most likely you won't find it." He turned to look at Puti, and said thoughtfully: "Fang Zhi is a good person, an upright person, the son of a peasant, better I think than intellectuals. Intellectuals are indeed self-centered, cherish their reputations—call it by the fine-sounding name of dedication to work—it is a weakness. I'm not talking about bloodlines, however."[6]

The three said nothing for a time. The moon spread a peaceful glow; the atmosphere was calm and cordial.

---

5. Since Han Lao was a good doctor, he feared he would be ordered to operate on an important person—with a serious penalty for failure.

6. At the beginning of the Cultural Revolution, some, particularly young people, advocated the theory that one was born "red" (revolutionary) or "black" (reactionary).

"Do you know Han Yi?" Huiyun asked suddenly, studying Han Lao's face.

"That's my son. You know him?" Han Lao's whole body twitched. "In the beginning he had a reputation as red and expert, developing well in every way. But in these past two years, he's developed a disease; it seems as though his soul is covered with a hard shell—"

"Hardening of the heart! Hardening of the soul!" Huiyun blurted. "These are the names we've given to that kind of illness in Spoon Court. My son, too, has caught that sickness. That sickness is contagious."

Han Lao did not speak. He seemed to be pondering the names for the sickness. Huiyun wanted to say something but checked herself. She gave Puti a glance, then could restrain herself no longer: "We are always in a situation of reform. We blame ourselves for everything. One day . . ." Huiyun shrank back, and looked blankly at the ground.

"At first I, too, was in the early stages of heart-hardening. It is only now that I have learned there is just this heart of flesh and blood, which will not change. It is the most authentic thing in life." Puti spoke slowly. Her heart was full of Fang Zhi. It was Fang Zhi who had cured her acute and chronic sickness and poured fresh water into her rigid heart. He had given her back her life; she should somehow use that life to repay him, to nourish him, to protect him. Actually, for a long time now, that life had not belonged to her, but to him.

"We also need to reform," Han Lao said, still deep in thought. Suddenly he smiled again and said: "You two are very interesting, devising quite a few newfangled phrases. Teacher Mei, you must still take good care of yourself." To Huiyun he said: "Your son may recover from his sickness; as to mine, it's hard to say." Presently he got up and took his leave.

As he walked to the courtyard gate, Puti was still standing in the shadow of the Everlasting Rock. "Han Lao! Wait!" she called out, and ran after him a few steps. "I want to go and see Fang Zhi. I'll follow you. Just make believe you don't know me, okay?"

Han Lao, still pondering, looked at her for quite a while, then said: "All right. For the most part there is no one watching him. However, you may run up against some situation. It's hard to say."

"I don't care," Puti said loudly. She ran into her room and picked up her handbag. After Huiyun had gone into her room, she locked up the courtyard gate and followed after Han Lao.

Going out from the courtyard gate there was no one to be seen. In the cool moonlight, in the mottled shadows of the trees, Puti felt as if she were going to a cemetery. Here too, dead men were more than plentiful. She and Han Lao, maintaining an agreed ten steps between them, arrived without mishap at Fang Zhi's door; Han Lao put out his hand, gestured, and simply walked off.

Puti gently pushed open the door, and was inside in a flash. She quickly closed the door and leaned against it, breathless. The light in the room was very dim; a small light at the head of the bed shone on Fang Zhi's head. He was just holding up the ink wash drawing of the bamboo and rock when he saw Puti's form and dropped the picture onto his body. He did not feel the slightest surprise, but simply looked at her.

"You came," he said in a low voice. He looked at her, the sight he had hoped for when he jumped from the building, the sight he had longed for during the lingering days and nights of his infirmity. He had known that ultimately nothing would keep her from coming: no criminal name, no sickness, not even death itself. All would give way before their love.

"I came," she answered softly, and put her hands in his.

They felt themselves so blessed, so strong. In this instant in time, their mundane lives were transformed into golden ones that nothing could destroy, transcending space, leaping over life and death. This clasp of four hands, this meeting of two pairs of eyes, would never be limited by time or place.

# 15

# The Departure

THE SWELTERING MONTH OF JULY PASSED. IN THE FIRST TEN DAYS OF AUgust, at the entrance to Spoon Court, what fragrant plantain lilies were left, after the calamity, put forth snow-white flowering shoots. In a few days these blossomed, emitting a sweet-smelling perfume.

Although authority in the Chinese faculty still lay in the hands of Zhang Yongjiang, an increasing number of people resented him. The words passed on by Xiao Ding were unofficial evidence of his involvement in moving the corpse, while Shi Qingping's use of all sorts of magnificent reasoning to ensure a change of residence appeared as internal evidence. Everyone was clear about it in their own minds. Some people in the June First Commune put up big-character posters about Zhang Yongjiang; Zhang, however, had his defenses. And there were those who argued against speaking on behalf of class enemies. Thus the posters came down again. So it was with many developments of the Great "Cultural Revolution." The Revolution itself was destined to wind down in eight to ten years' time.

In sum, Puti's situation improved considerably. Fang Zhi was gradually regaining his health, and this comforted her greatly. Zheng Liming came more than once to Spoon Court to talk with Huiyun and Puti about the struggles in the school and in society. He often remarked that Puti's illness could be regarded as disaster heralding happiness, since it had prevented her from being denounced continually, day in and day out. Huiyun's situation, however, still didn't improve. Every day, now, in addition to her work, she took pains over outfitting her son. Zhang Yongjiang's answer had been to let Qin Ge go and get his things. She pushed Cui Li to seek out her son, but they never met up with him.

The dwellings at Spoon Court were out of the way, far from the school's central areas. Because of this, some people enjoyed coming

159

to sit there for a bit. After Han Lao, Xiao Ding came when she had the time. Those who came all knew that no matter what was discussed, Huiyun and Puti were not likely to pass it on. They aired their grievances freely, then left in a calmer frame of mind. In any case, in those days time was at its least valuable. Strangely, visitors came often but never encountered each other, almost as though a schedule of appointments had been arranged.

The last days of August arrived quickly. Huiyun, returning home, brought the several remaining flowers of the fragrant plantain lily. "These are the last of the flowers." As usual she placed them on Puti's table. "I still haven't seen Qin Ge's shadow. Could he have left?" she asked Puti.

"He couldn't. Cui Li would know," Puti comforted.

Although the dog days soon ended and the evenings now brought a hint of coolness, they still sat out in the courtyard, entertaining friends who came to unload their complaints and worries. The freshly arranged plantain lilies' scent already gave off the odor of decay. As they sat in the courtyard, Huiyun observed: "Who knows who'll come for a talk this evening." Puti only looked silently toward the two stars at the top of the willow tree.

Astonishingly, the one who came for a talk was none other than the son for whom Huiyun had longed so unremittingly: Qin Ge. With one foot he kicked open the courtyard gate. In his hands he held a big messy bundle that resembled bedding, but did not completely contain it. He rushed in, and Huiyun and Puti had quite a scare.

"Son!" Huiyun's great dull eyes glistened and shone, as the street lights dimmed abruptly. "My son!" She immediately made a move as if to rush over and hug him, then halted timidly.

"Ma!" Qin Ge shouted, dropping the pile he was embracing on the ground. "Get them ready." He sat down with one buttock resting on his mother's little stool, looked around the courtyard, and commented: "So it's these two little worn-out rooms? Are you getting enough to eat? Ma!"

"Enough? Well, we still haven't died of hunger." Huiyun choked with sobs as she spoke. "You're much thinner, son."

"When we have food, we eat; when we have a place, we sleep. To struggle with class enemies, capitalist-roaders,[1] to struggle with contradictions and with one's own 'selfishness' is an ongoing process.

---

1. That is, persons in power taking the "capitalist road."

The revolutionary road is long—" As he spoke he suddenly noticed Puti. He stared at her as he continued speaking to Huiyun. "I've heard you live with the black author of *The Everlasting Rock?*"

Puti gave a start and shivered. She could clearly see under the light from the street lamp that this young man was one of the activists who had raided her house. It was he who had taken what she had saved, bit by bit; it was he who had smashed the mirror and the perfume bottle; it was he who, yelling with the others, had burned the books in the courtyard, thereby consigning a culture to the flames. His upright and handsome face had looked so ferocious in the raging fire's light that Puti had been unable to completely forget it.

But what could one say now? Puti only sat without participating. Huiyun implored: "Don't speak recklessly! Aunt Mei is my good friend."

"Good friend? How can you still be so muddleheaded! She's a murderer!" Qin Ge's face was flushed with anger.

Puti rose, unable to restrain herself, and cried: "I am not a murderer! You, on the other hand, raided my house! Stole my things!"

"So I raided your house! Your money was delivered to the bank, sealed for safekeeping. So what?" Qin Ge slapped his thigh and also stood up.

Puti very much wanted to shout out: "You pay me back! I need money to treat my illness!" An outcome of the Cultural Revolution was that whenever even the slightest bit of personal anger still lingered, it could take on a rude and unreasonable tone. But this was Huiyun's son, so she only glared at him and said nothing.

"You have the audacity to launch a counteroffensive!" Qin Ge had seldom seen a class enemy who had dared to shout back. This was simply inconceivable to him. He reached down and undid his belt.

"Stop!" Huiyun rushed over and grasped his hand. Great tears fell on that hand—her son's hand. "How did you become like this! If you want to beat someone, then beat me first!"

Perhaps mothers, at whatever time, will always remain mothers. Huiyun, especially, was that kind of mother. She restrained Qin Ge and turned her head toward Puti, with a look that beseeched her not to argue. Puti noticed that Qin Ge's eyes resembled Huiyun's—surely the beautiful big eyes of Huiyun's youth. She gave a sigh, turned, and went into the house.

The courtyard was quiet for a long time. Huiyun said softly: "You're going to stay here with Mama? There's a bench. Mama will sleep on the bench."

"No. I'm too tired, I couldn't sleep. I feel I have become hard, I'm getting harder, I'm turning into a rock. I'm no longer a man." His voice had a strangled quality.

"You are a now a man, my son!" Huiyun folded his head in her arms.

"I miss you, Ma," Qin Ge said. Suddenly he struggled to throw off his mama's embrace. This corrosive bourgeois influence was too much! He rose abruptly, and gave Huiyun a shove. "What if everyone were this kind of revolutionary? I can't lag behind. I must leave. I'm giving you this." He handed Huiyun a piece of paper, then walked off with great strides. Huiyun followed him, calling his old name: "Huaisheng! Huaisheng!" She chased him right up to the gate and out.

Puti quickly came out to follow Huiyun. Circling around the trash heap, she saw that Huiyun was standing alone beside the pitch blackness of the reed pond, staring dumbly after the beloved form of her posthumous child, already swallowed up in the night's dim light.

Puti gently drew her back toward Spoon Court. Beneath the lamplight they looked at the paper. It was a listing of the class status of families and of individuals in simple columns. There were also counts of sons and daughters, and opposite, a column for parents' opinions on their sons and daughters going to the countryside. Last was a circular announcing a district meeting for parents of young intellectuals going to the mountains or to the countryside.

They didn't know that Qin Ge had not come easily by this paper. In the tumult of those days, Qin Ge and some of his fellow students had already progressed from the fanaticism of raiding houses and making public denunciations. They were also tired of study groups, beatings, and the holding or putting up of slogans. They had been at a loss as to what to undertake next when the appeal "To the Great Northern Wilderness" had come. They had felt that here were fresh horizons for their by now much-regimented revolutionary ideals. The air of the Great Northern Wilderness would be pure and fresh, the winds of the Great Northern Wilderness would be vigorous. Revolutionary youths as well as worker and peasant associations all took guidance from Chairman Mao. To take root in the borderlands, to establish the borderlands, was so rich in romantic hues. Let alone that Qin Ge had all along nursed this kind of ambition. He and several fellow students had excitedly jogged to the district committee, casting off their jackets as they ran. Everyone had rushed to fill in applications, aching to start the next day on the new revolutionary journey.

Others had all passed through without a hitch. The person in charge had taken Qin Ge's application and turned it over. He had frowned and muttered to himself as he looked at it, vaguely and ambiguously observing: "For the borderlands, the political qualifications are somewhat higher." He had said to come back in a couple of days for further information. "Can it be that I don't even have the right to work?" Qin Ge had suffered discrimination on more than one previous occasion, but he had never felt this agitated before, nor had he felt this sense of righteous indignation.

At the beginning of his third year in middle school, the first time his fellow students had been permitted to shoot with live ammunition, there had not been a ration for Qin Ge. He had had to sit in the classroom along with another unfortunate student—an ultra-Rightist's offspring—wistfully looking out at the playing field. From that time forward he had had to give up any idea of serving in the People's Liberation Army, although that was the universal ideal of boys in New China. He had wanted "daily to move upward," he had wanted to obey the Party, to do his very best to behave according to the moral standards of that day's society. He had ceaselessly criticized the father he had never seen, although from start to finish he had never been clear about just what the Resources Committee was. Almost all of those drawn out of thin air and flung into the catastrophes of the Cultural Revolution were from families of the intelligentsia. According to limits clearly outlined by his mother, he had participated in all "revolutionary" operations, trying to be first in everything, but he had not even achieved a Red Guard armband. However, to go to the Great Northern Wilderness, to establish granaries for the motherland, this exactly fit Qin Ge's ideal. He had no fear of hardships, fatigue, mental or physical suffering. He knew that he needed toughening up and reforming. But now he was not even to be given this opportunity. What fault did he have, after all? In what way was he lacking?

After a couple of days he and some fellow students had once again gone to inquire at the district committee. The man in charge had still spoken vaguely, unclearly: "For the frontier, political qualifications have to be stricter."[2] After that he had said unequivocally: "You come back. We'll talk again with the next group." Qin Ge had almost wanted to unfasten his belt, but he had made the best of it and began to argue: how he had not taken his college entrance examinations because he wanted to go out and help establish farm

---

2. Since China's frontier areas were close to the Soviet Union, it was feared that "bad elements" might escape across the border.

villages, since that was where people were needed most. How he had studied Chairman Mao's essay on the May Fourth Movement[3] and knew that if the revolutionary youth did not cooperate with workers and peasants, they would have no future. He presented his views vehemently and tearfully, putting to use all the debating skills he had studied that past year. His fellow students had also backed him up from time to time. The man in charge had been quite embarrassed, but still did not have the authority to sanction a decision. Then an ordinary-looking man had walked in from another room. He was from the "Great Northern Wilderness Welcoming Youth Committee," and said straightforwardly to the district committee member in charge of the proceedings: "Accept him. I think it'll be okay! He can't run away!" The man in charge had no alternative but to put Qin Ge's application in, along with his fellow students'. The students had all cheered and jumped for joy, pushing Qin Ge back and forth. At long last he had been given an opportunity to offer the tribute of his youthful years to his country, to the motherland.

Huiyun first made a pencil draft, filling in the form once for practice. In the column for an opinion on sons and daughters going to the countryside, she had first written "no." Then she had thought it over: her son was bent on going, no matter what. Why not show a bit more wisdom, and make her son happy? So she wrote: "I firmly support his decision to go to the mountains and the countryside."

As planned, Qin Ge came early one morning to collect the application. He deemed his mother's thinking improved. Huiyun availed herself of the opportunity to say: "Huaisheng, do you really think Mama is a bad person?" Qin Ge did not reply, only busied himself looking at the tips of the willow tree. "If Mama were a bad person, if Mama did not love her country, would she have educated you as she has?" Qin Ge got up and walked off. At the courtyard gate he turned to look back at Huiyun, those huge radiant girl's eyes filled with confusion and sorrow. "Ma!" he cried, and left. After that he frequently came to Spoon Court, staying both to eat and sleep. Huiyun was tremendously elated. Mingled with her happiness, however, were periods of distress.

Then came the evening for the district parents to hold talks. Huiyun was afraid to attend the meeting. There would be many people

---

3. The May Fourth Movement was a major movement advocating the modernization of China; it was a reaction to the Treaty of Versailles, which ended the First World War in Europe.

there and she feared that she might once again become a target for denunciation. But if she didn't go, she didn't know what further charges might be brought against her. She and Puti discussed it for a long time, and she finally decided to go. She arrived early and sat in a corner, hoping that no one would notice her, and that as soon as the meeting was over she would be able to return home safe and sound.

The man in charge of the meeting lectured about the great "hows and whys" of going to the mountains and the countryside, exclaiming that this program had great anti-revisionist significance, that it had sprung from the great leader's appeals, and so on. He also held forth on the parents' attitudes, some of which were correct, some incorrect, and what the gap was between the two. He talked and talked, on and on, saying: "For example, we have Comrade Tao Huiyun, who is all alone, who needs her son to care for her, yet she has resolutely responded to the great leader Chairman Mao's appeal, joyfully supporting her only son's decision to go to the Great Northern Wilderness; she deserves to be a model." Finishing, he took the lead and began to clap.

When she heard her name, Tao Huiyun felt her heart jump abruptly. That name had always been linked to "seize for the stage."[4] When she heard the word "comrade" she was astonished. That word was so cordial, so precious, so vitally important, but could also be so easily and conveniently withdrawn. She had not been called "comrade" for well over a year. Even after she heard the word, she simply could not believe that it had been used to refer to her.

Then she heard the "comrade" in charge call upon her to say a few words. There were other people from Y University present. The atmosphere was not at all tense. There was nothing for it but for Huiyun to rise and say something. "All mothers hope their sons will be at their side"—she paused, thinking to herself: "What a mess! This humanism!"[5] She saw that everyone looked uncritical, so, stiffening herself, she said, with difficulty—"so that they can better be cared for. But if a son's going far away to the countryside can strengthen the nation, make the people more prosperous, I think many mothers will go along. Moreover, my son was bound to go. I had to give him my wholehearted support, to make him happy."

---

4. That is, where the victim will stand and be publicly denounced.

5. Humanism (*ren xing lun*) connoted bourgeois sentimentality. See Chapter 7.

These very realistic sentences evoked irrepressible smiles from everyone in the audience. At that time very few people spoke in such a down-to-earth way. However, right in the midst of the smiles, in another corner of the room, a real woman "comrade" got to her feet, very gaunt in appearance, her face deathly pale. She spoke in a very loud voice: "You should not term Tao Huiyun a 'comrade.' She's the counterrevolutionary of our school. Who doesn't know that!" The man in charge of the meeting had indeed not done any investigatory research, and immediately blurted out: "I didn't understand the situation! I didn't understand the situation!" When he inquired as to the name of the "unmasker" he learned that she was none other than Comrade Cui Zhen; her daughter had still not applied, but she fervently desired to send her daughter to strike roots in the borderlands, too. The person in charge hurriedly declared her to be the only exemplary model mother among those present. Huiyun still stood with bowed head, only sitting down when an old lady beside her quietly pulled at her jacket front. The meeting dispersed without resolution. Lining up, Huiyun went out of the door side-by-side with Cui Zhen. Out of pure curiosity, she was keen to know about Cui Zhen's health, but of course she said nothing.

She only reported what had happened in the meeting to Puti. Puti thought for quite a while before remarking that perhaps this would become a "new trend in the class struggle." However, she also expressed the view that they were already "meat on the hammering block," "fish under the knife," so to speak, so they had better concentrate on the present, and not worry overmuch about the future—since, in reality, worrying was futile.

Spoon Court now became much busier. Qin Ge came often, Cui Li even more often. The first thing she always asked as she came in the door was: "Is Qin Ge here?" If Qin Ge wasn't there, she sometimes stayed for a few words, sometimes turned around and left straightaway. Qin Ge believed that Cui Li lacked the determination to dedicate herself to the borderlands; her motives were not pure, and for her to go would not be beneficial. Puti and Huiyun also tried to persuade her to consider going with the second group. From day to day, agitated and uncertain, hesitant and undecided, she looked on helplessly from the sidelines.

Huiyun devoted herself wholeheartedly, with all her maternal instincts, to the task of outfitting her son for the journey. The most useful articles remaining from the Tao and Mei households were sorted out for Qin Ge. Bedding and cotton-padded clothes all were laundered; an old, fringed, sky-blue tablecloth was turned into two pillowcases, unique to behold. Huiyun also sought out a sturdy tree branch and polished it carefully for a long time, thereby furnishing her son with a prop for the lid when he opened his chest. Allegedly, every chest in the Tao family had been fitted out with this kind of "chest-stick," all naturally made from first-class timber. Puti could not in fact see why this should be necessary, but she had to acknowledge that this was the Tao family tradition and should therefore be respected. On the other hand, Huiyun felt much comforted when Qin Ge unexpectedly approved.

On the eve of his departure from Beijing, Qin Ge left the names and addresses of several friends with his mother, saying that if something cropped up, she should seek them out; that they might also come to the house to call. In actual fact, not one of them would ever show his face, and Huiyun would naturally never call on any of them either. It was by now already September: the days were much shorter and cooler. Cui Li came in the afternoon and they had supper together, the four of them sitting in Huiyun's room, each with his or her own thoughts. No one spoke.

Huiyun knew that Qin Ge did not care for Cui Li; moreover, his heart was with the revolution, and not in any way keen on romance. Thinking that time was short, she urged Qin Ge to see Cui Li off, to give them a chance to talk alone. Qin Ge had to comply and urged Cui Li to go.

Cui Li's wan and sallow face had an exceedingly timid look. She said to Huiyun: "Aunty Tao, tomorrow I'll go with you to the station."

"Great," Huiyun answered at once.

Actually, Qin Ge and Puti both maintained that it would be better if Huiyun did not go to see him off. Surprisingly, on this issue they shared the same opinion for once. But Huiyun was determined. "Not see him off! Outrageous!" Puti let the matter rest.

Qin Ge went out for a short while to see Cui Li off, coming back in mumbling to himself: "It's really disgusting! I'm glad she's finally left. To be so full of affection!" Huiyun looked at him sternly. He winked his big eyes mischievously, then set about dignifying his expression. Obviously not a few girls had fallen for those eyes. "Ma! You relax!" he said solemnly. "These past days have been as though I were intoxicated, but I won't turn bad, don't you worry!" He even gave Puti a smile. That smiling expression, betraying exhaustion, also resembled his mother's.

The people in Spoon Court rose early the next day—the sky was still dark. Qin Ge had already sent his luggage on ahead. Thanks to his mother, he was tidy and clean. He only carried a canvas bag on his back and a string bag in his hand. He looked full of zest. He was to go to the front of Tian An Men Square with his fellow students, to make a vow before the portrait of Chairman Mao. Huiyun very much wanted to follow him there, but tactfully restrained herself.

Cui Li hurried to accompany her to the station. There were still not many people there. Gradually, more and more arrived, many making no effort to wipe away the tears streaming down their faces, others sobbing freely. Huiyun and Cui Li did not know what was going on. They always seemed to be in somebody else's way, with people pushing and shoving them. With great difficulty they squeezed toward the side of a car near the front. Suddenly, they noticed that from out of the side of one of these cars someone was yelling "Ma!"

"Ma!" Qin Ge stuck his head out of the window, one hand beckoning, the other holding a steamed, stuffed dumpling that Huiyun had prepared especially for his journey. "Ma! You go back!" he called, sweat dripping from his pink and white face as he slipped the dumpling to the fellow student beside him.

Huiyun looked longingly at her son's young face. Who knew when, or even if, she would ever see him again: see once again that life born of her own flesh and blood! Perhaps in eight years', ten years' time. Would this, indeed, perhaps be the last time? Her heart contracted painfully, her head began its slight, uncontrollable shaking. "But I promised Puti!" she suddenly remembered, becoming aware of the situation, "I can't get sick!" With this thought, she leaned against Cui Li and calmed down.

"Qin Ge!" Cui Li cried, her face as pale as Cui Zhen's.

"Ma!" Qin Ge ignored her, only repeating "Ma! You go back!"

At this moment the bell rang for the train to depart. The hubbub at the station immediately quieted down. The scene became as serene as a deep and secluded mountain valley: there was no sound. Everyone held their breath. It was quiet for about half a minute, then all of a sudden sobbing burst forth, blending with the heaven-rending burst of gongs and drums sounding like a raging tide suddenly breaking against rocks, to send these sons and daughters off to the mountains and the countryside.

The train slowly started up, leaving the wailing and the deafening gongs and drums behind. Neither Huiyun nor Cui Li shed any tears. They only stood there looking after the departing train. Black smoke drifted upward toward the bright azure sky, that sky special to Beijing's autumn. Only when the station was completely deserted did they turn their steps toward home.

# 16

# The Radiant Rock

ON THE SURFACE, THE DAYS AT SPOON COURT BECAME QUITE PEACEFUL. The lives of Huiyun and Puti now centered around reading, writing, and discussing letters. Fang Zhi's handwriting in his daily letters became neater with each passing day. In one letter he wrote: "Lying here, I think of my soul as a spring, the source, with the entangling roots of Panxi's local people; I was nourished in the soil of my native countryside." Reading this, Huiyun was deeply moved by Fang Zhi's honesty, commenting to Puti: "It's remarkable he doesn't say you are the source and the earth."

"He can dismiss convention, that's all," Puti said, giving a little laugh.

Two letters also arrived from Qin Ge, describing his new life both simply and clearly. "The country people are really good. I seem to be much more normal here." He wrote: "Ma! I'm very busy, very busy!" Probably because he was very busy, his Chinese characters all looked as though they were on the verge of running away. Puti said she hadn't known Qin Ge could write such a good letter; she quickly recited it from memory.

One day Puti went back to Z Hospital for a routine checkup. Everything was normal. Going home, she followed the road to town to buy vegetables. After a while her arm swelled up and began to ache, so she rested beside a little bridge. Suddenly she saw Cui Zhen coming toward her, carrying a bucket of pasty liquid in one hand, and holding a brush and paper in the other. She glanced at Puti, then, without excusing herself, went under the bridge next to an old wall, and with the brush and paste affixed the papers to the wall. Apparently other people were to write the characters.

"Mei Puti!" She brushed and brushed, suddenly stopping, and turning to come up on the bridge. "How are you feeling? How come you're still not at work?"

"I have the doctor's permission." Puti looked warily at her.

"I feel very tired." Cui Zhen seemed to be muttering to herself. "Don't all cancer patients feel like this?"

"You should rest. Healthy people can get tired, too," Puti said kindly.

"I should fight off tiredness!" Cui Zhen said, grinding and gnashing her teeth. "I just cannot fall behind!" Nevertheless she sat down as she spoke.

"Brushing a bucket of paste, does this amount to not falling behind?" Puti thought pityingly. "It's a case of thorough hardening-of-the-heart!"

"You're selfish! You people can only understand your own concerns." Cui Zhen began to get excited, but her face remained pale.

"If the people really needed it, I would sacrifice myself in front of you!" Still speaking calmly, Puti picked up her string bag and left.

"You class enemies still go out to make reports, still spread your selfish philosophy! We cannot tolerate it!" Cui Zhen yelled indignantly at Puti's back, following this with a violent coughing fit. The more vehemently she coughed, the more satisfied she felt, thinking: "My illness shows that I am active!"

"I don't know whether she went back for a checkup or not," Puti thought quickly. "She needs a fluoroscopy. When Fang Zhi is better, she should also see him. But she will doubtless give us political labels. Fang Zhi, Fang Zhi, when will he be well again?" A feeling of frustration overwhelmed her. There was something murky about the sparkling blue sky of the fall day.

The gate to Spoon Court was not locked during the daytime. When they went out, they always had to secure it carefully. The gate was now slightly ajar: clearly someone had come in. Here was an unknown situation once again! Puti cautiously slowed her steps; her heart began to beat heavily.

Slowly she pushed the gate open—and saw Fang Zhi standing beside the Everlasting Rock, smiling at her.

"Are you well?" His deep voice was choked, his unkempt beard over an inch long. Only his gaze held its former steadiness. He looked at Puti with eyes full of trust.

For an instant Puti was struck dumb and made no reply. She quickly opened the door of the house and pushed Fang Zhi inside. "Come in! Lie down right away!"

Fang Zhi heeded her suggestion and lay down. His waist was already aching badly; he could no longer stand up. "How did you know I can't sit?" he asked, smiling. When he had first started to sit again, he had felt as though he no longer had any muscles, as if he were sitting directly on his bones. The pain had been intense. It was already much less so.

"I didn't know you couldn't sit. I just knew you should lie down." Puti stood before the bed. The two looked at each other without speaking. After a while, Puti turned and went out of the house, going over to the west wall, where she poked at the stove and put some water on to boil.

Lying there comfortably, Fang Zhi looked the friendly little room up and down. He hadn't seen it for over two months. It still held the same air of tranquillity, the same gentleness; even the dust on the window sill was familiar and lovable. Outside the window, some of the ivy leaves on the Everlasting Rock had already turned completely red. The colors of the Rock seemed lighter, brighter.

Puti came in, carrying a bowl of fried flour soup. "I'm sure you haven't had breakfast."

Fang Zhi beseeched: "Don't walk around, okay? Let me look at you."

Puti lowered her head and with a smile sat down beside the door.

Fang Zhi talked, telling her how he had already been to the orthopedic hospital; there a classmate had examined him and x-rayed him. Everything was all right. He hadn't let her know he was coming because he was afraid that he might not be able to come for a while. Although his health would not present any problem, it was hard to tell how the political situation would turn out. The greater or lesser demands of the struggle on the political scene aside, he was not aware of any objective criteria that might be held against him. "Originally, it was not my intention to provoke penalties, but only to conscientiously confess my way of thinking. It seems that this confession will have bitter consequences for the rest of my life," Fang Zhi said regretfully.

Puti began to remember how her father had spoken words such as these. He had recalled three phrases from Zhuang Zi: "Evil does not seek punishment, goodness does not seek fame, reason considers experience." But how to keep punishment at bay? If her father were here, she knew that his thinking would be the same as Fang Zhi's. What happiness if he could have known Fang Zhi's thinking! She looked at Fang Zhi's kind and honest face. Fang Zhi observed, apologetically, that he had not any hot water, and thus had no way of trimming himself. Puti did not take her eyes off him. As they looked at each other, the two of them smiled, without knowing why.

"Puti, I want you to carefully reconsider . . ." Fang Zhi swallowed slowly; there was something he could not get out. "My 'favorable situation' is not what it was. It's very possible I'll be assigned to go and work in remote districts on a medical team, to serve as a doctor at the most basic level. Although I am quite willing to take this opportunity to serve the people directly, I don't think you could endure this. I know that Puti is not afraid of suffering, but your body sets great limits upon you. You have literary talents, you have—"

"What are you trying to say?" Puti interrupted, tears shining in her eyes. Fang Zhi paused, speechless. There was no sound in the little room. The autumn sun cast the shadow of the Everlasting Rock in through the window.

Finally Puti spoke. "You want me to reconsider. Let me tell you my decision. I think the most important thing is for us to marry as soon as possible."

"Marry?" Fang Zhi sat up slowly. Puti quickly put the quilt behind his back. "But I'm not completely well—I would be a burden on you."

"It's just because you aren't completely well. I can care for you more easily if we're together. We should look after each other, we shouldn't be separated any longer, we need no longer endure the pain of longing for each other."

"Really?" Fang Zhi gazed at Puti, at that face transformed by the radiance of her emotions. Embarrassed, she took off her glasses and wiped them, lowering her eyes. A teardrop hung on each of the curving arcs; the lines at the corner of her eye were so fine and delicate he felt like reaching out his hand to touch them.

"Moreover, at any time either of us might be isolated for investigation. It's very likely. Right? So, we should secure our happiness legally, as soon as we can."

"Do you really think so?" Fang Zhi got to his feet, his look not leaving her radiant face for an instant.

"You don't need to look at me like that—you."

"You—you, dearly beloved—most dearly beloved." As he spoke, Fang Zhi spontaneously knelt, leaning his tousled head against Puti's knees. The two wept freely with happiness.

When Huiyun came back at noontime and learned the news, she was as happy as a child anticipating the New Year. The three of them talked; the wedding was set for mid-fall, according to the lunar calendar, September eighteenth on the solar calendar. Fang Zhi and Puti next approached their respective work units to ask for permission to marry, causing quite a stir in the Literature Department at

Y University, and the surgical department at Z Hospital.[1] This was especially so for Mei Puti, since this most important event in her life had been quite a topic of conversation and speculation in the 1950s. Quite a few people already knew about Fang Zhi's and her comings and goings. However, they had thought it unlikely that a young surgeon would go so far as to officially marry a cancer patient approaching forty.

When Zhang Yongjiang saw the application, he told Shi Qingping the news at the dinner table, saying: "That time you didn't write up the big-character poster: if you had made their comings and goings seem disgusting, maybe now they wouldn't be considering marriage." Recently Zhang and his wife had exchanged two rooms for one with a friend from their faction. That family had many members and they didn't fear monsters and demons.

Shi Qingping was irritated. She accused Zhang Yongjiang: "Why keep their marriage from going through? For what reason?" The scene when Elder Sister Qi had cut her throat rose before her; it still made her blood run cold.

After they had moved the corpse, Zhang, Shi, and the rest had heard that there were rumors about what the true situation had been. They knew that quite a few people were outraged at the injustice done to Mei Puti. Zhang Yongjiang had repeatedly tried to persuade Shi Qingping that it was not necessary for them to go so far as to move their residence to find shelter from such rumors. But Shi Qingping did not dare stay at home alone; Elder Sister Qi's ghost was much more to be feared than any frame-up charges. "What hadn't ensued from moving a corpse!" she observed. "Of the many big-character posters, eighty percent were mostly lies. Why shouldn't we have moved the corpse?" Zhang Yongjiang insisted, but he could not bend her. It had not occurred to him at the time that moving the corpse would entail such heavy responsibilities—it might even be claimed that they had thereby realized Elder Sister Qi's own unfulfilled wishes! She should have sought out Mei Puti in the first place! After people had first raised the issue, Zhang had gone through a period of worry. However, while many people harbored sympathetic feelings, they didn't want to speak out publicly for "monsters and

---

1. In China, couples must obtain permission to marry from their respective work units before it is legally possible to register. In most cases, parental consent is also required.

demons." Recognizing this, Zhang had stopped worrying and continued to engage in the revolution. Now, the number-one enemies in
their eyes were the mainstays of the June First Commune, such as
Zheng Liming. The "monsters and demons" had long since dropped
from discussion.

"Say that I do approve Mei Puti's marriage, wouldn't that be too
generous to her?" Zhang Yongjiang asked his wife.

"It doesn't matter. He's only a Rightist who's slipped through the
net." Shi Qingping looked disdainful.

"Really!—How can a Communist Party member marry a Rightist
who's gone unpunished?" Zhang Yongjiang was suddenly inspired.
"What kind of philosophical sentiment is that! What a position! It
can't possibly be approved!"

Man and wife chatting at the table had decided the matter. So-
called organizational authority had taken this kind of great leap forward. Living, aging, illness, death, marriage, work, judicial proceedings meting out punishment—all now hinged on one sentence from
the leader!

Fang Zhi's path was even more difficult. Xiao Ding and others
calculated that if, when the application was submitted, the certificate
could not be obtained or the "opposition" caused trouble, perhaps a
criticism meeting might develop, taking off on the "arrogance of
evil." Moreover, Fang Zhi was just regaining his health; why stir up
such an unfavorable situation? Xiao Ding commented: "Is there the
slightest chance with legal formalities? You two should take it as it
comes. You're obviously asking for trouble otherwise." Fang Zhi felt
that this kind of simplification was disrespectful of Puti. Not knowing
whether he was excessively under the influence of old prejudices, he
quietly took the words to Huiyun for her opinion. Huiyun said
coolly: "What do you think?"

"I think it definitely wouldn't work," Fang Zhi said earnestly.

"Good! Very good!" Huiyun started to yell in a loud voice: "Puti!
This is really a Spoon Court man! We will be guileless and upright!"

Their characters were as guileless as expected, their behavior
most upright. However, in this time of rampage against evil spirits,
such guilelessness and uprightness could only win them rounds of
blame and censure. When Fang Zhi finally applied to the "organization" to marry, Xin Shengda severely criticized him before the whole
of a revolutionary mass rally, haranguing: "Some 'monsters and
demons' still consider themselves to be 'people'! They have the im-
pudence to ask for permission to marry, they don't honestly confess
their crimes. What do these people think of the Cultural Revolution
led by Chairman Mao!?" He wanted to draw Fang Zhi into an accu-

sation. Fortunately, however, Sister Huo mediated, pointing out that since Fang Zhi was in the midst of treatment for his injury, they should not provoke further suffering. Sister Huo came especially to Fang Zhi's room to lecture and advise him. "Dr. Fang"—when there was no one else present she always returned to this form of address—"you have transgressed the limits of what's proper for a person in your position. If you allow yourself to be completely taken up with this matter, how can you satisfactorily reform yourself and admit your guilt? You are a good doctor. If they were indeed to put the hat of a 'Rightist-slipped-through-the-net' on you, your surgical skills would go to waste. Besides, as far as the university is concerned, it cannot be sanctioned either. It would be better to let this feeling die!"

When Puti pressed inquiry at her department, they answered that permission had not been granted. The reason was that "a Communist Party member cannot marry a Rightist who has escaped punishment." First they identified people as monsters and demons, then claimed they were Communist Party members who could not be like that! Puti really didn't know whether to laugh or cry at this preposterous logic. Zheng Liming and others were very indignant and promised to fight on her behalf.

Huiyun believed that they should make some kind of preparations, no matter how simple and crude. To create a sense of "newness," the old household furniture should be cleaned, the old bedding washed. Sitting on the little stool smoking, she said in dead earnest: "I'll take care of washing the bedding, but I can't remake it. You'll have to look for a person blessed with good fortune."

"Probably in China now, there aren't many persons blessed with good fortune," Puti smiled coolly. "Who knows how many families are still intact. Moreover, why would anyone blessed with good fortune come here to us?"

"In that case you'll have to sew them yourself.[2] Anyway, I can't do it." Huiyun obviously believed that an unlucky character like herself would bring bad luck to Puti. For good luck, therefore, it would be better for Puti to go to the trouble herself.

Puti took needle and thread to sew the quilt. When her arm began to ache she stopped, rested for a while, and then sewed on.

---

2. In China, winter bedding consists of quilts, which are filled with cotton batting sewn into a silk and cotton lining. In order to wash these, therefore, they must first be unsewn.

The old peach-colored silk quilt already had a ten-year history; it was indeed one Mama had looked upon. This thought comforted Puti. Thinking back to those earlier days when Mama was still in the world, she remembered how she would often return with some unnecessary clothes and urge Puti: "How is it you still have no friend? The trousseau is all ready." During those years, deep within her heart, Puti had often envisioned her wedding. But now, she had begun with the draft of a report to the Party organization: "Dear Party, . . . Comrade, Communist Party member . . ." This kind of report certainly never stated which Party branch. Love for the Party would ordinarily have moved her to write "Dear Party." Men she had met during the course of her lifetime had often not been given a second thought because they did not conform to her concept of Party standards. How was it, then, that she had never before even considered the fact the Fang Zhi was not a Party member?

"Fang Zhi is a man, normal, honest, and kind," Puti said to herself with satisfaction, yet with some distress. "Together we will conquer every kind of cancer cell. Our Party will also conquer the cancer cells. It can, it surely can."

Their application, however, did not receive the "organization's" approval. Right up to September eighteenth, they had no certifying letter in hand.

Several more days passed. Zheng Liming ventured an idea: if they really weren't going to get certification, they could simply go to the office and piteously entreat the official on duty, explaining the real situation. If they encountered reasonable, kindly persons, perhaps sanction would be given for the registration. The three— Huiyun, Puti, and Fang Zhi—discussed it. They considered the possibility that perhaps a new game would be played after the first of October.[3] They waited a few more days for the last possibility of certification, then decided that on September thirtieth they would try for a visit.

Early in the day on the thirtieth, Huiyun sat in the courtyard cutting up red paper. She cut great and small "happiness" characters, and a red paper lamp shade with fringes. She also took out a bunch of red thread, had Puti pull it, and wove a little braid. Puti didn't understand and asked what she was making. At this moment someone called "Mei Puti" from outside the court gate.

---

3. October 1 is the holiday celebrating the founding of the People's Republic of China.

It was Zheng Liming. He hadn't dismounted from his bicycle; with one foot pressed on a pedal, he handed her a paper: "It's your certifying letter!"

"How did you do it? You're really wonderful!" Puti gripped the paper tightly, as if only by holding onto it could she remain upright.

"A number of people felt Zhang Yongjiang was too unreasonable. He has clearly been making people suffer so as to suit his own personal ends." Old Zheng[4] lowered his voice. "I heard that before October 1 they will find a new target to focus on. Tao Hui should be careful." He finished and had no sooner put his foot down on the pedal than he was far away.

This was already the day before October 1.

When Huiyun learned they had the certifying letter, she was wild with joy. "This is a hundred times better than going with two empty hands to register. It's a good omen!" She behaved as though being set apart for targeting was nothing. She hurried to move the stool and polish the lightbulb. In a twinkling she had hung the red paper lamp shade on the bulb. Who knew where she had found a pair of glass bottles? Placing the braids of red thread inside, she poured in peanut oil.

"A pity," Puti observed, frowning; "it's still not as good as eating it."

Huiyun didn't listen. She looked a big rock up and down, found two insertion points to stand the bottles in, one a little above, the other below.

"When you finish registering, light them," Huiyun exhorted. She stepped back, looking right and left, showing her exhausted smile.

Only when Puti realized that Huiyun couldn't have found red candles to buy anywhere did she fully appreciate the substitution. "They'd look even better on the Everlasting Rock, Huiyun," Puti said. "We can light up the Rock with our three hearts."

"Oh! No!" Huiyun chuckled. "Keep those, for this life and the next—when they're burned down they'll be no more." The rims of her eyes reddened suddenly. She quickly turned to get out the bicycle, and left.

At about eight o'clock, Fang Zhi arrived. He saw that Puti wore a dark blue print shirt with a light gray jacket and dark gray slacks. "This is what you wore the first time you came to the outpatient service." His

---

4. "Old" (*lao*) can refer to a mature person of some status; it does not necessarily connote an elderly person.

heart overflowed with warm and gentle feelings. To him, the old clothes were incomparably intimate and lovable. Puti looked at him, and lowered her eyes.

"You are really good, you are my good man." She spoke in a low voice, and reached out a hand to pick a hair from Fang Zhi's shoulder.

They had expected to meet with they knew not what difficulties before they got to see the registrar. Unexpectedly, however, they only had to ask one person before finding the registration office. In the room sat only a wizened little old man; there was no one else. It was none other than Old Qi. When he saw Fang Zhi and Puti, he rubbed his eyes with his hand.

"You're really a very good couple," he muttered. "How is it we never thought of urging you to attend to this long before?"

Fang Zhi hurried to explain the situation at the hospital and the school and that they had only one certifying paper.

Old Qi, facing a gigantic likeness of Chairman Mao on the wall, drummed his fingers on the table. After thinking for a moment he said: "Dr. Fang, you're not a stranger. I could no longer work at the court, so I got this job. And I can't become completely mechanical, only issuing certificates when presented with letters. I know of the wrongs to which Teacher Mei has been subjected. I will be glad if you two can live as one family." His voice quivered as he spoke: his family had already turned to dust. "Done! I'll issue it!" So saying, he pulled out two great red marriage certificates and had Fang Zhi and Puti fill them out.

"Will this make trouble for you?" Puti asked anxiously. Fang Zhi, too, turned hesitantly toward him.

"I have no one supervising me here. If the hospital sends people to check, I'll think of a way. According to the regulations on marriage, why shouldn't I register you?"

The two each filled out a page. On the large red certificates were printed quotations from Chairman Mao and Lin Biao. The two applicants looked at each other and smiled spontaneously.

The certificates done, Old Qi affixed seals and gave each a copy. Again the two looked at each other, relieved, and gave long sighs. From now on they would be fellow travelers: However rough the road, they would take life's distances together.

Probably it was their serious yet gentle expressions that moved Old Qi; he seldom saw that kind of look come in. Clearing his throat, he delivered a short and simple speech: "As from now, you two are husband and wife. Your relationship as husband and wife is under the protection of the law." He then drew out an extremely dirty handkerchief and wiped his nose. "The law? Right! The protection of the law. You have worked wholeheartedly. Only now are you marrying. Actually, it's a model late marriage." He looked especially warmly at Puti. "No matter at what, one must always work, otherwise what would we eat? Or wear?" He changed the subject abruptly and said, still looking at Puti: "You're in the Russian Language Department?[5] You must struggle resolutely to take your family to an outpost of anti-revisionism, an outpost for the prevention of revisionism." He also turned to Fang Zhi: "You are a medical worker. You must grasp the surgical knife to serve workers, peasants, and soldiers, to serve poor and lower-middle-class peasants."

Fang Zhi and Puti had both thought he was going to say something like "I wish you happiness and prosperity," but he did not. He only shook his head in a satisfied way signifying that he had finished.

Fang Zhi seized his hand to thank him. Puti felt the handshake was also for her: there was no need for her to put out her hand, too. For the first time in her life she experienced a peaceful feeling of dependency. As they went out the entrance to the office, they again smiled instinctively at each other: they now walked in the world as man and wife.

On the road, they stepped lightly; neither spoke. Only from time to time did each glance sideways at the radiant face of the other, at the lifelong companion.

They soon came to the reed pond. Behind the luxuriant reeds, the vase-shaped entrance to Spoon Court showed in a thin line. The great willow tree was still green, the willow branches waving as if to welcome them home. Fang Zhi gently took Puti's hand and said: "Are you tired?"

At almost the same moment Puti turned to him and asked: "Does your waist hurt?"

At this moment, the gate to Spoon Court opened. They saw two soldiers wearing Red Guard armbands pushing Huiyun out. Huiyun held a wash basin in one hand, and grasped the gate frame with the other, seeking to delay them. She instantly saw Puti at the reed pond, with Fang Zhi standing beside her. She understood right away. In uncontrollable happiness she called out: "You're back? Congratulations!" The two Red Guards stared at Fang Zhi and Puti, and gave Huiyun a shove. Smiling, she waved her hand at them, and walked toward the school.

---

5. Puti was actually in the Chinese Department.

"Huiyun!" Puti rushed forward a couple of steps. Fang Zhi quickly restrained her, himself hurrying over to help Huiyun carry her things.

"Don't worry about me! You go in together!" Huiyun turned her head, halting Fang Zhi's advance with an angry voice as she walked off.

They stood silently for a moment. What could be done? This was only a prelude to full-scale isolation. One could be thrown into prison at any time, cut off entirely from the outside world. They had no alternative but to pass silently through the vase-shaped opening together, going to stand beside the Everlasting Rock.

Puti handed the key to Fang Zhi. Fang Zhi opened the door to the room and together they entered their home. They bowed toward the container with her father's ashes. Puti could not help sobbing as she leaned her head against Fang Zhi's chest.

She missed her father and mother greatly, and missed Huiyun. Returning home from registration at this moment of embarking upon their new life together, Huiyun was not there. How could her happiness be complete without her? Fang Zhi wiped away her tears and said comfortingly: "Massed isolation is always of short duration." Puti asked painfully: "How long will this 'short duration' be?"

The two were aware that they could not see the end of these sufferings of a short duration, and that their moment of happiness was only a twinkling. Neither knew what misfortune the next moment would bring. Puti quickly took out the matches, went out of the house with Fang Zhi, and lit the red threads in the glass bottles on the Rock. The light from the improvised candles pulsated over the irregularities of the red and green leaves, transforming the beautiful Everlasting Rock into something mystical. Solemnly, they gazed at the luminous Rock.

"The Rock is a candle" Puti said softly. The light shimmered inside the dark little room. The ceiling bulb, with the red-tasseled shade, lit up the whole room, bathing the newly married pair in a red glow.

They knew that from this time on, the distresses each bore would be halved: with pain thus shared, the cup of sorrow would be watered with the dear one's tears. They also knew that what happiness each enjoyed would not be similarly divided: life companions caring for each other could immeasurably enrich the cup of happiness. The strength of the two normal cells had been united. This was not an addition, but an infinite multiplication.

They gazed in silence out the window at the Everlasting Rock. Under the clear autumn sky the lively flames appeared diffuse. Yet in the shadow of death, those diffuse yet lively flames had been bright enough to light the road of life.

# About the Book

THIS POLITICAL AND DARKLY ROMANTIC NOVEL CENTERS ON MEI PUTI, A forty-year-old, unmarried professor of literature, who suffers because of her heritage as part of the old elite. Puti is sustained by her growing love for her doctor, Fang Zhi, as well as by a developing friendship with her neighbor and fellow "class enemy" Huiyun.

Puti's illness, the intrigues at her university, and the politics at Fang Zhi's hospital all evoke the ways in which China suffered during the turbulence and tragedy of the Cultural Revolution. Jealousy and betrayal, as well as modest heroes and brave friendships, propel the narrative of endurance and love—and we see how politics, history, and fear can influence the most intimate of human relationships.